DISCARD
FCPL discards materials
that are outdated and in poor condition.
In order to make room for current,
in-demand materials, underused materials
are offered for public sale.

The Air We Breathe

Center Point
Large Print

Also by Christa Parrish and available from
Center Point Large Print:

Watch Over Me

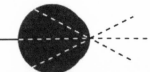

**This Large Print Book carries the
Seal of Approval of N.A.V.H.**

The Air We Breathe

CHRISTA PARRISH

CENTER POINT LARGE PRINT
THORNDIKE, MAINE

This Center Point Large Print edition is published
in the year 2013 by arrangement with Bethany House
Publishers, a division of Baker Publishing Group.

Copyright © 2012 by Christa Parrish.

Most Scripture quotations are from the Holy Bible,
New International Version®. NIV®. Copyright © 1973,
1978, 1984, 2011 by Biblica, Inc.™

Other Scripture quotations are from the
King James Version of the Bible.

This is a work of fiction. Names, characters, incidents, and
dialogues are products of the author's imagination and are
not to be construed as real. Any resemblance to actual events
or persons, living or dead, is entirely coincidental.

The text of this Large Print edition is unabridged.
In other aspects, this book may
vary from the original edition.
Printed in the United States of America
on permanent paper.
Set in 16-point Times New Roman type.

ISBN: 978-1-61173-656-4

Library of Congress Cataloging-in-Publication Data

Parrish, Christa.
The air we breathe / Christa Parrish.
pages ; cm.
ISBN 978-1-61173-656-4 (library binding : alk. paper)
1. Teenage girls—Fiction. 2. Female friendship—Fiction.
  3. Psychic trauma—Fiction. 4. Domestic fiction.
  5. Psychological fiction. 6. Large type books. I. Title.
PS3616.A76835A58 2013
813′.6—dc23

2012037129

To Carol Parrish, my grandmother—
Sometimes a love of words
grows in families.

The Air We Breathe

PART ONE

1

She wanted to poke out Elvis's eyes. He stared at her from the corner—the young King, not the old, sweaty, fat one—in his suit of shiny white, clutching a microphone in his wax hand, his molded face frozen in his signature twisted-lip grimace.

Louise had moved him out front because "The King" brought the tourists in. There weren't any tourists on Dorsett Island, in February, but her mother opened the wax museum every day of the year, except Thanksgiving and their vacation time between Christmas Eve and New Year's. Even if Uncle Mick hadn't required it, Louise probably would have done the same. She needed purpose to her days. All the dusting of displays and painting new scenery would be meaningless without the *potential* of someone coming through the museum doors.

Molly took a pushpin from the counter drawer, tore a page from her notebook, and covered Elvis's face with it, jabbing the pin into the middle of his forehead. His hair would hide the hole.

Maybe now she could finish her history homework.

Tap. Tap. Tap. Her pink eraser bounced up each time she thumped it against the oak counter. She held the sharpened tip between her pointer and thumb, graphite filling her fingerprints. She rolled the pencil along the wood; it limped unevenly because of its six-sided shape, and stopped, quivering before falling still. Molly rubbed her fingertips across a sheet of paper, smears of pencil-lead storm clouds forming on the white.

No one would come in today.

The wheeled stool squawked as she shifted on it. She moved again, perched almost birdlike on the padded seat, feet hooked in the metal bars. Another squawk. The building had all sorts of sounds to it—one big cacophony of air clattering through old pipes, of the television constantly playing in her mother's office, of shifting floors, and of toilets that didn't stop running unless Molly remembered to jiggle the handle.

Across the narrow street, Tobias parked in front of Island Pizza & More, his Civic dressed in magnetic signs declaring Free Delivery, the letters floating above a simple sketch of a red lobster holding a slice of pepperoni pizza in his claw. The *More* indicated typical Maine tourist fare—chowders and seafood salads and fried fish. Neon signs taped in the restaurant window advertised lobster roll platters for $11.99, plus tax.

She walked to the window and watched him through a palm-sized worn patch in the blue F of the window lettering—Lou's HOUSE OF WAX, with *Lou* written in script letters and balanced on the corner of the H in HOUSE.

During the summer, tourists came in demanding, "Who's Lou? Is there really a Lou?" and sometimes her mother would appear from the back and say, "You're looking at her." Uncle Mick's father had been named Lou. When talking to Mick about the caretaker job, her mother had told him her name was Louise. He slapped his dirty denim thigh and said, "Guess it's meant to be," and Louise pinched Molly's upper arm through the sleeve of her winter coat. A warning. *Keep your mouth shut.*

That had been a long time ago.

As he got out of his car, Tobias looked back at her, and she slipped her hand over her peephole. Moments later, the front entrance opened and he walked through, a cackle of menacing recorded laughter greeting him from the speaker in the corner above the door, angled downward so the sound tumbled atop his head.

"Man, I hate that, even though I know it's coming." He tilted a small pizza box at her. "Garlic knots. Frank got the order wrong. Again. Want them?"

"Okay, I guess."

"You guess? The best garlic knots outside

Brooklyn and you only guess you want them. I'm wounded."

She smiled, head turned away from him, tilted to the floor. The flat brown carpet was littered with little Ts of white, the ridges she plucked off the margin of her spiral-notebook paper. She brushed at them with her toe, trying to move them under the counter, but they stuck, stubborn and thin. "Do you have sauce, too?"

"Molly Fisk," Tobias said, setting the box on the counter and flipping back the lid, "for you, anything."

A small container of marinara waited in the corner. She popped off the cover, squeezing too hard, the chunky orange sauce spilling over her fingers. She didn't want to lick them in front of Tobias. "Napkins?"

"Well, not anything." He laughed, and Molly smiled for the second time that day. The only times that day.

Something fell from the ceiling into the pizza box, a black speck with legs. She nudged the shelled body over and onto its feet, exposing a tomato-colored back and four inky spots, like the tip of a marker dabbed onto the beetle's wings.

"I don't think you should be awake yet," Molly said, blocking its path with her finger. The beetle hesitated, then crawled onto her skin. She held it up to Tobias.

"Did you ever make a wish on one of these?" he asked.

She shook her head.

"Really? When we were kids, my brother and I would find ladybugs and make a wish, and then blow them away home."

"They're beetles, actually. Coccinellids. And there are more than five thousand different types."

"Of beetles?"

"No—ladybugs. There are like three hundred thousand species of beetles."

"They could take over the world."

Molly laughed a little. "Possible."

"How do you know all this bug stuff?"

She wanted to say, *my father*. "Wikipedia is my friend."

"You should be an etymologist."

"Entomologist."

"I said that, didn't I?"

"There's a . . . Yeah. You did."

Tobias scratched his head under his knitted hat, stripes of green and blue and brown and orange, his near-black hair shaggy to his collar. She had called it black once, and he insisted it was brown. "My mom's hair, now that's black," he'd said. But his eyebrows were definitely black, thick and untamed, as was the little triangle of beard he kept right beneath his lower lip, a patch small enough Molly could have covered it with her thumb. She thought about it sometimes, when she

15

saw him laugh, and she'd feel a jolt in her belly and had to clasp her hands behind her to keep from reaching out to him. Her mother hated his facial hair. *"When I see it, I want to lick a Kleenex and scrub it off."*

Molly had once asked him what his little beard was called. "I don't know," he said. "I just like it." So she went to the computer and, after searching various terms, found an ESPN article about speed skater Apolo Anton Ohno and his tuft of chin hair. Jazz dab, it was called when trumpeter Dizzy Gillespie sported it in the '50s, or soul patch. Soul patch. That fit Tobias. He wore his soul all over. She felt as if she had none, like one of the wax figures, empty, crumbling.

She remembered the box of tissues in the counter drawer, opened it and wiped her hands. Then she took a garlic knot and broke an end off, dipping the bread in the sauce. Tobias asked, "Can I?" and Molly nodded, saying, "They're yours."

He scooped one up and crammed the entire thing into his mouth. "No lunch today."

"Busy?" Molly asked.

"Came straight to work from class."

"It's Wednesday."

"Had to make up a lab this morning. Total pain," he said. "But just this last semester and I'm done here."

He drove an hour each way to the closest community college. To save money, he said, so

16

he could transfer to a real school—somewhere away—leaving his family's business behind. Leaving her behind.

She thought she loved him; at least she had all the symptoms portrayed in the romance novels Louise read, the boxes of used paperbacks Uncle Mick brought when he visited—more often lately, despite it being the off-season. Yes, she'd skimmed a few of them, picking out the ones with the most clothed cover models, mostly skipping over the racy parts. She had the flutters and the bumbling tongue-tied conversations. She had long talks with him in her mind, forgetting all she'd planned to say when he stood in front of her. She thought about him at night, when she changed into her pajamas in front of the mirror and wished she looked more like the women on those Harlequins.

She couldn't think about him going. "How is it out there? It looks gray and cold."

"Gray. Cold. Perfect. Come out to the beach with me."

She flinched, shrinking into her center, folding up, a magician's handkerchief stuffed into the cup made by his hand, pushed in by his pointer finger, and then, when he shook his hand open, it had disappeared. That's what happened when Tobias —anyone—prodded her for more information, for feelings, for something she couldn't do.

She disappeared.

"I can't. I'm . . . working."

"No one is in town, Molly."

"Not here. Well, yes, here. But also school-work." She nudged the history textbook on the counter. "I graduate in June, too, you know."

"Ayuh. I know," Tobias said, and he looked puffed up with more to say, dark eyes full, swirling with thoughts, questions. Molly heard the door open behind her, and he flattened a little. "Maybe another time."

"Tobias," Louise said, coming close enough for Molly to smell tuna fish and caution. "Can we help you?"

"Louise," Tobias said back. "I thought Molly might want a break. You know, take a walk, get some air."

Her mother looked at her. Neither made a gesture. No blink, no brow wrinkle, no lid flutter. Molly's thoughts spilled from brain to eye, all crammed up against her cornea. *Say no. Say no.* Louise had no trouble reading them.

"Molly has things to do. And I'm sure your parents aren't paying you to stand here all day."

"That they aren't," he said. "Later, Moll." And he left with the ghoulish laugh following him out the door.

For a moment, she and her mother existed in a vacuum, the emptiness within both of them pouring out, flooding the room. Then Louise coughed. "Shirley's lost her fingers again," she said, holding out two small, flesh-colored digits.

"We should just put gloves on her," Molly said.

"That's not what I asked."

"You didn't ask anything." Her words flew out, startled and confused hornets, stinging her mother on the way by. Molly had no reason to be angry—she had wanted Tobias sent away—and yet she hadn't.

Louise folded the fingers back into her fist, her heavy shoulders falling a little more. "I'll take care of it."

"No." Molly held out her hand. "Just give me."

Louise set the pieces on the counter. "I'll start dinner," she said, and went back into the office.

Molly took her repair bucket—butane lighter, sheets and Duplo-sized blocks of beeswax, artist's brushes, tubes of paint—and hurried through the exhibits to the Shirley Temple figure in the classic-movie room, between James Dean in a black leather jacket and Judy Garland dressed as Dorothy. Shirley was posed in a short plaid dress with white collar and cuffs, chest puffed out, ringlets perfect, and deep dimples near the corners of her mouth. She pointed to herself, hand fisted, thumb toward her chest, like she did in the movie *Bright Eyes* while singing "On the Good Ship Lollipop." Her other arm hung by her side, two nubs where there should have been fingers, like the buds babies have in the womb.

"Oh, Shirley. When will we get you to keep these on?"

When they'd started at the museum, Mick had given them some tips about repairing wax figures, but he'd inherited the place from his father and couldn't have cared less if the sixty-year-old attraction remained a wax museum or was bulldozed to the ground. He kept the place open only for some spiteful family feud Molly knew nothing about, wanting to lose money.

So Molly and Louise did their best. Her mother searched the Internet for information on wax-figure upkeep but found only news articles about Madame Tussauds' headless Hitler being sent out for repairs after some tourist decapitated it in Berlin. So instead she purchased books on figure sculpting. They experimented with techniques in the books, heating and carving and shaping wax at the kitchen table, giggling over the deformed faces they produced, the uneven biceps, the misshapen feet. Neither were artists, though Louise had loved art once, long ago. Molly managed the repairs better than her mother could, her own fingers thin and nimble as she worked. And she had something Louise didn't—a relationship with the wax people.

Each time Molly worked on Shirley's hand, the fingers became lumpier, more misshapen. Usually she just heated the broken ends of the beeswax with the lighter and squashed them together, holding them until they cooled and stuck. Today, however, she snipped off the heads of sewing pins, wiggled them into the hand, and pushed the fingers onto them. Then she softened a bit of wax between her palms and molded it around the seams. She mixed pink, white, and yellow paint on a pallet and dabbed it on the repairs. It blended well enough.

"There you go, Miss Curly Top," she said, and went back out to the front counter, flipped open her history book and tried to take notes on Vietnam. She saw movement in the corner of her eye, a flash of white through the worn F, and watched as Tobias pulled away from the curb in his car. He waved as he passed.

She hadn't tasted air outside the museum or apartment for three years, maybe closer to four. *Inhale, exhale*—the same dust over and over, the same sad sighs, the scent of tourists, their stories and laughter. Her secrets, her memories, she couldn't escape them; she breathed them out, they floated around and around the building until she breathed them in somewhere else—snapping photos of visitors in front of the Elvis figure in the lobby, back in her bedroom, the office, the storage closet. And each time they came back to her, the wayward memory flashed bright behind her eyes, only for an instant but with a full-color intensity enough to stop her, whatever she was doing. She'd blink and swallow them down into her lungs quickly, so she wouldn't cry, or run away to hide. And out they went on the next breath, gone for a while, floating, floating, until she sucked them in again at another unsuspecting moment.

She would go outside today.

Gingerly, she lifted her body off the stool so it wouldn't squeak and betray her. She crossed to the door, fast, planning to ram her entire body against the metal push bar and break into the street, but she stalled at the glass, stuck, her heart swelling in her chest with each beat, feeling as if any moment it would rip through her ribs, too large to be contained.

There had been another door once. *No, no. Don't think about it.* She started trembling, tears salty on her lips.

"Molly?" Her mother stared at her from the office door.

"I can't," she told her mother.

Louise went to her, pulled her close and rocked her. "Shh," she said, stroking Molly's hair. "I'm sorry, baby girl. It's okay." And she hummed a tune from the past—from when they were both different people and nothing had yet gone wrong. Molly desperately wanted the song to comfort her, the way it once had. But it didn't.

2

Claire
September 2002

When her alarm went off in a crackle of static, Claire hit the snooze button. It burst on again nine minutes later, and she turned it off, stretched under the blankets, a tickle of disconcertion in her sleepy brain. She brushed it away, yawned, jammed her feet into the worn terry-cloth slippers, and shuffled into the bathroom to pee, brush her teeth, and splash cold water on her face. She dressed in yesterday's jeans and a clean long-sleeved shirt—horizontal stripes of blue and green and gray—and white athletic socks, the kind with the arch support that hugged her feet.

Downstairs, she unwrapped an herbal tea bag, dropped it into a mug of water, and heated it for two minutes in the microwave. She toasted an English muffin, smeared peanut butter on it, and when she reached into the microwave to grab her tea she saw them—Caden and Amelia—flashing behind her eyes—mental ghosts, real ghosts, perhaps—and their faces surprised her so much she dropped her mug; the scalding liquid spilled on her thigh, the cup shattered on the ceramic tile.

"Mmm, oww," she cried, peeling off her jeans,

leaving them to sop up the tea as she ran upstairs to the bathroom and pressed a cold, wet cloth to the welt blooming on her leg. "Shoot, shoot, shoot."

She didn't care about the burn. She swiped at her sleeve, exposing the wristwatch Daniel had given her for their third wedding anniversary. Thirty-three minutes. That was how long she'd been awake, how long it took her to remember her children.

At first, in the days immediately following the accident, there wasn't a minute she was able to shake them from her head, not a second her grief didn't hang from her neck, choking her, dragging her down so sleep was her only escape. Even in the hazy moments before she woke, she still knew some part of her was missing, some ugly monster was waiting around the corner to pounce as soon as consciousness crept back in, and when it did she remembered her children were dead.

Three years. Three years without them, and now each morning it took a little longer for her babies to come to mind. Yesterday, twenty-nine minutes. The day before, twenty-eight. It wouldn't be long before she went a day without thinking of them. A week.

What kind of mother was she?

A childless one.

In her clean pants, she went back down the stairs but went through the kitchen to the living room, where the last photo of Caden and Amelia sat on the mantel. Her son, forever nine, with his black hair and dark eyes, his body rigid with all the intensity that was Caden, his arm protectively around his sister. Amelia laughed—she was born laughing, and for six years had filled their home with unbridled joy and wonder and trust—her nose small and flat in her chubby face, her tongue protruding between her teeth, white Brushfield spots flecking her irises.

"I'm so sorry," she said, stroking the picture, smearing her fingerprints across the glass.

She cleaned up the broken mug, dumped the shards in the trash with the uneaten muffin, stepped into her rubber mud boots—not because of the weather but because they slipped on easily—and in her jacket walked four blocks to the Newsstand, the small periodical and tobacco shop nestled between the barber and a florist on Broadway.

Malachi smiled as she pushed open the door. "Late today, Lady Claire."

"I spilled my tea on me this morning. Burned the skin off my leg."

"Glad it's nothing serious."

Claire laughed. "Thanks so much." She folded the *New York Times* under her arm without looking at the date. She knew it already; it had been creeping up on her since the beginning of the month. Determined not to think about it, she dropped two one-dollar bills into the undergrad's hand. "How are you doing?"

"It's all good. Know what I mean? I'm breathing. I got a girl. I'm passing physics. Barely. But D equals diploma. I can do that math, all right. 'Bout the only math I can do."

"Not so good for physics."

"Ah. That's why I'm a psychology major. Tell me, how long does it take you to do one of your puzzles?"

"It depends. My best time is two fifty-seven, but that was a Monday. I haven't managed a Saturday in under seven minutes yet."

"You are one determined woman," Malachi said, pushing two quarters across the glass counter. "I can't finish one in seven hours."

"I have a lot more time on my hands to practice," Claire said. "See you tomorrow."

"Only if you're sitting in the dreaded physics."

"D equals diploma."

"I hear ya, Lady Claire. I'll be back in on Thursday."

She felt calmer with the newspaper against her body, knowing in minutes she'd be home—the puzzle section folded in a tidy rectangle, the side of her hand and pinky bruised with ink as she filled in the small squares. She lived her life in those boxes, the point of her pencil jumping from one to the next, her whole world summed up in concrete solutions.

Safe inside her front hallway, she walked out of her boots, shrugged off her coat, and opened the paper with a shake, the musty newsprint smell fanning her body. She twisted one Ticonderoga pencil in her hair, clutched another in hand, sat at her desk, and set the timer.

She had her own technique, completing the across clues first, until she got stuck, and then she worked the downs.

1. Society newbies. *Four letters.*

DEBS

5. Disreputable. *Five letters.*

SHADY

11. Earthbound birds. *Four letters.*

EMUS

The phone rang, and with the first tone, Claire tried to ignore it. Planned to, moving through two clues before the second tone came, a gentle tweeting from the mobile in her pocket. Daniel's ring. She'd never changed it, and it still surprised her the rare times he called. Six times, maybe, during the two years they'd been divorced, and only once in the past six months. On Caden's birthday.

Hesitating, she flipped the newspaper over.

September 4, 2002.

She managed to dig her phone out and flip it open by the fourth ring.

"Claire, it's Daniel."

"I know."

27

"Yeah, of course. I'm sorry. I just . . . I wasn't sure you'd pick up."

"I thought about it."

"I'm sorry. Maybe I shouldn't have called."

"What do you want, Daniel?"

He swallowed loud enough that she could hear it in the five hundred miles and all the unspoken disappointments between them. "She would have been nine."

She said nothing.

"Are you still there?" he asked.

"I'm here."

"I'm sorry, I know I shouldn't have called, but I wanted to . . . I mean, I needed to remember her with someone who . . . understands."

"Lisa not cutting it today?"

"Claire—"

"You called me."

Daniel sighed. "Lisa is fine. Thank you for asking."

"She's due in February, right?"

"How did you—?"

"Your mother. We still talk, sometimes."

"I wanted to tell you. There just didn't seem like a good way to do it."

"No, I guess not."

"I'm sorry."

She sighed, jabbing the pencil point deep into every O in the newsprint. "You apologize a lot."

"I can't imagine I'll ever be done," he said.

Swallowed again. "Have you been to the, uh, you know—"

"No."

"But you are going?"

Forgetting, she'd discovered, was an art. People spent their lives mastering it, using all manner of techniques—prescriptions, delusions, a fifth of, well, any old cheap liquor from the discount warehouse—but she had a certain knack. Give her eighty clues and a pencil, and the world disappeared. Give her thirty-three minutes and her daughter's birthday . . . "Yes."

"Could you . . . tell them I love them?"

"Yeah, okay," she whispered, and hung up.

Claire swept her fingertip beneath her eye, expecting tears but finding none. She flattened the timer into the desk, number side down, and buried it under the newspaper. She changed her clothes, again. This time into a soft cotton dress—plain gray like her favorite rainy-day sweatshirt—and red flowered clogs, because it didn't seem right to wear jeans or mud boots to the cemetery.

She walked back down the street to the florist and bought three small bouquets of carnations—red and white and yellow, half still closed and wrinkled. She kept her eyes turned down, avoiding the faces of those she passed. Her feet, sweaty with the exertion, slid forward in her shoes, her toes grating against a rough inside seam. She removed her shoes and continued, barefoot, to Saint Victor's, walking beside the gravel path rather than on it, in the sharp broad-blade grass.

She could have found their stones with her eyes closed—all three of them, gray rectangles with glassy fronts, the unpolished sides gritty with tiny peaks and divots. She rubbed her hand over the middle marker—Amelia's—the dry skin on her palm catching on the rough marble. Rubbed until she felt heat, then pain. "Oh, my baby," she said, turning her head up toward the sun. She tried to suck the tears back inside her with a deep sniffle, but they came anyway, and she let them, wiping her cheeks with the cuff of her sleeve.

The cellophane crinkled, and she hugged the carnations to herself as if they were her children, pushing her face into the tops and breathing deep, imagining undertones of cherry ChapStick or Johnson's No More Tears or gingerbread houses in the floral scent.

Unwrapping the bouquets, she placed a bunch on each grave—first Caden, then Amelia, and then Alexis Rose, her baby born into God's arms.

No, I put her there.

She sat, and beneath her dress pulled her knees to her chest and tucked the hem under her feet to keep the cold September soil away from them. "Your dad called," she said. "He couldn't . . . make it, but he wanted me to tell you he loves you." How idiotic, trying to protect them from their parents' divorce. If they could see her and Daniel, they already knew. And if they couldn't? Well, then it didn't matter.

She didn't say anything more but stayed there, finding small words in the larger ones on the headstones, watching ants scurry around the stems of the carnations, exhaling down into her collar, into the tent made by her dress, to stay warm, dozing for a while, head clamped between her knees. Finally, when the white clouds turned pink and flattened along the horizon, she walked home wearing her shoes.

She unwrapped a Healthy Choice ravioli meal and heated it in the microwave. She didn't cook anymore, hadn't turned a burner on in months for anything except to make tea. One plate at the table, one serving in the pot . . . All that depressed her. More reminders of her failures. She ate in front of the television, watching a *Friends* rerun, black plastic tray balanced on her thigh, and when she finished she tossed her trash into the can with the day's paper, stuffing the wad into the too-full bag. Then she found one of her puzzle books on the bookshelf and filled in boxes with letters until she couldn't keep her eyes open anymore.

3

Hanna
May 2002

She wore dresses on Saturdays. Every other day it was jeans or leggings or shorts, but Saturdays were special. It was errand day for her father, and he took her with him. They would walk to the bank and post office, would pick up any odds and ends her mother decided she needed, and then he'd take Hanna for ice cream. Stewart's mint chocolate chip, usually, but on rare occasions she had a chocolate shake instead. Her father always had the shake, with extra malt powder, and he let Hanna have as much as she liked even after she finished her cone.

He'd tried to get her to have something else when the weather turned cold—the convenience store had hot dogs with free meat sauce, and chili, and sometimes chicken noodle soup, which was better than her mother's but she would never say that aloud—but Hanna stuck with the ice cream, despite her father's rhyme. *"Ice cream on a winter's day, will pneumonia bring your way."* Or whooping cough. Or brain freeze. Or warts. He substituted a different ailment every time, and Hanna would giggle and order an extra scoop for only fifty cents more.

She wriggled into her favorite polka-dot play dress without undoing the button at the neck, tugging and twisting until her head finally emerged, her fine blond hair alive with static electricity, clinging to her face and dancing in the air around her. Hanna licked her palms and smoothed her hands over it; and the strands settled as Hanna twisted an elastic around them, gathering it all at the nape of her neck. Though Hanna was eleven, her mother still babied her hair, combed it, blow-dried it, and called it corn silk.

She fumbled around the top drawer of her dresser, the one that kept her underpants and socks and half undershirts she pretended were real bras, and found her favorite pair of cotton tights. A rainbow wrapped around each leg from ankle until just above the knee, six thick colored stripes starting with red and ending with purple, skipping indigo completely. That's what her father told her each time she wore them. *"So much for Roy G. Biv."* Hanna didn't care. She liked stripes even more than polka dots.

"You look like the gypsies dressed you," her mother told her as she twirled into the kitchen. Susan crammed a handful of spinach into the blender on the counter in front of her, shook in some frozen blueberries.

"Nuh-uh," Hanna said, slipping on her fat, squishy beach clogs. Bright green. "Where's Daddy?"

"Here. Here," her father said.

"Well, let's go," Hanna said.

"It's warm out there. Like summer. You may not want your missing-indigo tights."

Hanna opened the back door. It was hot. "Okay, hold on a minute." She peeled off the tights in the downstairs bathroom, leaving them hanging over the shower bar.

Her mother hated that.

"Now I'm ready," Hanna said, pirouetting back into the kitchen. She grabbed her father's hand, tugged it. "Come on."

"So, I'll see you at Peg's for lunch?" Susan asked.

"We'll be there," Henry said, and before Hanna could get the words past her teeth, he lifted her arm above her head and twirled her down the hall and through the front door. "Let's make like a bee and buzz off."

"Dad."

"Sorry, Hanna-Bee. Scientists and funny do not mix."

The sun shone sharp and white, reflecting off most of the outside surfaces—mailboxes, car hoods, the thick, leathery leaves of her mother's azaleas. Hanna squinted, the light overwhelming her. Blue eyes were more sensitive than brown—she knew that, but she despised sunglasses. They pinched behind her ears and slid down her sweaty nose, and worse, they made everything around her look dull and dirty. Her mother tried all the time to get her to wear them, saying she should protect her eyes. Susan's baby blues were bothered by the sun, too, and she walked around with saucer-sized brown lenses dwarfing her thin face whenever she went outdoors.

"Why's she coming?" Hanna clamped her arms across her chest. She loved her mother, but so did Henry, and Hanna got lost in the shuffle of his attention toward Susan. She wanted her time alone with him.

"We want to talk to you. Together."

"You talk to me all the time." She paused and then said, in a puffed, almost teenaged voice, "Together."

"Don't get fresh."

"Sorry," Hanna mumbled. She kicked a stone off the sidewalk; it fell through the grate in the road. She looked through as she walked over it, but of course couldn't see the rock down there. All the grays and blacks blended together.

Divorce.

The word bloomed somewhere in the center of her mind—if she concentrated on it, she could see it, a seedling pushing through black dirt, right in the space behind where her nose and forehead met, that heavy space, the one that filled up first when she had a cold and never completely cleared away. She tried to visually stop the intrusion, but the idea grew larger, like watching time-lapse photography; the green plant-word unfurling toward the light, leaves stretching out, reaching, stem thickening, growing tall.

Don't be stupid. They never fight. Then again, Charlotte Conrad's parents split last fall, and she said she'd never heard them argue, never ever. Not even when they went into the bedroom for privacy; she knew because she listened at the heating vent that connected their room and hers. "They said they still loved each other but just grew apart, whatever that means," Charlotte had told her at the school lunch table as she licked a chocolate pudding blob from a plastic spoon.

Hanna didn't want to ask, but the thought was too large now, and if she didn't open her mouth the pressure would be too much, so she did and asked, "Are you guys getting divorced?"

Her father looked stunned for a moment, then laughed, his deep snuffle that sounded like the noise huge pigs make when pushing their snouts through the mud. "Of course not. What on earth gave you that idea?"

Shrugging, Hanna said, "What else can't you tell me without Mom?"

Henry slung his arm around Hanna's slim shoulder and squeezed her against his side. "It's good news. Trust me. At least I think it is. No one is dying, leaving, or moving. Or turning into a zombie."

Hanna giggled. "Okay. I trust you. But, can we still get ice cream after?"

"Oh, fine," Henry sighed an airy, exaggerated sigh. "If we must."

They walked through their neighborhood's sidewalked streets lined with large painted-lady Victorians and early 1880's brick two-stories and soon entered the area of the city where the houses were smaller, packed tighter together, vehicles parked on the side of the street because most had no driveways. Then the buildings grew into storefronts with three or four floors of apartments above as they approached downtown.

"Bank or post office first?" Henry asked.

"Post office."

Hanna pushed the button on the crosswalk light and waited for the little white man to pop onto the screen and displace the red hand, and when he did, she grabbed her father's hand and they walked through the intersection, Hanna tugging slightly and walking more quickly. She had always been afraid of getting stuck in the middle of the road when the light changed, vehicles zooming past her, honking and yelling for her to move out of the way. She knew that wouldn't happen, had seen drivers wait, both patiently and impatiently, for a straggling pedestrian to get out of the crosswalk. It didn't matter. The fear didn't go away.

The Avery Springs post office was an old stone building with marble floors, high ceilings, and rows of metal mailbox doors. The air was naturally cool inside, cooler still if she flattened herself against the wall, which she did as Henry chatted with the clerk and bought a book of stamps. She sucked in a few gulps of water from the fountain, wiping her mouth with the back of her hand to keep the drops on her chin from landing on the front of her dress, but they did anyway. She wanted ice cream now. Her skin, damp before coming inside, now felt tight with dried sweat. She would have washed her face in the fountain if there had been somewhere to dry it—other than her shoulder.

"Ready?" her father asked.

Hanna nodded and he held open the heavy door for her. She slipped outside, into the heat, and complained, "It's like a million degrees."

"Impossible."

"Dad," she said, rolling her eyes.

"There's a vending machine outside of the bank. Let's hurry there, and I'll get you a Brisk."

"How about a Sprite?"

"If you drink a soda now, you're not having one with lunch."

"I'll take the iced tea, then."

The gorgeous day had brought crowds downtown. People pushed strollers or dragged leashed dogs, couples walked hand in hand, children pressed their faces to the store windows, asking for something displayed inside. College students sat on benches playing their guitars, cases opened and displaying a smattering of change, or they congregated at corners, smoking and kicking hacky sacks to one another. Hanna and her father wove through it all, finally arriving at FSR Bank, in an area of downtown where there were only offices and professional businesses, and on Saturdays the street was nearly empty. He bought her a water, the tiny lighted message declaring Sold Out when she pressed the Lipton Brisk button, and they went inside.

There was a line. Henry stood at the end of it. Hanna fell into a red vinyl chair next to a table with pens and deposit slips stored in the appropriate cubbies. She picked up a stack and flipped the edge with her thumb, like shuffling a deck of cards. *Fffft.* She did it again, and again, until her father cast a sideways glance at her and she stuffed the papers back into their proper spot.

By the time her father arrived at the teller window, there was only one woman waiting for service, and two men with ball caps and sun-glasses sitting in chairs outside one of the banker cubicles. Their glasses were wire-rimmed with brownish-gold lenses, like pilots wore—at least in a couple of movies she'd seen. Her mother would have approved.

Hanna ducked under the red velvet rope and stood next to Henry.

"Hey, Hanna Banana," the teller said. It was Marie, the nice one with the birthmark on her chin and neck. The odd pink skin caught the corner of her lip, too, causing it to swell so it looked as if half her mouth pouted all on its own, even when she smiled. Marie wore a thick, etched wedding band—it covered nearly to her knuckle—and above that another ring of tiny clustered stones Hanna guessed were diamonds, even though they were more gray than clear. She wondered if there was something wrong with Marie's husband, too. Did he have a similar stain across his face? A limp? Three fingers on his left hand? She couldn't imagine some normal person marrying Marie, no matter how nice. Hanna's mother wouldn't have married her father if he'd been imperfect. At least, she didn't think Susan would have.

The gray-haired security guard put his key in the inside lock just as another sunglassed man yanked open the door and, panting, squeezed his obese body through.

"Just made it," the guard said with a laugh and turned the key. "Don't worry, I'll let you out."

The guy wiped his face on his ribbed shirt cuff, his hair covered in a navy blue bandana. "Thanks."

Henry chatted with Marie as Hanna watched the last woman customer leave—apparently so had the two guys in the aviator glasses, so it was only her and her father and the fat, sweaty man in the bandana who stood next to the Please Wait Here for the Next Available Teller sign. He shifted around on his big black Nikes, kept snuffling and clearing his throat. Finally, he said, "Excuse me, sir. I'm in a hurry."

"Oh, sorry, sorry," Henry said, tucking his deposit slip into his back pocket. "I'm here going on and you're waiting. Marie, lovely as ever. See you next week. Sir, she's all yours."

With his hand in that place between her shoulder blades, Henry moved Hanna toward the door, and she watched as Bandana Man stepped up to the teller. His hands shook. He slid an envelope under the glass window. As she opened it, Marie's smile trembled, melted. Her eyes flicked toward the old security guard, who was chatting with Henry about his gout. Hanna didn't know what gout was, but she knew something was wrong.

"Dad, let's go."

"Just a minute, hon."

"Mom's waiting."

"Hanna."

"No, no, don't let me keep you," the guard said. "I'm old. I can blather about my ailments until Christmas, there's so many of them." He fumbled with the key ring at his side, heavy with at least a dozen metal keys, and unhooked it from the clip on his belt. "You folks have a good day now."

"You too," Henry said.

The guard, about to stick one of the fat gold keys in the lock, suddenly looked up and noticed Marie. His hand slowly, silently, tucked the ring into his pocket and floated over to rest on the handle of his gun. "Marie, you all right there?"

At that moment the two sunglassed men burst from the restroom, each holding a pistol. The fat one at the teller also pulled out his gun from the waistband of his gray running pants.

"Okay, listen now," one of the men said. He was tall, bone thin, wore a Boston Red Sox baseball hat, brim rounded into an upside-down U. His voice was thin, too, with a bit of a southern drawl. He pointed his gun at the guard with a steady, unwavering arm. "We don't want anyone hurt, do we? So you, sir, are going to take your hand off your firearm and put them up where I can see them. All slow like. That's right."

The guard did as he said, and the thin man continued, "Now, Marie, how's that money coming? You have those bags filled?"

Marie didn't move, and the fat guy at her window shook and sweated, plump drops of perspiration blistering over his face like burns. Dark, wet circles spread from beneath his armpits. His navy bandana was almost black. "Man, this isn't right. She's buzzed the cops—I know it. We gotta go."

"No, Marie didn't do that, did you? Because you saw what was in that envelope my nervous companion slid across to you just moments ago. Photos of your little girl. Phoebe, isn't it? Photos of her at her school, in front of your home, at

Grandma's house. So, no, Marie didn't do anything at all."

Tears bubbled out of her eyes, catching the corner of her bloated lip, pooling there for several seconds, then spilling over, like spit, down her chin and onto her shiny pink blouse. Her head trembled side to side. "No," she whispered.

"See. I told you. Marie wasn't going to do anything stupid. Marie is going to finish filling those bags. Aren't you, now?"

"Yes." A hoarse, helpless whisper.

"Well, aren't we making some mighty fine progress," the thin man said, chuckling in a way that scared Hanna more than any shouting or gunfire. She cowered against her father, who had his arm tightly around her.

"Now, next order of business. You two fine gentlemen there are going to send that sweet little girl over my way."

The other man in the aviator glasses—short, compactly built, and wearing a cap from a team Hanna didn't recognize—whipped his head toward the thin man, so quickly she expected it to twist off and roll across the floor. If the thin man noticed, he didn't let on. Not even a twitch.

"No," Henry said, his voice plain and firm.

The thin man chuckled again. "Well, I thought you might say that. No daddy wants to turn his baby over to some . . . miscreant. But, I tell you, there's much less chance of you deciding to play hero if she's tucked away right by my side. It won't be for too long. Just until our lovely Marie completes her assigned task."

"No," Henry repeated.

"Now, okay, no need to be snippy. We've all been right friendly to you, and I'd hope for the same courtesy back. I promise nothing will happen to this dear angel if you instruct her to march right over to me. However," the thin man said, "if she's not here in thirty seconds, someone *is* going to get hurt."

"That wasn't in the plan," the fat guy said, his gun aimed toward the floor, arm jiggling. "You said no one gets hurt. You said—"

"Enough," the thin man snapped. "No one will get hurt *if* "—he raised an eyebrow—"people start listening."

The short one looked at his watch. "We need to get out of here."

Hanna had to pee; she felt the familiar warm tingle, the needling pressure. All her fear had settled in her pelvis. She concentrated on willing the urine back up into her bladder, but the more she thought about it, the worse it felt. She hadn't wet herself since first grade, and the idea she might humiliate herself in front of these men horrified her. She clamped her fist between her legs.

"Please," she managed to squeak out.

Her voice must have stirred something in the security guard. As quick as his old arm was able, he moved it from the raised position to his waist, tugging his weapon from the holster.

Boom.

The guard fell, his body jostling Hanna on its trip to the floor. A fine curl of smoke floated from the barrel of the thin man's gun. The fat guy swore. "You killed him."

Hanna felt her father's body tense behind her. She imagined a panther, ready to pounce, knowing he was about to use the moment of distraction to try to . . . What? Save her? Save them both? She wanted to beg him not to; the gun fired again and Henry crumpled on Hanna's feet. She couldn't see his blood, but something warm dripped through the holes in her beach clogs and between her toes.

Fat Guy wretched. "You stupid—"

"Shut your mouth or you're next," Thin Man told him. "Get the money, now." He jerked his head toward Hanna and said to Short One, "Get the girl."

"This isn't—"

"Get her," Thin Man barked.

Without another word, Short One picked up Hanna, her front against his, her chin on his shoulder. She watched her father's unmoving body as she was carried away, each step bouncing her field of vision, and felt a warm wetness spread between her and her captor's body that rapidly turned cold as he shoved her in the back seat of the waiting car.

4

Molly
February 2009

It rained so heavily the air looked jellied, denting around Tobias as he ran across the street, collar of his jacket pulled over his head and one hand holding it there, the other cradling two bottles of soda. Water erupted from the asphalt, flooded it, and then bubbled downhill and over the scraggy slope at island's end to be reclaimed by the sea. Molly watched—always watching, only watching—as the bottles squirted out of his arm, little torpedoes skidding across the pavement. He bent to grab them as he went, a smooth, perfect motion, and tucked them both into the waistband of his jeans before hopping up the steps.

"Hey, you open?" he called, knocking on the glass.

Molly unlocked the door, held it open for him. After he came through, she twisted the dead bolt again. Tobias shook off in the lobby, rain splashing everywhere. "No witch today?"

"I didn't turn the speaker on. And now I have to clean this mess. Mom will be so ticked if she sees it."

"At the water or me?" He grinned, the acne

craters at the corners of his mouth deepening.

"Your choice."

Molly grabbed the dingy string mop from the corner storage closet and swished it over the puddle. "You're not working today?"

"I am. But, you know, it's still early for deliveries. But we just got these flavored seltzers in Friday, and I know how much you like them, so I figured I'd come bother you and bring the drink along. Since I know how much you like them."

"And I know how much you don't."

"Nasty stuff," he said, taking them from his pants, and in a suave move flipped them from caps pointed down to bottoms, a soft-drink slinger, and placed them on the front counter. "I wouldn't open them yet, though."

Molly laughed. "I won't. Believe me."

"Weird weather, huh?" he said. "For February."

"I'm glad I don't have to be out in it."

On Sundays, like today, he came after church. His family made their way to mass early, so they could open for lunch, but he stayed back and, minutes before ten, sprinted down the street to the little Baptist chapel. She watched him go week after week, him leaving about the same time she settled in to watch a local service broadcasted on the public television channel.

During the off-season it didn't matter if she left the door locked until the televised service ended, but even in the busiest summer months Louise gave Molly that hour for worship. They didn't talk about religion, though, not anymore. Her mother wasn't able to peer inside and see what the Lord had done for Molly, the healing hands caressing her bruises, the gentle whispers to her soul. The peace that came over her when she cried out for it. The inexplicable hope, even though she stared at the same walls every day, the corners creeping with dark mold from the leaky roof. She could only regurgitate a handful of verses and the sermon notes she heard on the TV, and Louise came back with the same argument each time, the only one she needed.

"Where was God when your father died? Where was He when you—?"

She stopped there, always. Maybe she thought those words were enough, but Molly knew it was more than that; her mother had never gotten through to the realities lurking on the other side of that unfinished sentence.

"I think we can open these now," Tobias said, twisting the cap off his root beer. He opened the seltzer, and the foam oozed over his fingers with a hiss, carbonated water spraying both of them. "Sorry."

"You do that even when you don't drop it," Molly said. "Good thing there's no sugar in it."

He gave her the bottle. "I can go back and snag us a couple of slices."

"No, don't do that. You're already soaked." The

bubbles danced around her drink, kissing one another, clinging to the walls, swimming to the surface and disappearing before more took their place, much more lively than in Tobias's drink. Her stomach felt like that around him, all gassy and over-carbonated. He stared at her, and she wondered if his almost-black eyes saw something she didn't. She sipped her water; it fizzed up into her nose. "How was church?"

"Great. You should come with me sometime."

"I watch Pastor Gary."

"Not the same."

"I don't know if I could get away."

"On a Sunday? Come on, Moll, no one comes when it's cold and rainy like today."

"Uncle Mick wants the place open every day."

"Which is why you had the door locked."

"I hadn't gotten around to opening yet. I was going to."

"And the Closed sign still turned over."

She reached out and flipped the flimsy black-and-red sign hanging by a suction cup on the glass. "There."

"Your mother could watch the counter for a change. It's just one morning, Molly."

"She's not here. And I—" Molly heard a piddling sound, like a dog urinating on the carpet, looked around until she saw it, a thin stream of stray rainwater dripping onto Elvis's shoulder. "Oh, shoot."

She hugged the King around the middle, tried to slide his feet along the floor to move him, and stumbled backward. Tobias steadied both her and the wax figure, his arm around her waist and partly under her shirt, on her skin. The first time he'd touched her. And it wasn't like the novels, with electric sparks running up her spine, and her head spinning with excitement. No. Her stomach roiled with revulsion, the way a snake slithered, contracting and releasing as it moved up in her chest, jamming against the back of her throat until she had to bring her hands to her mouth to keep from vomiting. Elvis, his weight entirely on Tobias now, shifted forward and fell to the ground. Tobias moved fast, stood him back up, as if the damage would be lessened if the statue lay on the ground less time. But the King's arm fell out of his sleeve, breaking into pieces.

"You let go," Tobias said.

Molly pressed herself against the wall, arms buckled around her shins, teeth digging into her left knee—a safe pain, one she knew from where it came and how to stop, one she controlled with the pressure of her jaw, the angle of her mouth. Tobias's hand had been rough on her, like the edge of the corrugated pizza boxes he brought over. And it hurt, an old pain so deep she never thought she'd feel it again, but there it was, scuttling up from the past. It was as if his fingers were long, thin pins—straight pins, the kind she put through

Shirley's wax hand—sliding in deep and smooth.

"It's broken," she whispered.

"I'm sorry. I couldn't hold it by myself." He looked at her. "Are you okay?"

"Yes."

He held out his hand toward her. "Here. Let me pull you up."

"No," she said, shrinking away, shimmying to her right and pushing herself up the wall so she wouldn't come in contact with him again. "I'm good. I got it."

"Can you fix it?"

"I don't know." She crept around the pieces of the arm, far enough away from Tobias so that, even if he reached out, nothing of him would graze any part of her.

"You're mad at me."

"No. It's okay."

"I'll pay for it. I'll tell Louise I bumped it, knocked it over. Whatever. She hates me anyway."

She kicked at the broken arm pieces. "It's fine. Really. I think there's another arm in the storeroom I can replace it with."

"I'll help."

"No. Please . . . go, Tobias."

"Molly? What's wrong?"

"Nothing." She backed toward the door, until the dead bolt pressed into her spine, cool through her shirt, hard, menacing. "I just need to get this fixed before Mom gets back. She'll be here soon."

"You look weird. White. Scared." He pinched his little beard. His soul patch. "Does she hurt you?"

"What? No. What are you talking about?"

"You're practically a prisoner here, and—"

"I am not."

"I never see you go out. You always have some reason why—"

"Stop it, will you? There's nothing wrong."

"I don't believe you."

"You don't know anything."

He took a step toward her. "Then tell me, Molly."

She spun the bolt and, staying behind the door, pulled it open so she was trapped against the corner of the wall, the glass between her and Tobias. "Go," she said again. It hurt to say it, the word barbed wire in her mouth, because she wanted him to stay, too. She wanted someone to strip off her skin and look beneath, to the tissue and vessel and bone, and see everything that she kept hidden away—to prove she wasn't wax but flesh. She wanted normal.

Tobias looked at her through the glass, knocked gently on it with the second knuckle of his middle finger. His breath condensed, a film between them, and then, with his eyebrows crunched into the bridge of his nose, he shook his head and walked across the street.

She'd lost her only real, living friend.

When they'd first moved to Dorsett Island, there had been no lack of curious neighbors; no one can hide in a town of two hundred year-round residents. People wanted to know what tempted the Fisks to move *from away* to Maine, why Molly schooled at home, and what on earth convinced Louise to work for eccentric Mick Borden. Molly didn't know exactly what stories her mother fed them, though from snatches here and there she gathered they included fleeing some sort of abusive relationship and a desire to make a new start. People nodded and welcomed them, bringing homemade chowders and jams and neighborly wisdom in their loose-jawed accents. And for a precious short while, Molly thought the island could be home.

There were a handful of girls her age—newly turned twelve—and they came around inviting her to do twelve-year-old things. Molly tried to join them, but soon the waves outside became too loud in her ears, the wind too rough against her cheeks, and the wildness of it all forced her back through the doors of the museum, safe inside.

She only left with her mother.

And then not at all.

And the girls scattered to do their twelve-year-old things without her.

Molly didn't meet Tobias until later. She knew of him, of course—one of the reasons the island girls had been so eager to come around and befriend her had to do with the fact she lived across the street from his family's restaurant, he being an object of several of their almost-teenage crushes. Tobias had nothing to do with them, too busy working or hanging out with his own friends to take much notice of some girls a couple of years younger, dressed with too much eye shadow and too small bathing suits, strutting for his attention.

Molly's Bible had started things with Tobias. She wasn't quite certain what those things were, exactly—on his side of it, at least. It had been toward the end of last summer, a frantic weekend of tourists trying to cram in a few more hours of carefree leisure, a few more days of sun-induced forgetfulness. The museum was busy enough that Molly didn't want to duck back into the apartment to make a sandwich, and her mother couldn't get her lunch. Louise had locked herself in the bedroom, suffering from one of her "migraines"— those times when she couldn't cope and ended up chasing a few sleeping pills with spoonfuls of applesauce. It had been some time since Molly believed her mother had real headaches, and some time since Louise thought she was fooling her daughter, but they both still played along.

Molly had been starving, her stomach curling around itself and making noises worthy of the Chamber of Horrors. She decided to order some fried mozzarella sticks from across the street,

54

have them delivered. Tobias showed up not long after that, styrofoam container balanced in one hand. "Hey," he said. "Molly, right?"

She nodded. "How much do I owe you again?"

"Five thirty."

She gave him seven dollars from the cash drawer. As he reached for it, he noticed her Bible open on the counter. "Job, huh? I read that today, too. You working through the one-year schedule?"

"Yeah, the one online."

"Me too. Wicked cool." And he looked at her, the way she'd once looked at a drab, dusty brown owlet moth in her father's tweezers—him holding it up to the desk lamp, her at first finding it startlingly dull compared to the brightly colored butterflies in cases around the room and not any different than the hundreds of stupid moths that bumped around the porch lights every night.

But when Daddy told her this moth had special organs in their ears that could pick up bat sonar, and they flopped to the ground when they heard it so the bats couldn't eat them, the boring bug suddenly became special. And she saw it not as a pesky thing that stupidly chased the hallway lamp when she opened the front door, getting trapped in the house to die there, but as something with value.

Molly had that value now in Tobias's eyes. Before that day, he had waved a few times but was just as likely to ignore her. He'd delivered pizza or subs or calzones to the apartment every four or five months. But now, he said, "Maybe I can come over sometime and we can talk about the read-ings."

"Okay."

"Awesome. Wow. This was really a God thing, wasn't it?"

She had to agree it was. And since that day he had stopped in nearly every day, some excuse or another in his pocket, and Molly told herself that he was, like herself, lonely. He'd told her more than once he didn't fit with his family, that they were content on Dorsett Island and he wasn't, that they wanted him to stay on with the business forever, and he planned to go to medical school, Lord willing. "And," he said, "they're Catholics. So they totally don't get me."

Molly had been so thankful for a friend. And now she'd gone and ruined it.

She rammed the door shut, locked it again, and ran back into the museum, through the first three exhibit rooms, to the workshop door hidden behind a musty black curtain. Every time she moved it aside to get through, her nose filled with dust and she'd sneeze, like now, covering the bottom half of her face with her sleeved arm. She knew instinctively where the pull was to the light; three steps in she swept her arm through the air around her head until the balled chain caught her fingers. She tugged. On burst the light, and she flinched at the body parts strewn over the workbench, dangling on hooks, staring down at her from shelves. She still wasn't used to that initial inhuman sight.

The arms hung against one wall, with the legs, and she chose three she thought could be the right size, or close enough. Back through the curtain, another two sneezes—she always sneezed in twos —and into the lobby, where she undressed Elvis to the waist. Some of the figures were wax through and through, but others, like this one, had wax heads and arms, and occasionally legs, screwed onto mannequin bodies. She chose the replacement arm that seemed about the same length as the King's unbroken one. It was far more muscled, but no one would notice under his clothes. She screwed the appendage into his shoulder socket, wormed his shirt and jacket back on, and fixed his wig. In the closet she grabbed the mop again, and an empty bucket to put under the leak. Wiped up the water. Gathered the broken arm pieces into a plastic bag and hid them in the storage room, in a box labeled Scraps.

She didn't want to go back into the lobby, to sit across the street from the pizzeria, to watch Tobias tote pies and wings to his car and drive away, only to return empty-handed and do it again. She didn't want to sit alone with Elvis, listening to the *ting, ting, tap* of the water in the bottom of the bucket. She didn't want too much space around her. And she didn't want Louise to find her quite yet. So, after jerking off the light so hard she heard the chain bounce up against the bulb, she lay down on the cement floor and wriggled her body beneath one of the workbenches. Her eyes adjusted to the darkness, and when she turned her head to peer out into the room, she saw a patchwork of black and blacker, and all sorts of grays. Her nose nearly touched the bottom shelf of the workbench, and she smelled old wood. The peaks and points of the cement pricked her scalp, and she tensed her neck muscles to press her head harder into the floor.

Footsteps. Her mother was back. Molly heard the curtain flutter open and Louise's breath, but then the footsteps moved away. She stayed awhile longer, eyes closed, hoping to fall asleep, but she knew her mother would come looking for her again, would be nervous if Molly didn't show up soon. She kinked her neck to look down at her wristwatch, pressed on the Indiglo light; she hadn't been there ten minutes. Things felt so much longer in the dark.

Molly rolled out, went back to the lobby. For the third time that day she unlocked the front entrance. The sign in the door still read Open. Tobias got into his car across the street. He looked over but didn't wave or nod, and in that moment Molly felt as if she'd lost her chance at the normal she craved. Tobias had been her conduit to that. Now he wouldn't want anything to do with her.

Before pushing open the apartment door, she brushed away the balls of dust from her clothes. She didn't want her mother asking questions, not that Louise would. So much hiding between them. She knew her mother didn't ask because she didn't want to know—not because she was uninterested, but because it hurt too much.

Molly didn't want to give answers anyway.

She heard pans being pulled from cabinets in the kitchen. "Oh, you're home," she said to her mother, who slid a Pyrex baking dish onto the stovetop and opened another cupboard to get her favorite Better Homes and Gardens cookbook.

"Thanks for taking care of the leak," Louise said, intently flipping through the pages.

"I didn't do much."

"I'll call Mick tomorrow." She turned her head from Molly. Sniffled.

"Mom, is something wrong?"

Louise shook her head and tore a paper towel off the roll hanging on the wall, crumpling it against her eyes, sweeping it beneath her nose. "Sorry, baby. It's Linda Johnson's daughter. She was killed in a car accident this morning."

"The one on Beamson Island, who has the baby?"

"No. The one who moved to Hartford. I was there when Linda got the news. I didn't want to leave, but she said she needed to be alone. Stacey has a little girl, too, but wasn't with the father

59

anymore. Linda doesn't know what's going to happen to Dakota now." Her mother swore. "I can't find the lasagna recipe."

"Here, let me," Molly said. She flipped to the index. "Page 223."

"I just . . . can't imagine losing a child," Louise said. But Molly knew that was a lie. She could imagine it very well. "The least I can do is make a couple of meals."

"Want help?"

Her mother nodded, squeezed her hand, and gave her a box of unopened noodles. "You boil. I'll brown."

5

Claire
September 2002

They met in the basement of the Avery Springs Public Library the first Saturday of every month —the Puzzle Junkies, eight men and four women, mostly over thirty but a couple of eager college kids, too. Claire sat in her regular chair, at the end of the third folding table, where someone had carved three holes, each the diameter of a Bic pen, in the laminate top. *Eyes and nose,* she always thought, the picture made clearer by the fact someone had scratched a wide smiley arc beneath

60

the holes. She liked to stick her pencils in the holes, point side up, while she worked her puzzle.

Heidi burst into the room, travel mug in one hand, canvas bag slung over her forearm, and a pile of papers flapping in her other hand. "Oh my goodness. There was such a line at Kinko's."

"That's what happens when you wait till the last minute," Claire said.

"It's only last minute because of the lines. Had there been no one there, I'd have been here at least ten minutes early."

"When is there ever not a line at Kinko's on Saturday when you need copies made?"

"I like to think of each day as full of new possibilities," Heidi said, dropping her things on the seat. "Here. Your newsletter. Fresh from the copy machine."

Claire took it, folded it in half the long way. "Where did you get that one?" she asked, motioning to Heidi's blazer with black cross-word puzzle squares and numbers printed on the white fabric.

"On eBay," Heidi said. "Got a pair of pants, too, but I thought it would be too much to wear both at the same time."

"Along with your socks, your beret, tote bag, and earrings," Claire said.

"And my coffee." Heidi held up her cup, shook it around eye level, and laughed. "You know me too well."

The club's unofficial president banged his own ceramic crossword-motif mug on the table, and everyone quieted. The members took a few moments to share some of the most difficult clues they'd come across during the month—obscure foreign words and clever puns—and then all settled into solving the same puzzle. Claire finished first, in three minutes and forty-nine seconds. They discussed the American Crossword Puzzle Tournament in February, all trying to convince Claire to enter. She wasn't interested.

Though she did enjoy accumulating crossword-inspired accessories, Heidi didn't care a thing for working puzzles. She came to the meetings because Claire did, never finished even half the clues. And most of the ones she did fill in were wrong.

A good friend.

"Lunch?" Claire asked, packing away her mechanical pencils.

"Of course," Heidi said. "It's my turn to treat, your turn to pick."

"I don't think I paid last month."

"Yes you did," Heidi said, though Claire knew she hadn't.

"Okay, then, how about Scallions?"

Heidi looked at her watch. "I knew you'd say that."

They walked there, Heidi leaving her car in the library parking lot, noting the time she needed to leave the lot to avoid a ticket for breaking the three-hour rule. Last month she'd argued with the meter maid, trying to get out of the ticket the woman had been tearing off the pad just as Heidi ran to her car, pressing the automatic car door opener and throwing her tote bag onto the passenger seat. "But I'm right here," she had said, but the meter maid slapped the citation under her wiper and told her to take it up with city hall.

Claire always walked to the library, only a mile from her home.

She only recently began driving again.

They sat outside, at the tables on the sidewalk, the sun warm on Claire's shoulders, her dark hair, the autumn wind brushing her neck, sending shivers down her back, like a lover's breath. Daniel used to kiss her neck, little light puffs of lip from her earlobe down and around to her jugular notch. His thumb had fit in the hollow perfectly, resting there as he traced her collar-bone between his first two fingers.

She missed him.

No, maybe not him, though she'd loved him completely once. She missed more the feelings that came with being married—the security, the acceptance by those around her. Her married friends didn't know what to do with her now—she wasn't invited to the barbecues or game nights anymore. Oh, they tried, asking her to a couple of parties right after Daniel left, but it was awkward, tense, no one knowing what to say or how to say it. There was no place for a husbandless wife—or a childless mother—in the world Claire had once lived in, that of manicured lawns and church breakfasts and family vacations in Florida.

The waitress came. Heidi looked at her watch again. Claire ordered a grilled chicken salad, no onions, her friend a BLT with coleslaw on the side.

"Meghan is coming in a couple of weeks. With Landon," Heidi told her.

"You must be thrilled."

"I am. They're staying a week. I wish it were longer. I wish she'd just stay put here." Heidi stirred Sweet'N Low into her tea. "She's pregnant again."

Claire paused, unable to read her friend. "And?"

"It's not Travis's baby."

"I'm sorry."

"That girl . . . I don't know where we went wrong."

Unlike Heidi's younger daughter, Meghan had wandered through Canaan, was still wandering. She hit her adolescent years as her father was diagnosed with colorectal cancer, lived through his long battle with multiple relapses and rounds of chemo and an eventual colostomy bag, which tied him—and Heidi, for the most part—to the house; he was too embarrassed by the smell to go out in public.

Greg was also ashamed of the pain, how it drove him to the floor, sobbing. He'd lie in front of their bedroom door so Heidi couldn't come in and see him like that, his pajama bottoms soaked in urine, his faith twisted in a mist of agony and morphine. Heidi would sit outside the door, wet with her own tears, listening to her beloved cursing God with one breath, begging Him for relief with the next.

Meghan saw it all, too. Her sister, Jennifer, had been young enough that she floated around in her seven-year-old fog of Barbie dolls and Brownie bake sales, and hadn't quite understood all that went on. It was Meghan, though, who missed having her parents' attention—the guidance and instruction desperately needed by teenagers—and like the proverbial prodigal, she looked for it elsewhere. Her life had been layered with different men and jobs and ideas of what would bring happiness. None of it lasted very long, though Heidi had hoped Meghan and Travis would at least marry and settle down.

A man across the sedate downtown street waved; Claire looked behind her, but no one else occupied the tables outside the café. Heidi raised her hand and waved back, and the man crossed toward them.

"I hope you know him," Claire said with a little laugh.

"I do," Heidi said.

"Is there something you're not telling me?"

"Well . . ."

"Heidi! You're seeing someone and you never said anything?"

"Not exactly," Heidi said, breaking eye contact, and she stood to give the man a quick hug. "Andrew, hi."

"I'm late, I know," he said. "My eleven thirty ran over."

"Oh, that's not a problem," Heidi said. She didn't look at Claire. "Sit, sit. Are you hungry? Let me get the waitress."

Andrew held out his hand. "You must be Claire. Heidi has told me so much about you." He winced. "Sorry. That sounds . . ."

"Lame?" Claire said.

"Yes, absolutely. Lame it is."

He sat, and Claire determined not to look at him, or at Heidi. She fought with her croutons, stabbing them with her fork until they broke and then trying to scoop the crumbs up without using her fingers.

How could she do this to me?

Heidi forced conversation with Andrew, questioned him about his work (he was an architect at a firm specializing in not-for-profit building projects), his church duties (a deacon of more than ten years), and his son (some J name, still a preschooler)—each question constructed to give Claire all the basic dating

66

profile information. *This is a good one, this one has it together. You need someone like this.*

She finished the croutons and started on the grape tomatoes, then the cucumbers, which she sliced in half because somehow a round of cucumber bulging in her cheek seemed unattractive and piggy, even as she told herself she was in no way interested in impressing this man.

As Claire scraped the last bit of lettuce from her plate, she watched Andrew's feet through the mesh top of the café table, one brown loafer bent against the green metal leg, the other jiggled on the sidewalk, tassel wagging, a leather dog's tail. The toes of the shoes were scuffed nearly white. The shoes of a widower.

Heidi pushed her chair back, said, "I'm going to pay," and when Andrew stood and took out his wallet, she added, "No, my treat. I mean it." So he sat again, tearing off the white strip wrapped around an extra napkin and rolling it into a thin paper cigarette.

"Heidi didn't tell you she invited me," he said.

"No." Claire sipped her water, catching a wafer of ice in her mouth. She swallowed it whole; it slipped down her throat, the cold sensation melting away, disappearing into her stomach but leaving a slowly fading trail.

Andrew creased the paper in the center, creating a V, opened and closed it between his thumb and forefinger like a duck's beak. "I'm really sorry. I had no idea she was going to spring me on you like this. And then leave you alone with me."

Claire managed a small smile, finally looked up. "That's Heidi."

"Well, I'm sorry." He flicked the paper on his saucer, hesitated. "This is going to seem absolutely ridiculous and rude, given the last twenty minutes, but can I give you my card?"

"I don't understand."

"Just a thought."

"I'm not going to call you," Claire said.

"I know. And I won't hold my breath or anything. I'd just like knowing you have my number, in case you change your mind."

"I won't."

Andrew smiled. "I don't expect you will, Claire."

Her name curled off his tongue, and she liked it, a man saying her name. When was the last time she'd felt wanted? It had been so long.

There was a neediness that came from being abandoned by a husband, a desire to know that it wasn't her, but him. That she wasn't defective or unlovable. Yes, she knew Christ should be enough, but sometimes in a cold bed, He wasn't. She'd take the card as a reminder. *Someone else could want me.* "If you feel the need to give it to me, you can, I suppose. I'll make every attempt not to lose it."

Now he laughed. "I don't expect you'll do that, either."

He tucked the card next to his coffee cup. "Tell Heidi she owes me," he said, "and you, too, I bet," and walked with extra-long strides across the painted pedestrian crossing without looking back. Heidi came out of the café and said, "Don't hate me."

"How could you do that?"

"I know, I know. I just figured you wouldn't agree if I asked."

"Of course I wouldn't have agreed," Claire said.

"He's nice."

"So what?"

"You need someone nice. It's time."

"I think I'll know when it's time, thank you very much."

"Will you?" Heidi spun her teacup. "You're lonely."

"No I'm not."

"Yes. Lonely and alone."

Claire bit the inside of her cheek. "Speak for yourself. I don't see you out there."

"I was married to the love of my life. There's no one else for me."

"I could say the same for myself."

"If he was the love of your life," Heidi said, "he wouldn't have left."

"Don't do that," Claire said. "It wasn't Daniel's fault."

"It wasn't yours."

Heidi had sought out Claire after the accident. They'd had a passing acquaintance before—from an occasional Bible study, a small group, a fellowship dinner—but hadn't known each other. Heidi was nearly fifteen years older, with two grown kids; Claire was busy with homeschooling and running her children to piano lessons and gymnastic classes. But when Heidi came to her at the funeral, Claire recognized grief on her—the particular grief of death, a watermark seen only when held up to the light in just the right way, and only those who had gone through the same knew where to look. So when the sea of casseroles and prayers and encouragement cards retreated in the low tide, leaving all the debris of Claire's life damp and exposed in the sand, Heidi stayed.

She understood, having lost her husband of thirty-three years, never expecting Claire to just *snap out of it* and *get on with it* and *be thankful they're with the Lord.* She'd lived the paradox of believing in something bigger, something better, something beyond—alongside the smallness of her own human sight, a tunnel vision straight through to the ache of longing that didn't go away because a certain amount of acceptable time had passed.

Would enough time ever pass?

"I'm not ready," she said.

"I'm sorry. Maybe I shouldn't have interfered. But I worry about you. You sit home with your pencils and puzzles, beating yourself up over something you can't do anything about."

"It wasn't *something*. I killed my children."

"They died in a car accident. An accident, Claire."

"You don't understand."

"No, I don't," Heidi said. "But I don't think you do, either."

Claire pushed her chair back, stood. "You don't need a ticket today," she said, slinging her tote bag on her shoulder, walking toward home. Heidi didn't follow, or at least not closely enough for Claire to notice; she didn't turn around.

6

Hanna
May 2002

Thin Man kept her in a cage, six sides of square black grids. "A safe place," he'd told her. A kennel for a dog; for a large one, like a Labrador. He'd given her a cushion to sleep on, and a waffley baby's blanket, yellow with a washed-out Cookie Monster appliquéd in one corner. She could fit under it if she rolled into her chest and squeezed her chin between her knees. She wanted to sleep like that anyway, so she could reach her feet and rub them, as her mother used to when she was little, singing the song she made up—*"Hanna's feet. Hanna's feet. I love to rub Hanna's feet"*—tickling and pinching and patting and kissing her way up Hanna's entire body, ending with a bear hug and a pillow fluff before bed.

Sometimes singing the song was the only way she could remember her own name, after days of being called little girl by Thin Man. She didn't know how many days had passed. Two. Three. Ten. She had tried to keep track of how many times she'd gone to sleep but found herself constantly dozing on and off. They gave her something to make her drowsy—at least she thought they did—a clear plastic cup of fizzy liquid with a thick pink layer at the bottom.

Things kept disappearing on her—little pieces of her memory, coherent thoughts, things that made her more a girl and less an animal. She thought of the drawing hanging in her father's office, the evolutionary stages of man, from prehistoric to modern, each figure getting less hunched and less hairy. She was going backward, each day curling more tightly into herself, looking more like a pill bug, a spiral conch, an infant.

The only thing still clear in her memory was her father. Not the living, smiling, loving one. The dead one, facedown in a lake of blood. She clawed her eyes and yanked her hair and rocked against the wall of the cage. Nothing helped. That image stayed.

After they had taken her from the bank, the three men drove for some time, Thin Man and Fat Guy in the front seat of the car, Short One in the back with her. He'd covered her with a rough blanket that smelled like dog, and she breathed short, prickly hairs up her nose. Fat Guy kept talking, his voice sailing back to her in uneven rumbles. The other two remained silent. Eventually the car slowed and the interior became shadowy.

Thin Man turned off the engine. "Wrap her up," he said.

Short One did as he was told, winding Hanna's flimsy body in the blanket with only her eyes and mouth showing. He hefted her over his shoulder and maneuvered both of them from the car without hitting her head on the doorframe. Fat Guy was still talking, and Thin Man said, "If you open your mouth on the way to the apartment, I'll shoot you. You've seen I have no problem doing so."

Fat Guy rolled his lips over his teeth and bit down so he looked mouthless, only a slit in the skin between his chin and nose. The men climbed stairs, Thin Man ahead, Fat Guy puffing somewhere behind, and Short One's shoulder digging into Hanna's stomach. Her bladder released again.

Thin Man unlocked a door, and they all went inside. Short One put Hanna on the carpeted floor. "Now what?"

"She stinks," Fat Guy said, swore under his breath.

"I think the little girl here needs a bath," Thin Man said. "I'm more than happy to do so."

"I'll do it," Short One said.

"Always the gentleman," Thin Man said with a chuckle.

Short One unrolled Hanna and lifted her again, this time in a cradle carry, one arm under the back of her knees, the other against her back. Hanna offered no resistance or help, but as he took her down the hallway, her head fell against his chest. She felt his chest muscle twitching against her cheek, had felt the same thing when her father carried her, and she cried without sound, only tears and mucus and grief.

"Don't cry," Short One said after he closed and locked the bathroom door. "You'll get home. I promise."

He sat her on the toilet, undressed her, balling her soiled clothes in the sink. Ran water from the tub spout over his wrist before plugging the drain and squirting in some shampoo. "There," he said when the tub was half filled and he shut off the water. She didn't move, stayed slumped over, one thin arm across her chest, hand hugging her shoulder, the other arm tight against her lap. Legs clamped together. He hesitated and then took a towel from the hook behind the door and covered the front of her before lifting her under the armpits and easing her into the soapy, too-hot water.

He left the towel over her.

With a washcloth he cleaned her back in sloppy circular motions. She rested her chest against her folded knees. He didn't bother washing her hair, but the ends skimmed the water anyway, and when he pulled her from the bath she felt the sticky tendrils adhere to her skin. This time she obliged Short One by bearing weight on her legs as he set her down on a fuzzy pink bath mat, the kind she hated because it left lint between her toes. He eased a dry towel around her and tugged the bottom of the soaked one so she let go and it puddled at her feet. The damp weight reminded her of her father's body.

Looking around, Short One muttered under his breath. Then he stripped off his own gray Corona T-shirt and dressed her in it. It hung to her knees. He turned around in the small bathroom, again, as if looking for escape, picked up Hanna's underpants—pink with white daisies—rinsed them and wrung them out in his fist. He opened the drawers in the vanity, looked under the sink and found a hair dryer. It whirred to life when he slid his thumb over the switch and he blew the hot air over her panties.

"Here," he said, trying to hand them to her.

She didn't take them.

He hesitated again, knelt in front of her. Encircling one ankle, he raised her foot and slipped the underwear over her toes. He did the same with the other side and shimmied the still-damp cloth up her still-damp legs and, turning his head, snapped the elastic waist over her rump. When it became clear she wasn't moving on her own, he picked her up again and carried her back to the living room.

"Well, now, you've been gone quite a while," Thin Man said. "Did you two have a lovely time?"

"Shut up," Short One snapped. He set her in an overstuffed armchair and covered her with the crochet throw from the back of the seat.

"Sensitive, are we?"

"There's something really wrong with her. She's like, catatonic or something."

Thin Man stroked his hairless chin. "That seems about right, considering she's just watched her father gunned down in cold blood."

"No thanks to you," Short One said.

"And you weren't there, were you?"

Fat Guy chomped a cookie, chocolate dandruff fluttering from his lips. "He didn't shoot no one. What you have to go killing them for?" He swore. "We're in deep now."

"We have the money, correct? If I'm not mistaken, neither of you had much of an issue with the plan when you thought it would be solving your financial problems. And it did, did it not?"

"No one was supposed to get killed," Fat Guy

said. He crammed another Oreo into his mouth. The open package, almost empty, teetered on the arm of the couch.

"I believe you need to be going to work now. No suspicious deviation from routine, remember?" Thin Man said.

"Fine. I'm going."

He lumbered out the door, breathing gurgly, shallow breaths. Hanna listened to his heavy steps becoming softer and softer until she could only imagine the sound in her head, thumping to each heartbeat. That was all she heard until Short One finally said, "We need to do something with her."

"Perhaps I'll keep this little girl for a while."

"Don't even."

"Are you planning to play hero now?"

"I'll turn all of us in before I let you touch her."

"No you won't."

Short One didn't answer.

"Ah, such bravado. But don't despair. I have someone who'll take her off our hands, for a nice price. He wants this little girl . . . unsoiled. What a shame."

"What's wrong with just dropping her on a corner and letting someone find her?"

"Oh, my boy. You really are a genius, really. She's seen us." Thin Man twisted the cap off one of the green beer bottles on the end table, took a sip. "You want to be identified in a lineup?"

"She's wrecked."

"For how long? Modern psychiatry can do wonders. Look at me." He laughed, took another swig. "If you don't want another body on our hands, this is how we deal with it."

Short One pointed toward the collection of bottles. Thin Man picked up an unopened one and lobbed it to him. Short One caught it one-handed, covered the bottle cap with the hem of his shorts before unscrewing it. He swallowed most of the liquid without a break, wiped his mouth on his bare forearm. "You didn't have to take her at all."

Thin Man grinned. "But where would the fun have been in that?" He left his bottle. "You're here tonight, then."

"Do I have a choice?"

"Lock her in the dog cage."

"You're not serious?"

"We don't want her snapping out of it and running off while you're asleep. I'd say gag her, but one more kid howling in this dump isn't going to be noticed. I have difficulty believing a tenured professor would live in a place like this, I don't care how 'down' he wants to be with the 'common folk,' " Thin Man said, making air quotes with his fingers.

"When's he back?"

"August, before classes begin. At least Bogus was good for something. He'll be by again in the morning to watch her."

"How early? I have to be to work by eight."

"Well, you'll know when he gets here. And I mean it—lock her up."

Thin Man approached Hanna, stroked her cheek softly. "She really is a beauty." Holding up his hands as Short One tensed, he said, "I know, I know. I'm going. Be good, little girl."

Short One left her on the chair while he watched TV and finished the remaining Oreos. He heated a frozen pizza and drank more beer, fighting to keep his eyes off her, but finally put her in the kennel, trying to do so gently but banging his head on the top and eventually giving her a shove, closing the door against her legs and clicking the padlock into place. "I'm so sorry," he had said, words slurred.

And so the days went, Fat Guy during the day-time, with the television or video games blaring, ignoring Hanna except to give her the sleeping potion or to push in a bowl of Cocoa Puffs he served her in a dish inscribed *Fluffy*. He found that hilarious, as the cereal looked like dog food, and he gave her water or milk in the matching bowl. She used her hand as a cup and brought the warm liquid to her mouth only when Fat Guy went to the toilet or passed out on the sofa. In the evenings and overnight it was Short One, and he'd stopped looking at her after closing her in the cage that first night.

Thin Man stopped by a few times, but mostly

he was only there in her dreams. He called her little girl, and she could feel his finger on her cheek, cold and slimy like a leech.

This morning Fat One came in and switched on the television; he pressed the channel button, and Hanna saw a flash, a burst of sound as he searched for his favorites. He breathed heavier than usual, rubbed his arm. Swore. "I don't need this today," he said.

He hobbled into the kitchenette, leaving Hanna to watch a commercial for Time Life praise music, and then another for an Austrian crystal cross. "But wait, there's more. Call in the next fifteen minutes and you'll get two beautiful crosses for the price of one. Just pay shipping and handling. One to keep, one for a friend." And then some man in a suit stood in front of a shimmering wall of water and pointed to the sky. "Have you asked for Him to help you? If you don't ask, why are you surprised you don't receive? 'Ask and it shall be given to you.' Amen. So, right now, go ahead. Say, 'Help me, Gee—' "

Fat Guy flipped the channel. "Stupid nonsense." He rubbed his forehead. "It's hot in here. Stupid windows painted shut. Stupid uncle who doesn't have air-conditioning."

On the TV a man jumped up and down when the announcer called his name. "Come on downnnnn!" He wanted to win a new refrigerator. Hanna wanted to go home.

Help me, Gee. Help me. Please, please help me, Gee.

Fat Guy bent toward her, bowl of cereal shaking in his hand. He set it on top of the kennel, fumbled with the keys on a red string around his neck. Found the right one. After three attempts he managed to slip the little gold key into the padlock. The lock sprung open. He panted, stood, dropping the keys back into his shirt. "I feel . . ." He took two steps away from the kennel, dropped onto his knees, and fell backward.

And Hanna waited. *The Price Is Right* went off and on came *As the World Turns*. Fat Guy didn't move. Then *Guiding Light*. Hanna's stomach growled. Fat Guy still didn't move.

She stuck her fingers through the metal squares and maneuvered the lock off the hasp, pushed the latch aside, and nudged the door with her shoulder. It swung open. She crawled out, carpet beneath her fingers, sticky, matted with footprints and the milk she'd spilled yesterday. Her hair fell over Fat Guy's face. The man still didn't move. Hanna poked him in the neck.

Nothing.

She knelt, rubbing her thumbs over her fingers, squeezing her hands opened and closed. And then, in one quick motion, she reached down Fat Guy's shirt, grabbing the key hanging on the red string between the soft mounds on his chest, tugging it over his frizzy head.

Hanna touched Fat Guy's blue-gray lips, knowing deep down he was dead, in that same way she knew it was because of her words to Gee. She thought she should cry but didn't. Her tears had dried up. If she got home, her mother would be happy; she never liked Hanna crying, always told her to stop. Her daddy hadn't minded, though. When he was alive.

She stood too fast and grabbed the arm of the upholstered chair until the clouds stopped swirling in her eyes. Then, with shaky fingers, she slid the key into the door's inside lock, metal scraping against metal, and stood there staring at the silver key protruding from the gold oval, her toes curling in the carpet. She felt Fat Guy mounded up behind her, the stillness echoing in her ears. Her pulse bubbled behind her knees, in the crooks of her elbows. She turned the metal stub—*click*—her entire body flinching with the sound, afraid of finding Thin Man on the other side of the door. With only her fingertips she turned the knob and brought it toward her until she thought she could fit through.

Help me, Gee.

It had worked before.

She slipped her thin body between the door and jamb, not touching either of them, stepping into a short hallway. A banister, dark wood slick and curving like a serpent, twisted down a flight of stairs. She touched the cool, lacquered wood, following it down the bare-board stairs, following it around the corner into another hall with one door, a big brass C on it. She scurried down another flight of stairs, around another corner, another door, more steps, until she reached the entranceway, tiled with tiny white octagons and uneven gray grout. The door was glass in front of her. She saw the street, rippled cars parked along it, distorted in the speckled glass. And then she opened the door and ran.

Her naked toes dragged over the sidewalk, her hair bounced like a Slinky around her shoulders. She could not run far, her ankles hurting and her lungs aching and her toes cold. After two blocks, she had to walk. She looked at every man who passed her, stealing a glance behind her if she heard approaching footsteps, searching for Thin Man or Short One, but didn't see either of them.

What would happen when they found her gone?

As the sky darkened, not yet with night but with long, thin cloud fingers, the people around her darkened, too. First to creamy caramel and throwing words like darts around her. Spanish words; she recognized some from *Dora the Explorer*.

"*Mira, mira. Mirela. ¿Cuál es su problema?*"

Mira. Look. They were looking at her, walking the streets with her cornflower hair and Corona T-shirt. No pants. She crossed her arms to keep the cooling air from dipping down her shirt, kneaded her shoulders and elbows as she stepped through some invisible barrier back into an English-speaking part of the city, where people were darker still, where she heard them talking about her—"What's wrong with her? Where did she come from? Man, she's whack."

A woman, solid midnight, came off her stoop and stopped Hanna. "Dear, sweet Lord, girl. What happen to you?" She had an accent, like the people in the movie about the bobsledders from the tropical island.

Hanna opened her mouth, waiting for the words in her head to drop into the cavern at the back of her throat and fill it, but nothing came.

"We get you help," the night-woman said, her teeth and eyes bright. "Come into my home. We get you clothes, and help."

Hanna stared up toward the door, where other children and people sat and stared back. Someone touched her from behind, and she spun, waited for her hair to fall before she saw a huge man with a bowed-out belly. His hands were on her, and the fight inside her she had choked back into some deep place right after Henry had been shot came roaring up, and she clawed at the stranger, even as he said, "Calm down, little girl. We want to help you."

Little girl. He called me little girl.

She went deaf to him after that, and when his arm clamped across her breastbone, she lowered her chin and bit him as hard as she could, until she tasted blood on her tongue and he let go. Then she ran again, wiping her mouth as she ducked between people, turning one corner, then another, crossing the street and dodging a car, before she tired again. She pressed herself into a narrow alley to catch her breath.

She looked down at her feet, black with the day, and shivered. Tired, her stomach gurgling as it shrunk in hunger, she tiptoed through the alley, avoiding broken glass and beer cans and stray papers and potato chip bags, and emerged from the other side, onto a quiet street with building lights glowing in the fading day.

She needed to find a place to rest, a warm place. A small place. She felt dizzy in the hugeness of the outside. The tall brownstones she passed grew up from underground, having basement doors in stairwells below street level and iron fences around them so people wouldn't fall in. At least, that was what she thought they were for. It didn't matter; the twisted black iron looked like her cage, and that soothed her somewhat.

She snuck down into one of the stairwells, careful to crouch down, even though she was shorter than the windowless door's peephole, and squeezed in between two gray trash cans. But the cold ground hurt to sit on and her teeth chattered and she could see her breath, feel her frozen nose against her not-so-frozen knee. She stood, planning to find somewhere warmer to sleep. The one garbage can was full, a white bag pushing open the hinged lid. Hanna opened the other can; one bag of trash filled the bottom. There was plenty of room for her.

Holding on to the metal railing, she climbed the wall and swung her legs into the can. She dropped down, something sharp in the bag poking into the sole of her foot, and then she folded into the darkness, pulling the lid closed. It was warm, but with the smell of rot and fish and soiled diapers, she couldn't breathe. She pressed her nose to a tiny hole in the side, the size of a nostril but perfectly round, and took in thin breaths of outside air.

She dozed, woke, shifted, slept hard, woke, and dozed again. Light flooded in, and Hanna slapped her hand over her eyes, heard someone say, "Oh," heard the lid clatter to the cement. She squinted, tilted her head up but saw only shadows between her eyelids. "Are you okay? Are you hurt?" And then hands were on her, and she slapped them away; her flailing and kicking knocked the can over.

She crawled out, crashing into the jean-clad legs in front of her. A woman fell down next to Hanna as she tried to scramble by, grabbed her. "Shh. It's okay. Honey, it's going to be okay. Calm down." But Hanna didn't stop wriggling, jerked her head back into something hard, and the woman cried out but didn't let go. And then Hanna was half lifted, half dragged through the basement door.

"Trey, hurry," the woman called as the door closed, and Hanna fought harder, trapped again inside an apartment. Something dripped on her neck. "Help. Trey, come quick."

"Joanna, what—? You're bleeding," the man said, towel around his waist, water slipping down his bald, brown head.

"My nose. It's nothing. Just call 9-1-1."

The man dialed the phone and disappeared with it down a hallway. He returned dressed. "They're coming. Let me take her."

"No. I don't want to let her go. Get her that blanket," the woman said.

"It's her, isn't it?" the man said, covering her with a fringed throw from the back of the rocking chair.

The woman smoothed it over Hanna, rocking her. "I think so."

7

Molly
February 2009

When Tobias finally came back, it was with a girl. A petite, pretty girl with shaggy amber hair she wore tied back in a wide olive ribbon, the sides falling out and around her face. She wore a scarf of wild colors around her neck, looped twice, the tasseled ends hanging mid-thigh.

She matches him, Molly thought. They looked like they belonged together.

"Toby, this place is fantastic," the girl said, her Down-Easter accent much stronger than his, more like the old-time Mainers. Like Mick's. "Just like you told me."

"Molly," Tobias said, "this is Kristina."

"Hey," Kristina said. "Wow, this place is like something out of a movie. I love it."

"It's nice to meet you," Molly said, her tongue dry as Velcro.

"Oh, you too. Hey, you have a brochure or something?"

"Uh, yeah. Sure. Of course. I'm sorry." Molly handed her a pamphlet from the counter. Tobias gave her a twenty and a ten.

"And a map," he said.

"Right, of course. Sorry."

"Don't keep apologizing," he said.

Kristina grabbed a couple of postcards from the tall revolving rack near the door. "I have to have these, too. Toby says you're homeschooled?"

"Yeah." Molly slid the cards into a thin paper bag.

"That's fascinating. You seem normal, but, boy, no prom? No other kids? No boys to look at all day? And you're okay with all that?"

"I guess. I never really thought about it."

"Who teaches you?"

"It's an online school. Sometimes there are videos to watch. Mostly it's just reading and writing papers. And taking tests."

"Fascinating."

"Kristina's a psych major. Everything's fascinating to her," Tobias said.

The girl giggled, on cue, wrapping both her arms around Tobias's one, which he had planted in his pocket, his elbow bent and winged out like a chicken. "Ayuh. Got that right. Come on, let's get through. I have E.C.D. at two."

They stepped through the black curtain together, and Molly stared hard at the words she'd written in her history notebook, numbered and bulleted with lopsided asterisks and thick dark arrows pointing to key ideas. She would only remember it long enough to take the test, and then it would be gone, disintegrating into the mound of other things she needed to know only for a grade, and it would be on to the next handful of useless information. She didn't see any use for history.

"Those who cannot remember the past are condemned to repeat it." The George Santayana quote was printed in the front of her textbook, the one Louise had bought used online. But Molly thought both parts of the quote didn't matter. People held on to their pasts all the time, and it didn't make the future any different. And people forgot all the time, or tried to, and what did it

change? Nothing. The *repeat* part would always exist. There was nothing new under the sun.

Her rib cage felt as if someone had wound a rubber band around it, over and over and over, so tight that when she tried to take a deep breath, it hurt. Tobias was back in the museum with that perky girl. He was in college and going places, cool and charismatic, the kind of guy who drew people to him. Molly wasn't perky. She wasn't much more than the mop she cleaned the lobby floor with, a pole of wood and dull cotton tresses.

She wanted him to notice her.

Silly, silly.

They came through the other side, laughing about something, and Molly dove into her work, scribbling sentences about Nixon and Watergate. About betrayal.

"That was fascinating. Thanks. To think I've lived fifty miles from this place and have never been here," Kristina said.

"No problem," Tobias told her. "Will it work for you?"

"Absolutely."

"Let me walk you to your car. I know you have to get going."

"Such a sweetie. Molly, nice meeting you."

Molly swallowed. "Yeah, you too."

Tobias opened the door, the recorded cackle mocking Molly. *Hahahahahahaha. You don't get him. You don't get anyone. You're stuck here forever.* She was. She knew it. She'd be thirty years old, selling admissions and living with Louise, and she didn't think her mother would mind at all.

She watched them through the window, hugging, Tobias opening the car door for Kristina. Kristina picking something out of his hair. She kissed him on the cheek, and he closed her into the yellow VW Beetle. A new model, not the original. Kristina looked like a VW girl, all bright and tiny and full of character. The kind of girl Tobias would want.

Stop it, Molly. Stop it.

She wasn't one to pout. She didn't often sit and think about things she didn't have, never saw the point of it. God gave what He wanted, and He wanted her in a run-down wax museum, alone. There was a reason. She didn't understand it, but she trusted it. Had to.

Tobias jogged back across the street, opened the door.

Hahahahahahahaha.

"Hey, Moll?"

"Yeah?"

"Got a minute?'

"I guess." She closed her notebook inside the history text, keeping her place.

"About the other day . . ."

"Sorry I flipped out on you."

91

"No, don't. It's nothing about that. I mean . . . Molly . . . don't you even get it?"

"What?"

"I like you."

Everything inside her stilled. "I like you, too."

"No, Molly. I. Like. You. Like, like you. Like . . ." He took a breath. "Like, really like you."

She'd been wanting to hear those words, imagining him saying something like that for the past six months—since the mozzarella sticks and the one-year Bible schedule. But with the real words in front of her, it sounded ridiculous. She shook her head, snorted. "No you don't."

"Yes I do."

"No."

"Yes."

She laughed again. "No."

"Molly, stop telling me what I feel. You're great. Pretty, of course. Smart, funny, kind. Always have something interesting to tell me about bugs. The real kind, not the lobster kind. Always think what I say is important. You see me. You . . . Molly, why do you think I come here every day with my meager offerings of seltzer water and leftover garlic knots? I've wanted you to notice me." He rubbed at the hair beneath his lip with his middle finger. "Will you notice me now?"

Molly shifted on the stool. She tugged at the collar of her shirt, a flushed feeling coming over her. The compliments. She couldn't handle them. They made her feel as if some huge, hot spotlight had settled right over her head, close enough to burn her scalp, lighting up every pore and imperfection Tobias hadn't seen before, but would see—if he spent any amount of time with her. She couldn't let him close. If she did, he'd know she was none of the things he said about her— not smart nor funny nor kind nor interesting, nor worth three cents on the dollar. She was empty.

"Tobias, stop."

"No. I had to put it out there. It's been driving me crazy not knowing if you were ignoring me or if you really didn't see. But you don't see, do you? You don't see how wonderful you really are."

"I'm not."

"Let me be the judge."

"No."

"Why, Molly? What's inside there that you don't want anyone to know?"

"Nothing." She shifted on the stool. "What about Kristina?"

"She's a family friend. We go to OSCC together. I mean, we ran around in our diapers together. She wanted to check out the museum for a paper she's writing." He stopped. "You were jealous."

"Tobias—"

"I admit it. I was hoping for that."

Molly ran her pencil along the metal notebook spiral. *Zip, zip.* "I can't be what you want."

"How do you know what I want?"

"Whatever it is, I can't be it."

"I don't want you to *be* anything. I want to spend time with you. I want to get to know you better. I want to take you to the movies, to dinner, to church. I want to walk on the beach with you. I want to talk. That's all. I want a chance."

"I can't."

He sighed. "Louise?"

She nodded. How much easier that was than the truth, letting people believe their own truth. It required no floundering for a convincing story.

"Then I'll take what I can get." He bowed low, holding out his open hand. "M'lady, may I escort you through the museum?"

"You just went through."

"Not with you."

"Someone might—"

"No one's coming in today." He twisted the dead bolt and flipped the Open sign to Closed. "I'll pay again."

"Tobias."

"I'm not leaving until you say yes. Or Louise kicks my butt out of here. Whichever comes first."

Molly sighed. "Fine."

He held the curtain open for her, and she slipped through, him following close enough she smelled him. Not cologne. Laundry soap. And his hat—sweaty, unwashed wool. A gray smell, sort of dark, earthy, like decomposing logs in the woods. She remembered that smell from the times her father took her exploring when they went camping, turning over dead stumps or peeling the bark off to find the insects there—beetles and centipedes and ants and grubs. He had been an entomologist at the New York state university, his office filled with dead insects under glass, encased in resin, floating in jars of fluid. He'd taught Molly the scientific names, pointing them out, asking her to repeat them. She did, and unlike history the insects stayed with her, and she couldn't think about bugs without his face appearing.

After her father died, Louise had boxed up all the insects he had at the house and dropped them off at the school. Molly wished she could have kept just one collection, her favorite, a display of twenty-six butterflies and moths, the colors and patterns of each lepidopteron forming a letter of the alphabet. Molly knew her mother sent them away because she loved him. The reminders hurt more than being without his presence.

That's the other thing she remembered about her father, and her mother, too. They'd been in love, went everywhere together when they could. Sometimes they brought Molly; often they didn't. She didn't mind, not so much, because when her parents got dolled up to go out on the town—the sparkly dresses, the handsome black suits, the jewelry, the slick hair and red lips—they had a way of looking at each other that Molly loved to see. She would sit on the toilet and watch her mother apply her mascara in the bathroom mirror, darker than workdays, thicker, adding eyeliner and shadow well up to her brow.

When the doorbell rang, her mother would say, "Run down and let the baby-sitter in," and Molly would, hoping either Francine or April would be standing on the other side of the door—not Stephanie; all she did was watch MTV and talk on the phone for hours—because they were the nice ones, the ones who played games with her and sometimes let her braid their hair. And then Molly would watch her mother walk down the stairs, her father waiting at the bottom for her, and they would tell Molly not to eat too much junk and not to give April a hard time. And then they'd go, and she wouldn't miss them, not until bedtime, when she longed for her father's bearded kiss on her cheek.

Would Tobias feel that way about her, with a kind of love that glittered on date nights?

They went through the classic-movie room, the TV-show room, the hall of historical figures. Molly pointed out some of the statues, telling Tobias how she had repaired the lips on this one or had sewn a new skirt for that one. Or that George Washington had once been on display at Madame Tussauds, or Shirley Temple's pet dog in

Bright Eyes also played Toto in *The Wizard of Oz.*

"You do like Wiki."

"No. I read that on the sign in front of the display."

Tobias laughed. "Man, you must think I'm numb as a stump. I can read, you know. Promise."

Molly shook her head, stared a little too long at him, and he at her. He leaned forward, his face coming a little closer to hers. She turned away. "The Chamber of Horrors is next."

"What about the museum's secrets?"

"What about them?"

"There must be some."

"You should ask Mick the next time he's here. I don't know any."

And then they stood there, in the Chamber of Horrors, staring at the Frankenstein monster's grotesque form on a table, curly wires coming out of his head, his chest. A light bulb blinked as the mad scientist, posed over a large switch, prepared to pump electricity through the stitched-together body. It was Molly's favorite scene, the creator giving life to his creature. The spark that pulsed through one's body when Christ touched it. She thought of Milton's poem, quoted in Shelley's novel—

Did I request thee, Maker, from my clay
To mould me Man, did I solicit thee
From darkness to promote me?

—and of her mother. It was her cry, her "How could you do this to me, God?" Molly never felt that way. She'd watched enough Pastor Gary sermons to know God had a purpose for the sadness.

She wished He'd clue her in to what it was.

She thought about telling Tobias, giving him a bit of her, a thought she'd shared with no one, but he turned and looked at her with such sorrow in his dark eyes that she had to turn from him. Instead, she said, "I used to talk to them."

"Who? The figures?"

She nodded. "When we first came here. I was lonely."

"Are you still?"

"I don't talk to them anymore, if that's what you mean," she lied.

Tobias rolled the hem of his hat up so it no longer covered the top of his ears. "Come outside with me. I hate seeing you stuck in here."

"My mother—"

"That's not what I mean."

"Then, what?"

"It's all dead."

"It's wax."

"It's dead. All the characters and people shown here, none of them are still alive. This place is a mausoleum, and you're spending your days wandering around it. You glow with life, Molly. You should be somewhere else."

Molly shrugged. "I don't know. Like where?"

"Well, where do you want to be?"

She thought about what he said, about the statues. She didn't think of them as dead, or living. They were her secret keepers. She shared her stories with them—not because she thought they were real, or they understood or would speak back, but because they were all she had. "Nowhere."

"I don't believe you."

"What do you know?"

"I know my grandfather has lived his entire life five miles from where he was born, took over his father's business. My own pops is the same. I don't want that." He kneaded the back of his neck. "I got accepted to Cornell as a transfer in the fall."

"Oh," Molly said. "That's not around here, is it?"

"New York."

"Oh," she said again, quieter this time. "That's good, right?"

"It's good." He paused. "You could come with me."

"I don't even know you."

"I don't mean that way. Apply to school there. Or any of the other schools around there. There's a ton. I'm sure you'd get in to one of them. We could rent a trailer, load up my car, and drive together. You'd know someone. So would I. It would be really great."

"I'll probably just do college online."

"Why?"

"It's cheaper. And Mom needs me here. To help."

"She doesn't, Molly."

"Yes, she does."

"No."

"Tobias, stop. You don't understand."

"You keep saying that."

"Well, you don't."

"Then tell me."

She wanted to. For the first time since that horrible day she wanted to pour out her story to someone who wouldn't melt with the heat of a butane lighter. But she couldn't tell him, not really. He would be horrified—by her past, the lies, the Chamber of Horrors she kept in her head. She would lose the little bit of him she had.

"There's nothing to tell."

"Molly!" He yanked off his hat, dark hair partly matted to his head, partly standing up in greasy spikes. "I don't know what to do here."

"You don't have to do anything."

"So you keep telling me."

"It's the truth."

"It's not. You know it, and I know it." Tobias shook his head. "I guess this place has a few secrets after all."

8

Hanna
September 2002

She slept with her mother every night now.

When Hanna had first come home, Susan would tuck her into the twin bed, stroke her hair, and whisper sweet words to her. When her mother tried to leave, Hanna shook and squeezed Susan's arm until she climbed under the blankets and said, "Baby, I'll just stay until you fall asleep." If her mother tried to get up before then, Hanna would whimper and cling some more until, eventually, Susan dozed off and Hanna settled into some half-slumbering state where she was as aware of each house-shifting creak as she was of her own dreams.

It was hot and crowded in the twin bed. Her mother—struck unaware by sleep and missing her father—cemented to Hanna's back, creeping in closer and closer so Hanna had to move into the crack between the mattress and the wall to get away from her. She liked that cramped space, though, the wall cool against her, the scent of paint and dust and the memory-foam topper Henry had bought for her—before . . .

When it became clear Hanna wouldn't be

staying alone at night anytime soon, Susan put her to bed in the master bedroom, and they would both fall asleep in the glow of MSNBC.

Hanna was still getting used to the new mother. For eleven years, Hanna had only known the other Susan—the one who was affectionate and attentive, who worked as the curator of the university museum but still always made it to Hanna's classroom parties and choir concerts. The one who cut her peanut butter sandwiches into hearts and wrote little notes on her napkins to find at lunchtime. The one who bought the Disney Band-Aids instead of the plain tan ones, even though Henry complained it was a marketing ploy and decried consumerism's effect on society. Her mother would laugh and pull a *Lilo and Stitch* toothbrush from the shopping bag.

The new Susan looked mostly the same, though in past months had taken to pulling out her hair. Sometimes on her head, but mostly on her arms and face; her eyebrows were wide and patchy, and she hardly had eyelashes. She cleaned constantly, moving tornado-like from room to room, scrubbing walls and washing drapes, and cleaning the dust from the piano keys with Q-tips. Hanna had followed her around at first, until one day Susan snapped, "Can't you find something else to do besides stare at me?" After that, Hanna spent more time in her room alone, even though her mother apologized. Susan spoke to her less, touched her less. *Saw* her less.

And she never, ever laughed.

But neither did Hanna.

They used to giggle all the time, making silly poems about the things they saw, talking in Mary Poppins accents around her teddy-bear tea parties, teasing Henry about what they called his absent-minded professorisms—like shutting his car keys in the refrigerator or forgetting his shoes under the seat of the airplane when he'd taken them off while flying to Toronto.

Dr. Diane said the laughs would find their way back. Maybe sooner, if Hanna would talk.

She wasn't not speaking on purpose. She tried sometimes, but the letters jumbled and their pointy edges stuck in her lungs, because even though the words were in her head, the sounds came from her chest, her diaphragm quivering up and down, trying to push them out. She felt them all the time, though, all the unspoken words lumped together and filling her up. Dr. Diane said she might explode if she didn't talk. Hanna believed her.

It had been four months almost since her father died. She couldn't remember much about the two weeks she'd been held captive. She vaguely recalled her escape but had clear pictures of being in the hospital after she was found. The aides had restrained her with thick Velcro after she tried to bite the nurse with the big nose. Despite being older than Hanna's mother, that nurse moved faster than the young one in the Mickey Mouse shirt. Hanna managed to gouge some skin out of her cheek when she stuck in an IV needle. Several pairs of hands held Hanna down while others strapped cuffs on her arms and legs, and then the big-nosed nurse gently slid a syringe into her upper arm—it didn't hurt at all, not even a pinch, unlike the IV, which had felt like a dull nail hammered into her vein—and shushed her softly.

Not long after, Hanna became all rubbery and soft. She wanted to wipe her eyes, but being tied to the bed, she could only wiggle her fingers. She tried to picture them growing long, curving up to her face so she could wipe away the sleepiness, though the image did nothing to satisfy her itch.

She didn't want to close her eyes. *They* might come for her.

She had twisted her wrists in the restraints until her skin stung. It kept her from dozing off.

Hanna's wrists. Hanna's wrists. I love to scratch Hanna's wrists.

She remembered the curtains being drawn around her bed, but the big-nosed nurse hadn't pulled them until they met in the middle, so Hanna could peek through the window into the hallway. Then she heard the door open, and her mother yanked one side of the curtain. Susan wrapped herself around her daughter's body, kissed her hair, her forehead. When she realized Hanna hadn't hugged back, she looked down, tore open the restraints.

Hanna still didn't lift her arms.

"It's okay, baby. It's going to be okay."

Her mother looked like her mother but smaller, as if all her bones had shrunk while Hanna was gone, and her skin—too brown from the tanning salon already—had wrinkled in with deep creases. Her eyes were deeper in her head; if they sunk back any more, she'd lose them in her skull.

After Susan came, there had been questions from police officers and doctors she didn't answer. There had been X rays and blood work and a physical exam. And there had been that *other* exam, with her feet in the stirrups—like the women having babies on television—and the white sheet over her legs, and the hawk-nosed nurse poking around *down there* while her mother had held her hand and silently wept.

"Morning, baby," Susan said, waking, hugging her too quickly against her blouse—she'd fallen asleep in her clothes. "Breakfast?"

Hanna nodded.

"Meet you downstairs."

Hanna scurried to her own bedroom, put on socks and a pair of leggings under her nightgown. Then she wriggled into a sweater, the nightgown falling like a skirt from her waist to knees. In the kitchen she found a bowl of Lucky Charms with milk. Before, her mother would never buy sugar cereal, except once a year for camping trips; then she let Hanna have those little boxes with Fruit Loops and Frosted Flakes, the ones where her father cut back the flaps and Hanna ate right out of the box.

"You don't see Diane today," her mother said, shaking coffee into the maker. "I thought we could bake cookies. Or we could try a walk again."

Hanna scooped some cereal onto a fork, was lifting it to her mouth when someone pounded on the front door. She jerked, the soggy marsh-mallows jumping onto the table, sticking to the front of her sweater. Susan tensed, too. When the knock came a second time, she told Hanna, "Wait here," and went to the door, where Hanna could see the shadow of a person behind the white cotton panel covering the long glass pane.

Her mother moved the curtain aside, then unlocked the chain and dead bolt.

"Mrs. Suller, how are you this morning?" Detective Woycowski said.

Susan relocked the door after the detective stepped inside. "Fine. Can I get you some coffee?"

"No, I'm good. I was hoping I could talk to you for a moment. Privately. And then maybe to Hanna, too."

"You've found something."

"Maybe."

"I wish you would have called." Her mother looked at Hanna, sighed, and directed the officer to the room that used to be her father's study. "Give me a minute."

Back in the kitchen, Susan ran water over her hands and combed her fingers through her hair, used the pads of her thumbs to wipe the crusted sleep from the corners of her eyes. She tucked her blouse into her jeans and wiped a napkin over her teeth. "Finish your cereal," she told Hanna.

And Hanna waited, listening to the cloudy murmurs from the study, behind the pocket doors, low at first, then her mother's voice louder and tenser. Finally footsteps in the hallway, and the detective came in with Susan. He sat in the chair next to Hanna. "How are you today?"

She mixed her Lucky Charms around.

"Hanna, your mom and I were talking, and I'd like to show you some pictures again?"

Hanna swallowed. She churned the cereal faster. A tingling swept over her, like she was being washed in tiny red-hot stingers, starting at her feet and working upward, to her stomach, chest, face. She'd been stung by a wasp once; it felt like that all over. She nodded again, because she had to, because her mother was looking at her, wanting her to.

The last time she'd looked at Detective Woycowski photos was two weeks after she'd been released from the hospital. Two weeks after her escape. He had come into her bedroom, sat on her bed next to her, his weight causing her to dip toward him, and showed her six pictures. She recognized the one in the uppermost left-hand corner. *Fat Guy.* Her eyes had snapped to Detective Woycowski, and he nodded. "I know you see him, and I know you were able to escape when he had a heart attack. It's hard, Hanna, but please, just point."

Hanna had touched Fat Guy's face with the tips of her first three fingers.

"That's a brave girl," the detective said, and left the room with Susan. The door still open, Hanna had heard them clearly, her mother cursing Fat Guy, whose uncle was a professor at the same university at which her father had taught. It was the uncle's apartment where they had kept Hanna; the neighbor had reported an odd smell and the police found Fat Guy, also known as Bobby Bailey, or Bogus to his friends. Residents at the apartment had also noticed at least two other men coming and going, though no one had paid close enough attention to describe them much past male and white and in their twenties or thirties.

"We'll keep searching," the detective had promised Susan. "Maybe when she starts talking . . ." And the twisted feeling in her chest, the one that felt like her lungs were being wrung out like the dish towel her mother used to wash their van, had slowly tightened. They didn't know about Thin Man or Short One, but were looking for them.

108

She wasn't gonna tell.

Susan now took the fork from her. She fisted her hands, pressed them hard against the woven sisal place mat. Detective Woycowski gently moved her bowl to the center of the table, replaced it with a sheet of paper. "Okay, Hanna, just look at these pictures, and if you see one of someone you know, point to it."

Help me, Gee.

She scrunched her eyes shut, opened one with the tiniest slit, seeing blurry faces through her eyelashes. She opened her lid a little wider, focusing on each face. Shook her head.

She didn't recognize anyone.

"That's okay, sweetie. You did fine," the detective said. He went back to the office with Susan, and Hanna heard her mother's raised, frustrated voice and the placating tones of the police officer. Hanna picked the marshmallows from her bowl, pressing her pointer finger into each wet clover and diamond and rainbow; they stuck, and she licked them into her mouth.

The front door opened and closed, then her father's study door. The blue numbers on the microwave changed—first five minutes passing, then ten. Hanna left the soggy cereal on the table and went to her bedroom. She lay on her bed, staring at the ceiling. Eventually her mother would be in to check on her. How long that would take, she didn't know. Every day the space between her and Susan grew. Her mother hated the silence, couldn't bake enough cookies and deadhead enough perennials to make the hours go by fast enough. Hanna—her wordlessness, her phobias—kept Susan a prisoner in her own home.

Hanna covered her eyes with her forearm, pinching a nerve somewhere in her shoulder. Her fingers went numb first, and then the pins and needles began marching their way up her hand, past her wrist, her elbow.

Finally her mother came in and said, "Get your sneaks on, baby."

She had to use her other arm to lift the numb one off her head; it flopped like one of those rubber chickens magicians sometimes have. Well, at least the comic ones.

Hanna reached out with her big toe and kicked at her sneakers—white with a green swoosh and tied with green glitter laces. She had yet to wear them out of the house. Her mother had bought them on clearance, a seventy-dollar pair for fifteen, and had pulled them out of the storage bin soon after Hanna returned from the hospital, hoping they would entice Hanna to walk outside. Susan was a fiendish bargain shopper, even though it had never been a financial necessity.

Hanna's mother looked looser as she came into the room, all the tiny, tense muscles in her body suddenly letting down their guard. Her face sagged a bit more; her shoulders fell forward.

She tried smiling as she picked up Hanna's sneakers. "Come on. It's a beautiful day," she said. "Let's take a walk around the block, okay?"

Hanna didn't want to go outside and considered dropping in a heap at the front door as she'd done on other occasions her mother wanted her to leave the house. But something in her mother's eyes made her pause—caged-animal look. Hanna had seen it before when her second grade class had taken a trip to a local animal show and the tiger paced back and forth in its enclosure, bumping against the bars and snorting.

If she didn't go willingly, she knew her mother would drag her out.

Kin. She's kin to me.

She loved that word. *Kin.* So tidy and easy to say; she didn't have to move her mouth at all, just give her tongue a little flick and breathe out. They'd been reading a book of Greek myths in Ms. Watt's class and come across the word in a story. "That means family," the teacher had said. Hanna wrote the word on a strip of paper and folded it into her pocket, along with *squeamish* and *cyclops*. And after a week of Hanna calling all her relatives kin this and kin that, her mother had finally said, "Cut it out. You're driving me nuts with your *Little House on the Prairie* talk."

Hanna decided she owed her mother something for taking care of her, so she took the sneakers from her mother's outstretched hands, placed them carelessly over her toes, and shook them around to settle them on her feet. One fell back to the carpet. Sighing, Susan finished putting on her shoes and told her to hop off the bed, and they both put on windbreakers and stepped onto the front porch.

It felt big outside, the cool air swirling around Hanna, and she imagined little parts of herself floating away in all different directions, like hundreds of balloons released into the sky. The whole first grade did that once, all the kids tying notes to the ribbons, each hoping his or her balloon would drop into the backyard of some faraway child. Hanna had watched the colors spreading away from one another, getting smaller and smaller as the breeze carried them off above the clouds, no longer visible.

Feeling a panic rising up in her, she grabbed on to the wooden ball on the porch railing; it came off in her hand. She dropped it, clutched the railing itself, afraid to be lifted away.

"Come on," her mother said, taking her other hand. She tugged Hanna down the two steps, and they made their way around the block, Susan mostly leading her, pulling her along. It was one of those times when Hanna had no *juice* in her and just wanted to stand still and let the world spin around her, ignoring her. Other times all the fight exploded all over, in spitting and scratching and tears.

If she closed her eyes and looked inside herself, she could imagine every feeling inside her as a little person, those naked, plastic troll dolls, a different color hair for each—orange for anger, blue for sadness, red for pain, pink for happiness, green for something she couldn't quite put a name to—and they took turns popping in and out of their holes at the strangest moments, making her jump in surprise. Hanna had no control over them, couldn't choose which troll to let out and which to hold down. She just had to wait and hope the good ones came and the bad ones didn't, even though Dr. Diane said none of them were bad.

Dirt smudged her sneakers. Hanna licked her fingers and bent over to wipe the brown marks away.

As they walked, her mother babbled, filling Hanna's silence with grocery lists and random childhood memories, asking questions without pausing for answers. They managed to get around the entire block, and when they returned to their house, Susan waved to Mrs. Davis across the street.

Every time Hanna saw her, she remembered the time her mother had fainted and fallen down the stairs. She'd been six at the time, and Susan, pregnant. Hanna had run across the street to Mrs. Davis's house, forgetting to look both ways, pounding on the door until the elderly woman finally opened up and, after listening to Hanna, called 9-1-1. She kept Hanna as the ambulance took Susan away, fed her meatballs and Heavenly Hash and tucked her into a musty-smelling bed in the back of the house.

Her father had brought her mother home three days later with no baby and two Beanie Babies for Hanna, who didn't tell them she already had those same ones.

"I'll make you a grilled cheese sandwich," Susan said, opening the front door and nudging Hanna through. "You want tomato? I don't think we have any. There's ham, though. I'll make grilled cheese and ham, okay?"

Still talking, Susan buttered bread and dropped it into the huge cast-iron pan she always kept on the stove. She narrated each step—"I'm adding the cheese now. Two slices or three? Yes, three. I'll split the top piece in half so all the cheese is even. Two pieces of ham? Okay, you got it"—and Hanna wondered if she needed to run across the street again. Then her mother dropped the spatula in the pan and turned, stared at her. "Say something. Please just say something."

Hanna wished she had one of her words in her pocket now, and that she could take it out and read it and make her mother happy. Instead she stood there, staring back, trying to talk with her eyes. Susan went to her, fell to her knees, and wrapped her arms around Hanna's waist, squeezing until it hurt. Her head jammed against Hanna's middle, she started to cry, and all Hanna could think of was her mother's head pushing through her skin, into her stomach, the tears rinsing all the dirtiness away. And Hanna saw her mother hadn't colored her hair recently, brown roots on either side of the part. She touched the place where the dark and light met, the line dividing happiness and sadness, a time before Hanna knew the difference between the two, and a time after.

Susan pulled away, took Hanna's hands and kissed them. Stood.

"I think I burned your sandwich," she said. "Let me make you another."

And Hanna at sat the table, waiting for her lunch.

9

Claire
September 2002

The playground pulsed with streaks of green and gold and blue, children running from monkey bars to slides, laughing, crying, jabbing shovels in the wood chips beneath the equipment. Claire huddled in the midmorning sun as Heidi bumbled behind her chubby-legged grandson, Landon scooting away from her with all the enthusiasm of a two-year-old each time she tickled his ribs with a gentle poke. "I'm gonna get you," she said, and the toddler squealed, grinning as if nothing mattered except his grandmother's attention.

Claire watched the scene uncensored, allowing all her envy and anger and sadness to pool low inside her, in the empty place between her hipbones; the emotional soup swished with each Landon giggle, and finally she said, "Enough." The young girl on the swing beside Claire's bench looked up from the pile of chips she'd built with her sandaled feet.

"I think I'm getting too old for this," Heidi said, dropping next to her. Neither she nor Claire had mentioned the Andrew Brenneman incident again, but both knew all was forgiven.

With the side of her hand Claire tucked her skirt between her legs until it looked as though she wore pants. "You'll say that until Meghan leaves with him, and then you'll be lost."

"You got me," Heidi said. "Are you okay? You look—"

"Tired. Just tired. I didn't sleep all that great last night."

"Any reason in particular?"

"No," Claire said, meaning *yes*. Meaning *always*. Meaning *I can't tell you because you're happily running around with your grandson and I'm alone.*

After their years of friendship, Heidi knew not to believe her; she opened her mouth and in went the breath of question beginnings, but Landon came and, gripping his grandmother's first two fingers, tugged her off the bench. "More," he said, dragging Heidi to the bottom of the twisty slide to wait for him. She stood there, waiting for him, and when he came down she caught him, whispered something in his ear. He went running to the sandbox and waved for her to come. She did.

Beside her, Claire sensed the slightest sense of motion and saw the young girl still looking at her, the swing quivering from the child's weight suspended there. Her white-blond hair puffed out from a purple plastic headband, the kind Amelia had complained pinched behind her ears, and her skin seemed almost translucent, as if it hadn't been seen by the sun in a long time.

Claire didn't think it odd she wasn't in school, though the girl looked at least ten, maybe eleven, and strangely familiar—she had homeschooled her own children and often took them out mid-morning but doubted that was the case here. She wouldn't have been surprised to find the girl was battling some sort of long illness. She had a frailty about her, a glassiness. Perhaps she was too weak to pump the swing.

"Can I push you?"

The girl looked over her shoulder, to a woman who stood perhaps ten feet away, speaking to another woman, gesticulating, eyes wet, mascara smudged at the corners. Then the girl nodded.

Claire stood but not wanting to put her hands on the girl from behind, she stood in front of her, took the chain in each hand, low, where it met the rubber seat, and gently pulled forward. The swing rocked back and forth, and the girl held out her legs, straight, so Claire could push the bottom of her feet. She used to swing Caden like that, listening to the same squeaky rhythm of the chain in the metal eyehooks, the same light thud against the palms of her hands. Suddenly the girl leaned back as far as she could go, eyes closed, hair dragging on the ground, and Claire didn't touch her. After three passes, she sat up again, skidding her feet through the mulch to stop.

"Your necklace," the girl said, voice brittle. Uncertain.

Claire touched the crystal cross she wore every day beneath her clothing, dropped it back into her shirt. It must have fallen loose when she bent over to start the swing. "My son gave it to me."

"I saw one like that before."

"In the store?"

"On TV." The late-morning light revealed fine, nearly transparent hairs on the girl's legs; her face was expressionless. "It hurts you."

"What does? The cross?"

"When you say about your son."

Claire squeezed the cross now, feeling it prick her palm. *The nails. His nails.* "How do you . . . ?"

She stopped, and then in a moment of confusion and defeat, of transparency that seemed to descend on her, coming from outside her body, said, "Yes."

"My mom," the girl said, cool blue irises flickering toward the woman with the smeared makeup, "looks at me like that, too."

"Hanna?" The woman crossed to the swing in heavy, defensive steps. "What's going on? What did you say?"

The girl lowered her head.

"You said something. I heard you. I know I heard you." When her daughter didn't respond, she moved in toward Claire, desperate, seeking—she, too, seeming vaguely familiar. "What did she say to you?"

"She asked about my necklace," Claire said, not intending to lie, not really. But the little girl didn't seem to want her mother to know her words, and Claire felt the same. What had been exchanged between them went inexplicably deeper than a handful of short sentences about some ugly cross Caden saved for to buy with his own money, one she wore every day because it came from him. She'd told him she wore it under her shirt so it could stay against her heart, and he liked that answer.

In all honesty she hadn't wanted anyone seeing the tacky pink crystals, recognizing it from the late-night infomercial declaring it somehow special—holy, even—because one could peer into the secret center window and read the Lord's Prayer.

Again, she felt pressed down upon from . . . above? The situation before her had a weight she didn't understand.

"Who are you? Why are you near her?" the woman demanded, her earlier fear now anger.

"I was just sitting here," Claire said. She took a step away, the back of her knee bumping the bench. "I asked if your daughter wanted a push. She said yes. That's all."

The woman dug through her green leather bag, flipped out her cell phone. "Don't move." Claire thought she might call the police, but after dialing, she said, "Dr. Flinchbaugh," and waited, pulling at her eyebrows and blowing the tiny hairs from her fingers. A tinny mumble came through the phone, and the woman said, "She talked."

More distant words Claire couldn't make out.

"I don't know. She didn't say it to me," the woman said, then, after listening a moment, held the phone out. "Here."

Claire looked at it. "I don't—"

"Take it."

She did, wiping her hand over the keys and screen to clear away the smeary makeup residue, the sweat. "Hello?"

"I'm Diane Flinchbaugh. Hanna's therapist. And you are?"

"Uh, I'm Claire. Claire Rodriguez."

"Mrs. Suller said Hanna spoke to you."

"She didn't say much."

"Not much is everything. Hanna hasn't said a word in four months."

And then Claire remembered why the little girl looked so familiar. Her photo had been on the front page of the newspaper, along with the story of how she'd seen her father gunned down in that bank robbery downtown and then was taken and held for two weeks. The mother had been on television, pleading for her daughter's return, her hair blond and perfectly smooth, her clothes chic, her hips thin. And Claire had passed judgment, unable to understand how someone in such torment could look so good.

She had hacked three inches of dead ends from her hair last week after years without attention, and most of her "skinny" clothes had long since been donated to the community center, though she held on to some of them—the ones with meaning—in the off chance that someday she'd pull herself together long enough to diet back down into them.

Most women wanted back into their pre-children sizes; she'd have given anything to be able to fit into the pants she'd worn when Caden first rode a two-wheeler, or the sweatshirt she had tied around her waist when Amelia said her first sentence. She looked nothing like she did when her identity wound around the words *mother* and *wife*.

And Claire could now see this woman up close, hiding behind her flowing silk, wide-necked blouse, her canary yellow peep-toe skimmers, her manicured fingernails *and* toenails. She had the *look* Claire recognized, of someone whose world had imploded and there were no pieces large enough left to pick up and try to fit back together. Only dust.

"Ms. Rodriguez?"

"I'm here."

"I need to know what Hanna said to you. Her exact words, the best you can recall them."

Claire hesitated again. The little girl sat unmoving on the swing, startlingly so. Not a muscle tremored; her chest seemed neither to rise nor fall. She fixed one unblinking eye on Claire, the other buried deep beneath her bangs. "I'm not sure she wants me to say."

Silence on the other end of the line, and then, "I understand. Would you be willing to come and see me?"

"I suppose," Claire mumbled. She didn't like it, the feeling of being dragged into their situation. A traumatized kid. That meant drama. Pain. She'd had enough of that already.

"Hanna's next appointment is tomorrow at ten. I'll put you through to Barbara. She'll give you directions."

She waited on the line; the secretary prattled off street names and traffic lights, and Claire pretended to pay attention, giving the appropriate uh-huhs when needed, planning to look the address up on the computer later. She closed the phone and held it out to the woman, who took it, squeezed it.

Then the woman gathered Hanna against her, arm around the girl's shoulders, and lifted her from the swing. "C'mon, baby," she said, leading her away, Hanna's rigid body propping up her own. She strapped her daughter into the middle seat of a Windstar van, slid the door closed and turned back toward the playground. But she was too far away for Claire to make out her expression, her face a flat, pale thumbprint in the distance.

"Ready to head out?" Heidi asked, coming up next to Claire and carrying a cranky Landon, dirt crusted around his mouth, one shoe on, the other sticking out from his grandmother's back pocket. "This one needs a nap."

"No bye. No bye," Landon cried.

"Let me take him," Claire said. She lifted the toddler onto her hip; he ground his face in her shoulder, leaving a slimy trail of mucus on her sleeve.

"Who were you talking to?" Heidi asked.

She rubbed her thumb against the writing callus on her right ring finger; she held her pen wrong, always had, no matter how many times the nuns whacked her knuckles with their rulers in the Catholic elementary school her devout grandmother insisted on sending her to. All she wanted to do was get home, where peace came in little black-and-white boxes, all neat and patterned and numbered. Where she measured her own well-being in clues and obscure words people used only in puzzles. "No one."

10

Claire
October 2002

She sat in the small waiting room, more a hallway, four antique chairs with rich fabric seats on a floral Oriental rug. The psychologist's office was in an old Victorian home, long since divided up for offices and apartments, and the thick, white woodwork and paneled doors made the waiting area feel small, as if the walls kept pushing closer and closer together. A small black button surrounded by a brass plate stared at Claire from beside one of the doors, a thimble-sized light bulb above it. When the mother and the girl had arrived—only two minutes ago, even though Claire had been sitting here for the past ten— Susan poked the button with her pointer, and

124

the bulb glowed dull gold in the shadowy hall.

The girl sat next to her mother, swinging her legs, head down. Susan pinched her eyelashes between her fingers, then sat on her hands. Claire looked at her own hands, scraping at the corners of her fingernails, pushing back the cuticles, pinching away pieces of dead skin, which she flicked onto the floor. The white flecks settled on the rug, snow on the woven tulips. She turned her head, counted dogs on the toilé wallpaper.

The doorknob jiggled, and when the door opened the light blinked off. "Ms. Rodriguez, you came. Thank you. I'm Diane Flinchbaugh." The tall, blocky woman held out a square hand. One of the gold buttons on her polyester suit jacket hung from a single thread and jerked like a yo-yo as she shook Claire's hand. Her unseasonable linen skirt fell in wrinkles just below her knees, and her slip peeked out from the hemline.

"Nice to meet you," Claire said.

"Good, yes. Why don't you come in first, and then we'll join Hanna in the play area, where we usually meet. Hanna, Ashley will take you back in a moment." She extended her arm into the office. "Please, make yourself comfortable."

The office was thick and fussy, as plush as the waiting area, with crystal lamps and Queen Anne sofas and ornate frames on the walls. Claire stood until Diane returned. She motioned to one couch, and Claire sat; the psychologist sat in a chair across from her. "Now, tell me what Hanna said to you yesterday."

"She said she saw a necklace like mine on television."

"Necklace?" The psychologist squinted at Claire's collar.

"This one," she said, pulling it from beneath her sweater. "I told her my son gave it to me."

"Anything else?"

Claire hesitated. "She said her mother looks at her the same way I looked when I mentioned my son."

"And how is that?"

"With hurt."

"Did she say that?"

"Yes."

Diane crossed her legs. A scarlike run in her panty hose snuck out of her shoe and up the inside of her calf; a thick patch of something shiny—clear nail polish, Claire figured—glopped at the top of the run. "What happened to your son, Ms. Rodriguez?"

"He's dead."

The psychologist wrote something on a yellow legal pad. "How did the conversation begin?"

"I asked Hanna if she wanted a push. On the swing. She was just sitting there."

"And she said yes."

"Well, she nodded."

More writing, and then Diane stood. "Would

you mind coming with me, into my session with Hanna?"

Claire cleared her throat, stayed seated on the couch. "I really don't know how much I want to get involved in all this."

"You approached her."

"To give her a push on a swing."

"There must have been a reason. Or are you in the habit of asking the same question to other children you don't know."

"I was being nice," Claire mumbled.

"You're a religious woman," Diane said, or asked; all her questions sounded like statements, with psychological assuredness Claire found disconcerting. She'd gone to a shrink—two, actually—after the car accident. Alone, at first, at Daniel's prodding. He'd hoped the counseling would work some voodoo magic on her, snap her free from the depression that coated her, keeping her in bed, indoors, in the same flannel pants for days at a time.

She'd gone for seven sessions, maybe eight. They'd asked her about her faith in God and assured Claire her babies were in heaven. Platitudes. Prayers. None of it worked to lessen the guilt. And when, fourteen months later, Daniel declared he couldn't take it anymore, they'd gone to counseling together—his way to assuage his own guilt, since he'd already had one leg out the door for weeks, already fancied himself in love with the woman in the next cubicle at work. After a few sessions of counseling, he asked for a divorce and she signed the papers, not caring one way or another. He deserved a new life anyway. Who would want to stay with the woman who'd killed his kids?

"Are you religious?" Claire asked.

"No. But you are. And so you would believe there is a reason you spoke to Hanna, a reason you're here today. A reason she connected with you. Would your God want you to abandon this child?"

"You're manipulating me."

"I'm speaking your truth. Do with it as you will."

"Fine." Claire sighed. "I'll stay."

She followed the psychologist into a yellow room with a cerulean rug. Child-sized recliners huddled in one corner, shelves of toys in another. At a kidney-shaped table surrounded by plastic chairs in primary colors, Hanna sat poking holes into a flattened mound of blue Play-Doh, a college-aged woman beside her. Diane nodded at the woman, who moved from where she sat to a chair in the corner. Diane replaced her, touched Hanna's hands. "Would you draw me a picture today?"

Hanna nodded.

Diane rolled up the dough and gave her paper and markers, looking gargantuan in the too-small chair, knees bumping the edge of the table. Claire stood against the wall, unsure of her place.

"Can you show me where you saw Claire's necklace before?"

The little girl's eyes flashed toward Claire, who smiled. Hanna nodded again, reached for a black marker and twisted the cap off. She drew a rectangle, and a smaller one inside it, coloring between the lines she made. Then she took a pink marker, drew a cross shape inside the box. Claire thought she had finished, but Hanna drew a yellow circle on the paper, below the black rectangle, and then lines coming off it. She added a blue body shape, yellow hands and black feet. She slid the paper in Claire's direction.

"Is that the man who watched you?" Diane asked.

Hanna nodded.

"The man who kept you locked away?"

Looking at Claire, Hanna moved her head up and down, once, twice. Claire saw something in her face, a hint of untruth, a secret. Saying what others wanted to hear—Claire knew that well. She'd been doing it for years. *Oh, yes, things are well, thank you. You're right, God does heal all wounds. Thanks for asking, I barely think about it anymore.*

She wanted to wrap her arms around the girl, pray over her, rock her and hold her. Claire felt the Spirit expand within her, pressing against her insides, pushing up and out through her eyes, falling in tears of grief. *Oh, God, why? She's just a baby.*

Hanna walked her hand across the table, her fingers legs of a spider, and touching the corner of a clean sheet of paper, pulled it back to her and uncapped a brown marker. She drew a triangle with curved corners, with deliberation, not loose lines and carelessness like the last picture. She colored it in, adding darker squares, topping it with a scoop of mint green, dotted with chunks of black.

"Ice cream," Diane said. "Did you eat ice cream where you were?"

The girl shook her head.

"Do you want ice cream?"

She nodded.

"Well, we can send Ashley to find some. That's easy. That looks like mint chip, yes?"

"I want her to take me," Hanna said.

The psychologist flinched, and for one stunned instant seemed to grope for words. She recovered, saying, "Well, I'm sure that's a fine idea. When we're done here, you and Ms. Rodriguez can go for ice cream before you both head home. I'll make sure it's all right with your mother."

Across the bottom of the paper, Hanna wrote *kin,* over and over again, until she ran off the edge. Looked at Claire. "Do you like ice cream?"

"Sometimes," Claire said. "But, Hanna, I don't think—"

"I need to ask you."

"About . . . ?"

Her eyes shifted toward Diane. She puckered her lips closed, skin dimpling in her chin. After sticking the lid back on her marker, she opened a can of Play-Doh, pink this time, and mashed it onto the tabletop. Diane tried to engage her some more, but other than a few curt nods at benign questions, Hanna had closed herself off from conversation. Ashley scribbled notes in the corner, yellow pad on her knees; it matched the one Diane used in her office.

Finally Diane said, "Okay, Hanna, I suppose it's ice cream time. Wait here a moment."

The psychologist left, returning with Susan. "Hanna, you and your mom are going to drive to the ice cream parlor, and Claire will follow in her own car. The two of you can eat your cones there, and your mom will wait in the van, if you'd like her to."

Hanna nodded three times, slowly. Her mother curled her arms around her purse, a large chartreuse leather thing with pockets and buckles and metal studs, cradling it against her ribs. She looked at her feet, kicked one against the vinyl floor, sole squeaking, moved one arm from the bag to her daughter and led her from the room. Hanna turned her head back, briefly, peered at Claire through her milky hair before disappearing down the hall.

Picking up her own bag from against the wall, Claire said, "I don't know how to do this."

"Just talk to her," Diane said. "She wants to talk to you."

"But what if she brings up . . . you know? I have no idea what to say to that. What if I make it worse? I'm not—"

"Yes, you are." The psychologist handed her a small white card. "Next appointment, on Friday. We'll discuss it then."

Claire took the card and slid it into her back pocket. She left, got into her car, backed out behind the minivan waiting in the parking lot driveway with its left turn signal on. Her palms secreted perspiration onto the steering wheel. She didn't make left turns, not since *that* day. Had only started driving again last summer.

But the van pulled into the street, and Claire willed her leg, clamped down hard on the brake, to relax, and the car crept forward, front bumper protruding only inches past the sidewalk. She could see the van stopped at a traffic light not a quarter mile down the road. Her vision muddied, and she fought to keep from hyperventilating as every blood vessel constricted. Her hand fumbled with the directional, pushing the lever up— right—and she turned from the driveway, around the block, half stopping at the signs, and ended up three cars behind the minivan, which parked in a Stewart's Shop lot. Claire followed, stopping, walking to the mother's rolled-down window. The woman handed her five dollars. "For the ice cream. Hanna will wait here until you come out."

Claire went into the store and bought two single-dip mint chocolate chip scoops—on sugar cones, like in Hanna's drawing. She carried them back outside, and Hanna slid out of the van. Claire held out one of the cones, but Hanna didn't reach for it; she walked to the outdoor picnic table and sat, her back toward them. It was one of those mild autumn days that teased people, and they dug out their T-shirts after packing them under their beds for the winter, only to wake the next morning to frost on the windowpane and a load of spring laundry to rewash and refold into storage.

"I'm watching," the mother said.

She nodded, climbed over the wooden bench, settled across from the girl. Now Hanna took the cone. Closed her mouth over the top of the ice cream and sucked, creating a green dairy cowlick. She dug chips out with her tongue.

Claire waited, licked around the bottom of her own ice cream, pushed the softening mound deep into the cone so it filled down to the bottom and there would be cream in every bite. As she peeled the cone wrapper off, Hanna said, "If you do that, it will leak out the bottom."

The girl was right. A sticky drop rolled down the inside of her hand; Claire wadded a napkin against the point. "You've had these before."

Hanna tore her own wrapper off in strips, an inch or two at a time, unwrapping more only when she'd eaten down to the paper. When she finished, she wiped her mouth and held the napkin in her balled fist. "I need you to tell me about Gee."

"G? Like the letter."

Hanna shook her head. "On the television, the man said Gee would help me if I asked."

"What man?"

Shrugging, the girl rolled the napkin back and forth beneath her palm, against the table. "He was glittery, and he shouted and wiped his face with a white cloth a lot."

"I don't know, Hanna."

"You have to know," she whispered, her lower lip quivering. "They showed a necklace just like yours on the commercial, and then he came on and told me to say, 'Help me, Gee.' I did. Not even out loud but in my head. And the fat guy died. And I ran away."

Claire suddenly understood, her body bathed in a head-to-toe shiver. She'd heard the stories, of course. Of the missionaries, of prisoners for Christ and of powers. Or when someone told her about a friend of a friend of a friend who came home from a revival with solid gold tooth fillings, or had a cancerous lump evaporate after being anointed with oil. Claire had always listened to these tales with a mixture of disbelief—how could anyone believe that nonsense?—and longing—

why couldn't God work that way in her own life?

But she'd never seen a real out-of-the-ordinary miracle, until today. This little girl sitting before her, who prayed to some misheard name she didn't know, because some seedy TV preacher had told her to. And, in response to her childlike faith, He answered. "The man didn't say Gee, sweetie. He said Jesus."

Hanna swallowed. "The one on the cross?"

"You know about Him."

"I saw a statue once."

"But you don't know anything about Him?"

"He made Easter. And He keeps people from going to the hot place. Well, some people. The ones who go to St. Catherine's."

"Who told you that?"

"Katie Torino."

"A friend?"

Hanna nodded.

"Well, your friend should listen better in church, I think. Jesus is our friend. He does more for us than we can imagine."

"Why?"

"He loves us."

"Why?" Hanna asked again, her white-blue irises, marble-sized and icy, floating nearly invisible in her wide eyes.

"Because—"

The van horn honked behind her. Hanna stood, climbing over the picnic bench, and Claire turned to see the mother motioning her to come. "I have to go," the girl said. "I'll see you again, right?"

"Yes," Claire said.

"He wants me to see you again."

And Hanna climbed into the van. Her mother shut her in and drove away as Claire watched, autumn leaves scuttling over her feet.

11

Molly
February 2009

Uncle Mick came with more books and beer and a tub of Kentucky Fried Chicken. Molly had known he was on his way because her mother wore the expensive dangling earrings he'd given her—gold-tone disks the size of clementines, the metal etched with an Aztec design. With an expression of expectation Louise looked like a woman who hadn't been hiding for the past six years. Molly was glad for it.

"Come eat, Mollidoodles," Uncle Mick said, shaking the box of biscuits at her. She wasn't hungry but sat anyway. She liked the life Mick brought to her mother, to the apartment. And, yes, to her. He was outside of them, unattached to their past, a buffer between then and now. And he made them laugh.

Louise hadn't trusted him in the beginning, especially when he started sniffing around them with gifts and flattery and all the "Call me Uncle Mick, not Mr. Borden" talk. Molly didn't remember when it changed, had no idea why, but figured her mother's loneliness played a part.

No one wanted to be alone.

Mick wasn't anything like her father—not book smart, not handsome, not fastidious. He was the kind of guy who was rich enough people pardoned his obnoxiousness, but his money came without culture or style. His favorite clothes were Carhartt jeans, stained from work, T-shirts, and dusty steel-toed boots. He lived in an oceanfront house about a half hour's drive from the museum, the siding covered with old Shell Motor Oil signs and reproduction fishing nets; she'd seen pictures on his Facebook page.

He seemed to genuinely care about her mother, though. Louise had nothing to offer him except herself. And when he was around, she shined a little bit like she used to when Molly's father was alive.

Her mother had sacrificed for her, more than any mother should be asked. They weren't living the life Louise wanted or deserved; it wasn't some consequence for her past sins. She did what she needed to do for her daughter's sake, and had been successful—mostly—in giving Molly as normal and happy a life as possible.

When they first moved to Dorsett Island, Louise had tried to make it a home, a new start. She painted all the paneled walls a pale, cheery yellow, purchased bold art prints and hung them in every room, and made real dinners almost every night—meat loaf, baked macaroni and cheese, spaghetti with buttery garlic bread.

During the off-season they'd done school in the office between the lobby and their apartment, with the museum sign turned to Open—Molly working through her first encounters with Pythagoras, her mother listening for the telltale cackle on the rare occasion someone came through the door. In the summers, Louise worked the counter and Molly kept the candy stocked or gave brochures to those who wanted them, never far from Louise's watchful eye.

They'd laughed at their disastrous attempts in wax working. They remembered, sometimes, Molly's father, and Molly would find her mother squinting through wet eyes at the only photo she had of him, a small, fading candid shot taken during one of their camping trips that Louise had cut to fit her wallet.

It had only been since autumn that things had begun to crumble, like a preserved moth specimen, wings shedding crumbs of chitin each time it was touched, no matter how delicately. Louise's *headaches* increased in frequency, about one a week now, and when she wasn't in bed she was redecorating the living room or making grand plans to improve the museum.

Distraction had always been Louise's most trusted escape route, and Molly, for her part, also retreated into her own spaces. She daydreamed about Tobias, hope and impossibility mixing into a sludge of depression. She felt time pressing down on her, and the uncertainty that had been there all along grew more dense as it was squeezed into the short weeks until he left for Cornell. The pressure made her irritable and choked off her mother's attempts to reconnect; she snapped at Louise more, spent more time in her bedroom or the museum.

After dinner—Mick eventually goaded Molly to eat half a breast, and she picked apart a biscuit, too—Louise pulled all the board games out of the cupboard under the television and she and Mick debated what to play. She wanted Trivial Pursuit, he Pictionary. "Moll, you decide," her mother said, and she told them she'd rather just watch a movie. So Louise stuck a disc into the player and snuggled under Mick's arm, her feet folded up on the cushions and pressed against Molly's legs, his on the rattan chest they used as a coffee table. Molly crooked her arm and rested her head in it, falling asleep to Tommy Lee Jones chasing Harrison Ford on the screen.

She woke on the couch, covered with the quilt from her bed, neck stiff. Louise hummed from the kitchenette area, the water in the sink running. Molly stretched, her breastbone cracking. She smelled bacon. Uncle Mick must have brought it; it hadn't been in the refrigerator yesterday.

"Morning," her mother said, coming out to sit next to her. "I tried to wake you last night, but you were zonked."

"I guess."

Louise reached under the blanket and started to rub Molly's feet.

Not ready for her mother's attention, Molly squirmed and said, "I'll get dressed, get out to the desk."

"Wait," Louise said, tightening her grip on Molly's feet.

She looked at her mother. "Okay."

"Mick asked me to marry him."

"I thought he was married."

"His divorce finalized in August. We've been talking about it . . . for a while." With her thumb Louise twisted the new ring on her finger. Her other hand was still under the blanket. "What do you think?"

"What am I supposed to think?"

"I don't know."

"You already said yes."

"But I'm still asking."

Molly closed her eyes, focused on her mother's touch, now at her ankles, a little above. "I don't know."

"He wants us to move in with him."

Her chest tightened. "When?"

"Whenever we want. Soon."

"Before the wedding?"

"We're not having a wedding—just going to the JP." Louise closed one eye, her fingers plucking at her skin, seeking lashes that weren't there. She'd pulled them all out a long time ago. "So probably in the next month or so."

"What about the museum?"

"Mick will find someone. Or, there's another option. I thought . . . well, that you might want to stay here."

"Alone?"

"You're eighteen. And, you know, I wasn't sure if you'd want to be living with Mick and me. That maybe you'd be ready for your own place. Mick would still pay you, and we'd hire more help in the summer. I know you've been talking about online college. You'd have time to do that, and I'd be close. I mean, what am I going to do all day? I'd probably be here more than there."

I don't think you can leave this place, Molly translated. *I'll bring you groceries each week, and check in on you, and make sure you're still breathing. I'd rather pretend it's about you growing up than deal with the fact I've let this go on too long.*

"Do you not want me to come?"

"Of course not, Molly. It was just an idea. If you

come, Mick will find somebody else to work the place. If you want to stay, well . . . Whatever you decide."

She wanted to stay. A half hour away sounded like halfway around the world. What would she do there, anyway? Take some online courses. Clean the house. Stare out windows. Disappear. In all the years they'd been on the island, neither of them had considered what came next. Now *next* bore down on them, the square headlights of a speeding car in the darkness, and Louise's idea was her only way of lunging out of its path. Avoid, avoid, avoid. They were so skilled at it; that was where all things began. Never *how do we handle this?*, but *how can we fold ourselves up small enough so it won't be there anymore?*

"What have you told him?" she whispered.

Louise tugged at her new ring. "Everything."

Molly shook off the blanket, stood, the tender time between them swallowed up by reality. It had a way of doing that, consuming each moment of her life that resembled a bit of the past, a scrap of the *before*.

"I need to think about it," she said.

Her mother strode toward the kitchen, stopped, left hand gripping the molding. She didn't turn around. "Take as long as you need."

So Molly went the other way, into her bedroom, blown there by Louise's words. She was held hostage, not by her inability to go outside but by her failure to get the things within her *to* the outside. Guilt. Shame. Hurt. Anger. Fear. Her emotions bloated her so much now she could no longer fit through the front door.

She dug her Bible out from under her pillow. It was the last thing she looked at before switching off the light clipped to her headboard. She didn't have a nightstand, and it didn't seem right to put it on the floor, so she slept on it at night. She didn't want to read it now but opened to the title page and read the inscription:

God says, "Thou shall not steal."
But we want you to take this book!!!!!
It can change your life. If it does, let us
  know, please.
Write to P.O. Box 1286, Colorado Springs,
  CO 80906

Molly had stared at those words for years. The penmanship looked, to her, like teen print—a girl's, maybe thirteen or fourteen, still trying to find her place through the letters she wrote, forming each *a* with a fancy curl and each exclamation point with a star instead of a dot— enough flourish to set her apart from everyone else out there. There was more there, perhaps a name, scribbled out under blue-black permanent marker. Molly had been twelve when she found the book in the drawer of a hotel, smuggled it out of the room with a sense of deceit, even though the previous owner had apparently given her permission.

Maybe God still considered it stealing. She didn't know.

She thought about the person who left it. She'd written many letters, probably once a month, and kept them all, though now she couldn't imagine sending any of them. Once she'd addressed an envelope and snuck a stamp from Louise's desk, but she chickened out. So whenever she wrote a new one, she folded the letter into the envelope and carried it around with her in the Bible, using it as a bookmark, until she wrote another, and then she'd trade them out, adding the old one to the growing pile she kept in a folder labeled English in her backpack.

Sometimes she looked back through the letters. The first ones were tentative, a few lines of formality. *Hello. I found your Bible and took it. Thank you for leaving it for me. I really like reading it and I love God, too.* As she got older, and as she imagined the person—a girl, she was certain—who left the Bible growing older, as well, her letters became more like a living journal, and the girl became a friend. Her only friend, outside of the wax figures, before Tobias.

She wrote about what she'd read and why it touched her spirit, about her mother and the arguments they had, about her schoolwork, her job at the museum, and the strange tourists who came through in the summer. She wondered if the Bible leaver might have ever vacationed on Dorsett Island, if they had seen each other and not known it.

Her mother told her stories like that, about how she and Molly's father, as children, went every year to the same Brooklyn restaurant for Mother's Day dinner because it had been a favorite of both their grandmothers. They were sure they'd seen each other then, at some point, before they ever met. Louise said her mother had complained about the noisy family with six kids, which described Molly's father and his siblings. In a borough of two million people, it seemed rather serendipitous. At least Louise thought so. Molly called it romantic.

Lately she sometimes mentioned Tobias when she wrote. She asked the girl questions about her life, too. And, on occasion, she wrote about the past, telling things she'd never told anyone else before—well, not anyone living. Though in a way, the Bible pen pal was no more real than the wax figures.

She opened her spiral notebook and tore out a page, stared at the blue lines, like veins, there to hold the life of the letter. The words. But she didn't have anything to say.

12

"I want to go into a church."

Her mother looked at her, sparse brows wrinkled together. She still seemed startled when Hanna spoke, as if trying to connect the voice to the girl before her. "Okay. It's nice today again. When we take our walk, we can stop at St. Catherine's. It's open every day."

"No. Claire's church."

"Why?"

"I just do."

"Baby, I don't know where that church is."

"Call her."

"Do you have her number? I don't."

Hanna sifted through the basket on the stool beneath the phone, a narrow oak seat that doubled as an ironing board. Her mother had bought it at a craft fair when her father was still alive, even though he told her she'd never use it. He'd been right. It sat under the telephone and collected things, like mail and laundry that needed to be put away but her mother didn't want to carry up the stairs at that moment, and screws or little plastic pieces Susan could no longer match to what they went to, but kept anyway, just in case.

Hanna thought about how her mother had changed since *that* day. Some days she tore through the house, scrubbing doorknobs and beating the dust from all the drapes. She baked her healthy carrot cookies and canned salsa after buying pounds of tomatoes from the farmers' market, and rearranged the furniture in the family room. Other days she sulked and slept, piled mail on the table and ignored it, left the laundry in the washing machine wet and then had to rewash it when she went looking for a pair of jeans days later because it smelled of mold. Those were the dull days, and they had become more frequent than the go-getter days.

And Hanna knew it was all her fault.

She pulled the phone book out of the basket. "Here."

Susan crossed her arms. "I don't know her last name."

Hanna did. Dr. Diane had said it twice in front of her. She opened the phone book somewhere in the middle, the coupon section, pages of green-bordered deals on haircuts and carpet steaming. Leafing backward, the pages rustling like leaves, she found the R section.

"Rodriguez, Claire."

"We've bothered her enough, Hanna."

Hanna thought about that. When Claire came to the appointment yesterday, she didn't say much of anything, but neither did Hanna. Dr. Diane kept trying to get Hanna to talk, but she didn't want to, not to the therapist. Not that she didn't like Dr. Diane. All she kept thinking of was Gee. No. *Jesus.* She'd hoped Claire would have taken her for ice cream again, but Claire didn't mention it. Hanna didn't think it was because she was feeling bothered, though.

"I'll call."

"No. Give me that." Susan took the book, and it flopped closed, the right page disappearing into all the wrong ones. Her mother thumbed the edges and set the phone book on the table, opened to the ROB-ROT page. Dialed. "Ms. Rodriguez, please excuse us for bothering you. This is Susan Suller. Hanna's mother. Hanna was wondering if we might attend church with you tomorrow, but we understand if that is inconvenient, or if you wouldn't feel comfortable with it. If you want, you can call us back at 266-9083. Thank you."

She hung up and slid the book back into the basket. "Get your jacket. And wear your mud boots. There's puddles today."

Hanna climbed up the staircase, holding on to the banister with both hands, pulling as if she climbed a mountain and the banister were her rope. In her bedroom she found her boots, pink rubber with bright dots, clamped the plastic price tag string between her teeth and pulled. The tag popped off in her mouth. She threw the paper in the trash but chewed the plastic part, like gum. She missed gum. Her father had chewed it all the time, the stick kind that didn't make bubbles—Juicy Fruit and Doublemint. He showed her how to lick the minty wrappers and stick them on her forehead until they burned, and when Hanna pulled them off, there was a big pink rectangle on her skin. She and Henry would howl in pain and laughter, and Susan would call it that "weird nerd stuff," but soon enough she'd have a wrapper spit-pasted to her head, too.

Her mother had bought the pink boots just two days earlier, at Target. They were the only pair left in Hanna's size. Well, not really her size. A couple of sizes too big, but with rain boots it didn't matter because they always flopped on her feet anyway. Hanna walked around her bedroom a few times and decided to add another pair of socks.

Downstairs, Susan waited on the porch, then locked the door when Hanna came outside. She never used to lock the door, but now she said she didn't want to come home and find someone waiting for them inside. Her mother kept her so close now, afraid she'd be taken again. Hanna loved her for that. She loved her for so many things, even though she thought Susan might not love her quite as much anymore. Hanna figured that was okay. Some of her mother's love died with Henry, and if she knew the *whole, real* truth she might stop loving her at all.

My fault. Daddy is dead, and it's my fault.

They walked close together, their feet bumping every few steps. Hanna didn't avoid the puddles, but she didn't splash in them, either; just trudged through quietly so the water wouldn't jump up into her boots and soak her socks. Her mother used to yell at her about jumping in puddles. Splashing in sneakers was the worst, Susan told her, because the water would make them smell like an old man's boxer shorts. Or so she said.

Hanna had never smelled boxer shorts.

Her mother pressed her lips together, sniffled, her eyes turning pink. She swiped her fingers beneath her nose.

They passed St. Catherine's, and Susan slowed for a moment, her steps shortening. Hanna slowed with her, looking at the building, the gray stone blocks stacked on one another, the glass windows, colored not with pictures of people in togas with white birds fluttering over their heads but with bright patterns of seemingly random hues. Two sets of wooden doors—tall enough for giants— were fastened with black metal straps instead of hinges. She knew the building was old; she felt the oldness radiating from it as she walked by.

She'd been inside a couple of times. The first was when her great-aunt Madelyn was in town for Christmas with her grandmother and she wanted to go to midnight mass on Christmas Eve. Hanna had only been four and didn't remember much, except the smell—thick and spicy and cough-inducing—and that she fell asleep on her father's lap. The other time was in first grade when she'd slept over at Katie Torino's house and Mrs. Torino had asked if Hanna wanted them to take her home before mass or after. She said she'd go with them, since she didn't want to go home because Henry was away lecturing for the week and her mother would expect her to help clean the house—their Sunday routine, and Hanna got stuck with the toilets and the dusting.

But the main reason she wanted to go to mass was because Gregory Husker had told her earlier that week at lunch that if someone who wasn't a Catholic went into the church and touched the holy water to his lips, he would be struck dead.

"No lie," he told her. "My CCD teacher told me."

She knew nothing of Catholics, other than what her mother had said of them, mostly complaining of the traffic they caused on Sunday mornings when she was trying get to Price Chopper. "If they cared that much every other day . . ." she mumbled as she drove. Her mother and father did not believe in God. She asked once, and her father told her religion was for the irrational. Her mother said nothing good came from such foolishness.

But Hanna had been curious, so she went, not phoning her parents first. She and Katie rushed up the steps, beating Katie's brothers, and Hanna hung on to the metal handle and leaned back with all her weight to open the front door, but not before tracing the leafy carvings in the dark, veined wood. She had the sense of having been there before, but dismissed it as simply the memory of that midnight mass and peeked through the second set of heavy doors.

"Go, go," Katie said, poking her in the back as Hanna hesitated in front of the marble bowl waiting at the back of the church. She watched people dip their hands into the water and touch their foreheads, their shirts. They sat behind an old woman with a funny doily on her head, like the ones her mother put under cakes when she took them to someone's house. But the woman's doily wasn't paper but lace and was held in place with dozens of bobby pins. Hanna counted the windows, each with a shiny gold plaque underneath.

On the wall at the front of the church, high above everything, hung a statue of a man, his arms outspread, his legs overlapping at the shins, muscles and ribs carved deeply into the figure. There were diamond shapes in his palms and on the top of the foot Hanna could see, and a wreath on his head. She thought it was creepy and beautiful all at the same time.

"Who's that?" she whispered.

"Who?" Katie said.

She pointed. "That."

"You don't know who Jesus is?"

"How would I?"

"Because everyone knows."

Hanna didn't, though. The only time she'd heard His name was when her mother or someone on the TV said it. She'd thought it was just a word grown-ups got to use, and kids got yelled at for using. Not a real-life person.

"Why's He floating up there like that?"

"He's hanging on the cross."

"Why?"

"So we could have Easter. And so we won't go to . . . you know. The hot place." Katie smacked her lips. "Well, I won't, at least."

"Girls, shhh," Mrs. Torino said.

Through the hour, Hanna sat and stood and knelt when everyone else did and listened to the chimes and the organ. She waited in the bench with Katie when her parents and older brother went up front to eat the body and drink the blood. "I know. Gross, right?" Katie said. "But my brother got a hundred bucks when he made his Communion. I get to next year. And it's really just wine, anyway."

On the way out of the church Hanna stuck her fingertips quickly into the bowl of water and then scurried through the doors to the parking lot. There, she licked the water off.

She didn't die. Didn't even get a stomachache

or a cold sore. And the next day in school she had told Gregory Husker that he was full of baloney. She didn't, however, tell her parents she had gone to church.

Hanna wanted to go back inside today. But she didn't want to go in with her mother.

She wished she could go in with Claire.

Once the church was behind them, Susan picked up the pace and Hanna kept up. Both of them were fast walkers, wanting to get where they were going, moving with purpose. They continued around the long block, and then the short one, and after a brief detour onto the main road—the shoulder was very wide, and the cars moved over the middle yellow line as they went by—they turned down their own street and climbed up onto the porch. Her mother unlocked the door and, as she took a bottle of Dr Pepper from the fridge— another thing not allowed in the house when her father was alive, soda—Hanna saw the number one blinking on their answering machine. She pecked at the button with one finger.

It was Claire. Of course they could join her at church tomorrow morning. She'd wait for them in the vestibule at ten o'clock.

Hanna's first thought at seeing Claire's church was one of disappointment. New Life Christian was nothing like St. Catherine's. It was a flat, dull building of brick—and not even the nice brick like at Stewart's, with all different shades of brown and red and black and white, but one unvarying color—with plain windows. When she and her mother went inside, Hanna saw the ghost of old lettering on the door. *Hughes Insurance Agency.*

"You made it," Claire said when she saw them. "I'm always afraid I give bad directions."

They followed Claire into a large room with padded seats instead of benches, plain walls, and two fake trees in the corners up front. Someone had strung white Christmas lights through them, and the shiny, too-green leaves mirrored the glow. There were announcements at the beginning, some singing with instruments and microphones, but no elaborate rituals of kneeling and touching and speaking in unison. No smells, except for the coffee brewing on the table in the lobby.

Hanna tried to listen to the man who spoke; he wore normal clothes and brushed his hair forward so the ends became his bangs. She was trying to grow out her bangs—Susan had always kept them trimmed before—and they were long enough now that sometimes they got stuck up in the folds of her eyelids when she blinked. Today her mother had combed them out of her face and fastened them to one side with a pink plastic clip, her hair so fine she could still wear barrettes meant for toddlers.

The speaking bored her. She didn't want to know about spiritual gifts, whatever those were;

she wanted to know about the Jesus who helped her escape, the one who floated on the wall of St. Catherine's, who had diamonds in His palms and love in His heart. Maybe Claire would tell her.

In the end, though, she didn't ask. Her mother kept shifting around in the seat next to her, using the pencil from the holder on the chair in front of her to draw sticks and circles in the margin of the papers someone handed them when they walked in, to poke holes in the paper and her pants, until the point broke. Hanna had heard her on the phone with Dr. Diane yesterday afternoon, asking why her daughter was "obsessed with religion" and was the psychologist sure she should be encouraging it. Apparently the answer was yes, because there they sat.

Hanna reached for a pencil, too, and the card in the pocket next to it.

I would like a pastoral visit.
I would like more information on New Life.
I have made a decision for Christ today.

She drew a steady X on the line in front of the second option, since she didn't know what a pastoral visit was and didn't know what kind of decision Christ needed her to make. Susan snatched the card from her, folded it in half and tucked in under her thigh. That was what she did with things she planned to throw out but didn't want to put in her pocket or bag because she might forget about it there. And then she kept turning around to look at the clock on the wall above the exit.

When the time was up and everyone stood to leave, her mother grabbed her by the arm and pulled her from the seat. "You have things to do, I'm sure," she told Claire.

"Stay, please. There's coffee and donuts."

"No," Susan said. "We have things to do, too."

"Okay, then. I'll see you Wednesday, Hanna."

She nodded, and her mother pulled her through the people talking, through the ones eating donuts and drinking coffee, Hanna as far behind her mother as their linked arms would stretch. On their way past a table piled with pamphlets and booklets and flyers, she reached out and snagged a small brown book stamped New Testament in gold letters from a basket with a handwritten Take One sign taped to the front. So her mother didn't see it, she dropped it down the side of her mud boot, and it bounced against her ankle with each step she took to the van. When she got home, she carried her boots with her as she ran up the stairs and, standing in the middle of her bedroom, searched for a place to hide the book.

"Hanna?" Susan called. "What do you want for lunch? A bean burrito or leftover ravioli?"

When she didn't answer, her mother came after her, and Hanna climbed onto her bed, sticking the book between the stuffed animals crowded into the netted hammock holding them.

"What are you doing?"

Hanna waved a wooly rabbit. "I wanted Mr. Checkers."

"Well, get him and come down to eat."

She nodded, bounced down onto the mattress, landing on her backside, and slid beside her mother, taking her hand. Susan squeezed back. "I love you, baby."

"I love you, too."

Her mother didn't say it—*"I love you three"*—like they always used to do, counting up until her daddy told them to stop—*"You're driving me stinking nuts"*—or they grew tired of all the syllables it took to say the whole thing. *"I love you one hundred and twenty-seven"* was a mouthful, but they only got that high when they were driving in the car and it was boring and they were sick of playing I Spy or listening to stories on tape from the library.

Instead, Susan took both her hands. "You can talk to me, too, you know. More than anyone else. More than strangers. More than angels or things you can't see. Because I know you, Hanna-Bee. No one will ever love you like I do."

But she couldn't. She spoke with Claire because of the cross and the television and something inside her that tingled when she saw Claire on the bench that day, something she thought about every night as Susan slept beside her. She couldn't understand why she sometimes felt closer to a woman she met only a few weeks ago than she did to her own mother.

She talked to Dr. Diane because she had to, and even then not so much. She didn't remember the things the psychologist wanted to know. Sometimes she tried, and there was a big black splotch over the picture in her head, and when she concentrated on it to move it away, she started trembling and her armpits flooded with sweat and she wanted to scream. And then Dr. Diane would tell her it was okay, but Hanna knew it wasn't.

And that's why she couldn't talk to her mother, because Susan wanted her Hanna-Bee, and Hanna didn't want her to know she wasn't coming back.

13

Claire
November 2002

Claire started with a blank sheet of gridded paper. Many constructors used computer software, and sometimes she did, too, if she was in a hurry, but for the most part she liked pencil and paper, enjoyed the process of tracing the lines and shading cells, the scraping sound of the boxes being colored in by the side of the graphite point. Liked the challenge of coming up with her own words. She kept two pieces of lined paper near her, one for the across clues, one for the downs.

She drew her grid, fifteen by fifteen, wrote in her three theme answers—each playing off of an ice cream flavor, filling in an entire row of open boxes—having thought of them last night, in bed. The clues, of course, allowed for a double meaning.

Path having most boulders?

THE ROCKIEST ROAD.

Hanna had inspired the puzzle.

Scattering some dark squares around the puzzle but still keeping the grid's one-hundred-eighty-degree rotational symmetry, she counted the number of letters she needed in all the across entries and, on her lined paper, indicated those in parentheses.

Snickerdoodles, in beige?

COOKIES AND CREAM.

It took her three to five hours to finish a puzzle by hand, and if it was published she'd be paid between fifty and three hundred dollars, depending on the publication. Most paid less. She had sold three Sunday puzzles to the *New York Times* at one thousand dollars each. But those were surprises, blessings, all coming at a time when she'd had a large financial need—the furnace had to be replaced, the transmission in the car went, an unexpected leak in the roof when the ice backed up under the shingles one particularly difficult winter—and she clung to the God who provided.

Daniel had given her the house in the divorce and he paid a small amount of alimony; though there was still food and utilities and property taxes, which were unbelievably high, she had been able to make ends meet. It didn't take much work or self-control because, for the longest time, she wanted nothing—except the impossible, which cost nothing.

And then Hanna came along.

Cocoa-covered sparrow?

CHOCOLATE CHIPPY.

She finished the puzzle in just over three hours and, later that afternoon, left the house for Hanna's Wednesday counseling appointment. Diane Flinchbaugh said Hanna was more responsive when Claire was there, and while she didn't want the girl to become completely dependent on Claire, it did help once a week to have her around. And on Saturdays it was ice cream and something—a walk in the park, a trip to the library, a crossword puzzle at Hanna's home. Susan always drove Hanna, and Claire met them in her own vehicle. And then the mother would wait in the van or follow behind—far enough to give her daughter the privacy the psychologist insisted was important during these times, but close enough to step in should any problem arise. Hanna hadn't asked any more questions about

Jesus—in fact, she spoke very little when they were together, and about seemingly random things—but the girl wanted to say more. Claire saw that clearly. She could only wait until Hanna decided to speak what was on her mind.

She didn't blame Hanna's mother for her distrust. Who would let their child out of her sight after all Hanna had been through? But distrust wasn't the only thing there. Claire thought it was jealousy. She wished she could say to Susan, "Look, there's nothing to worry about. I'm not trying to steal your daughter away from you." Or, more bluntly, "Your daughter chose me. This wasn't my idea." But neither was completely true.

No, she wasn't trying to take Hanna's affection from her mother, but she liked being needed. Liked it so much, in fact, that *she* found pockets of irrational jealousy brewing when Hanna spoke to Susan. And while getting involved with the girl hadn't been her idea initially, she couldn't imagine life without her now. She was certain God had put them together, for whatever reason. She hoped His plan was for Claire to help Hanna heal. Maybe it was, maybe it wasn't. Most days, though, it seemed Claire was doing the healing, Hanna the salve beneath the bandage.

At the psychologist's office, Hanna remained withdrawn. Diane tried to prod her in different ways, asking her to explain past drawings, introducing the possibility she would return to school in January, asking her if she missed her friends, her teacher, homework. Hanna seemed content to tear paper into strips and write words on them. When Diane leaned over to read them, though, she folded them tight and put them in her pockets.

"You're quiet today, Hanna. Secretive."

The girl shrugged.

"Is something bothering you?"

She shook her head, traced her hand on a clean white page.

"Have you ever made turkeys like that?" Claire asked, leaning closer to see.

Diane's head snapped up, but when Hanna said, "A long time ago," the psychologist moved her chair to the periphery, giving Claire permission to come closer.

"One year we made strings of paper handprint turkeys at Thanksgiving and hung them over all the windows," Claire said, tracing her own hand in brown. She added black eyes and feet, a yellow beak, a red wattle.

"We?" Hanna asked.

Claire exhaled. "Caden and I. My son."

Hanna abandoned her handprints and cut another sheet of paper into strips. On one, in green marker, she wrote *together*.

Diane said, "Hanna, I'll be back in a few minutes. I need to speak with your mother."

Claire knew, because the psychologist had told

her, that during these "parent-doctor conferences," Diane actually went into a small viewing room where she could watch Hanna's interactions with Claire through a two-way mirror. *I need to see the two of you interacting on your own. It gives me insight I cannot get when I am in the room.* So Claire agreed, reluctantly, because the psychologist said it would help Hanna. And Claire wanted that more than anything.

"I noticed you write words," Claire said.

"I like words."

"What do you like about them?"

"How they sound. Mostly."

"Mostly?"

"Sometimes how they look. Sometimes what they mean. But mostly how they sound."

She nodded toward the strip Hanna held. "What about that one?"

"What it does. That's what I like about it."

"I don't understand."

Hanna uncapped a blue marker with her teeth. She smoothed the paper strip in front of her and drew lines between the letters—*to/get/her*. "It means something different when it's in pieces."

Together. Safe, firm, comforting. Break it apart and all the comfort disappeared. *To get her*. Claire thought of being chased.

Diane would have pushed. She couldn't. "I like words, too."

"Really?"

"Yes," Claire said. "I like them so much that I use them in my job. I write crossword puzzles."

"You must know a lot."

"I use a dictionary and thesaurus a lot."

The girl folded the paper strip and tucked it down into the little fifth pocket of her jeans. "My mom's a museum curator. My dad . . . he's dead."

"I'm sorry."

"He worked at the college."

"As a professor?"

Hanna nodded.

"He must have been very smart."

"He was. He knew everything about science. But my mom, she knows everything about everything." Hanna paused. "She's talking about selling the house. She thinks I don't know. But I heard her on the phone."

"I'm sorry. That sounds hard."

"Did that happen to you, when your son died? Did you have to move somewhere else?"

"No," Claire said. She wanted to choose her words with care, but Hanna was a perceptive child; she'd know if Claire was being dishonest. "But other things changed."

Hanna traced her hand again. This time she turned the paper around so her fingers were feet, her thumb a tail. She drew a long neck and head, and colored inside the lines yellow, adding brown spots. A giraffe.

"Very clever," Claire said.

165

The girl shook her head. "Not me. I saw it on television."

"Well, I like it."

"My mother . . ." Hanna paused. "She wants to go back to work. She hates being home. With me."

"No, Hanna. That can't be true."

"You don't know," she whispered. "She loves me. And she hates me. I see it."

Claire waited, but Hanna said nothing else, scribbled something on the paper, tore around the writing and rolled it under her palm into a tight, pointy scroll. The institutional clock on the wall ticked off the minutes. Diane came back into the room; Hanna's time was over.

"Think about school," Diane told the girl, and Claire left the session with her and her mother.

"So, Saturday?" she asked.

"We'll call," Susan said.

"Can we have ice cream today?" Hanna asked.

"Baby, we have errands. I told you that."

"Claire could take me."

Susan froze, and Claire knew that put-on-the-spot feeling. No answer was the right answer. Susan's fingers tightened on her daughter's shoulder, dimpling Hanna's purple down coat. "Not today. Claire has things to do, too."

Hanna turned to her. "Do you?"

Crossword puzzles? Washing the kitchen floor? Claire hated to lie. More than that, she wanted to be with the little girl. "Listen to your mother,

Hanna. It sounds like today is a busy day for her."

"But I have to ask you something."

"Go ahead. I have a minute."

"I have to ask you in private."

Claire looked at Susan; the woman's cheeks pulled in, her lips wrinkling, chin jutting forward. She looked back, her eyes demanding Claire to just tell Hanna no, but Claire couldn't do that. She heard the urgency in the little girl's voice. Something was bothering her. She wanted to tell Claire. Not her mother. And Claire wanted to know. The possessive feeling inside her grew, and instead of cooperating in what she knew was right—that is, urging Hanna to mind her mother—she said, "It's up to your mom."

Susan's gaze shifted down to her daughter, who stood quietly, her pale eyes focused back on her mother. Hanna didn't have any sort of pleading look on her face; she didn't wiggle and whine like most children would, like Claire had seen Caden do a hundred times. She didn't fold her hands together as if in prayer, waving them in front of Susan and begging, "Please."

"Not today," Susan said.

She put Hanna in the van, slammed the door, and turned to Claire. "I do this for her, because the doctor says it's best."

"I understand."

"Do you?"

"Yes, of course."

"I don't think you do. Just remember your kid is already dead. You're not getting mine."

And Susan brushed past her, bumping her out of the way, climbed up into her own seat, and slammed the driver's side door, too. The tires squealed as she sped from the parking lot, making a left—oh, so easy for her, for everyone else—and leaving Claire with the sting of a real mother's words.

She drove home, let herself into the empty house, and flung her purse on the hallway table. It overturned, fell to the floor, contents spilling out onto the ceramic tile because she'd been too lazy to fight with the zipper. She knelt, jammed lip gloss and rumpled receipts and pennies back inside by the handful. Thinking she'd gotten everything, she stood but then saw a white card half tucked under the molding.

Andrew Brenneman's card.

She snatched it up, crumpled the thick paper, and in the kitchen stepped on the garbage-can pedal. The stainless-steel lid opened, mouth-like, ready to swallow her meager offering. Claire looked at the card again, thought about what she'd be doing that night—more puzzles, another Healthy Choice meal, reruns on television. Things had changed since her children died, but she'd never thought, three years later, she would be able to count the number of black plastic trays she'd stuck in the microwave—nearly one for every night of the week.

She dialed. The phone rang twice. "Hello."

"Is Andrew there, please?"

"This is he."

"It's Claire."

"Claire?"

"Rodriguez. From lunch last month?"

"I know who you are, Claire," Andrew said. "I was responding in shock, not confusion."

"Oh."

"What can I do for you? Need an architect, I suppose?"

She took a breath. "Actually, no. I was thinking of a . . . well . . ."

"Date?"

"I thought, maybe, more along the lines of, you know, a . . ."

"Date."

"No." Claire twisted the phone cord around her wrist until it cut off the circulation in her hand. She unwound it. "Okay. Yes."

Andrew laughed, his voice crackling with static because her cord was loose in the receiver. "You're a tough one, Claire. But I'm glad you asked."

"I'm not asking. I'm accepting. You did the asking."

"Am I also doing the planning?"

"I suppose."

"Good. Then I'll pick you up Friday night at six, if that works for you."

"Do you need directions?" she asked.

"No. I'll find you."

He took her to Comanche, a swank bistro on the lake—reservations only during the summer and racing season but half filled most nights after Labor Day. Andrew wore casual pants and a blazer and unpolished shoes, probably what he'd worn to work. Claire had broken down and, as much as she didn't want to give Andrew the wrong impression—the impression of caring—put on black patent heels and a knee-length dress, long sleeves, empire waist, flattering over her figure. But she kept her tapestry-patterned jacket on all night; the little bit of cleavage that looked good in her bathroom mirror seemed much too much as she caught sight of herself in the mirror hanging over the entry table near the front door of her house as Andrew pulled his car into the driveway. No time to change. She'd buttoned the top two buttons, leaving the rest open, hoping somehow she'd look like she was making a purposeful fashion statement, rather than hiding.

He ordered grilled salmon, she fettuccine Alfredo, which she regretted as soon as the words were out of her mouth. Yes, it was one of the least expensive items on the menu, but it was also one of the messiest. The sauce would be in her lap by the end of the evening.

They made small talk for a while, trying to find a comfortable groove, or more likely trying to wear one in. She asked about his job; he wanted to know about hers. They kept it light and impersonal, staying away from former spouses and children and anything controversial. No politics. No religion. Finally, Andrew said, "I have to know."

"What?"

"What made you call?"

Claire twirled noodles around her fork, set it on the edge of her bowl. "I don't know."

"Yes you do."

"Hanna," she said.

"Who's that?"

"This little girl who . . . It's a long story."

"I have time." Andrew took his napkin from his lap, wiped his mouth and set it on the table, near his place. "Told the sitter midnight."

"Do you remember last spring that bank robbery where a man got shot and killed, and his daughter was taken?"

"Yeah. Horrible."

"Well, the girl who was there . . . ? That's Hanna."

"What about her?"

Claire told him the story—most of it. And when she finished, Andrew tore a roll in half, swiped

171

it around his plate, and said, "That's amazing."

"I know."

"God is good, Claire."

Her shoulder twitched. She picked up her water goblet, stem between her middle fingers, glass cradled in her palm. Sipped. The ice bumped against her lips.

Andrew ran his hand down his tie, smoothing it. "Was it something I said?"

"What do you mean?"

"Do you not think God is good?"

"Of course He is."

"But you got quiet."

"Sorry. I didn't mean to."

"I think you did," Andrew said.

Claire wadded the napkin from her lap and put it on the table. It uncrumpled by itself, as if it lived. "Don't presume to know what I mean and how I feel."

"I know because I've been there."

"And where is that?"

"Confessing with my mouth but not my heart."

The waiter came, refilling their water glasses and taking their near-empty dinner plates. "Can I interest you in dessert?" he asked.

"No, just the check," Claire said. "Thank you."

"Is that my cue?" Andrew asked, as the waiter turned away. "Time to say thanks for the conversation and maybe our paths will cross at the grocery store sometime?"

"If you say so, since you seem to have it all figured out."

"I've certainly been given the cold shoulder by a woman before. I pursued my wife for six months before she said two words to me, so I know what a brush-off looks like."

"I'm not brushing you off," she said. "I had a nice time."

"Just not nice enough to see me again."

The waiter slid the leatherette check folder on the table; Claire reached for it, but Andrew snatched it from under her hand. "A brush-off and a clear 'I can take care of the check myself so he doesn't think he wasted his time or money on me.' "

"I wouldn't want to assume you're paying."

"It's a date, Claire. Of course I'm paying. Dense I may be, but I am not a Neanderthal." He slid several bills into the clear plastic pocket. "Come on. I'll take you home."

On the drive to the restaurant they'd barely spoken, but Andrew had kept the radio on, so it hadn't felt as uncomfortable as the return to her house, in the silence, Claire listening to the rattle of the road beneath the tires, the buzzing of the wind through the slightly unsealed door. Andrew glided into the driveway, shifted his Toyota Prius into park, and unhooked his seat belt. "I did have a really great time tonight. And I would like to see you again."

"I don't think so. But I appreciate the dinner. It was—"

"Nice. I know."

"I'm sorry, Andrew. I guess I'm just not good for this yet."

"For what? Eating food? Talking in a car? Making a poor widower feel like he's about as interesting as a bowl of cold oatmeal?" He fiddled with the key chain hanging in the ignition. "Maybe you'll give me a few points for making you laugh."

"It's not you. Really."

"Will you at least let me walk you to the door? It will keep my gentlemanly sensibilities inflated."

"I can do that."

She pushed open the door, and he came around to the passenger side to close it for her. He walked behind her, and when she climbed the one step onto the patio, he didn't, remaining on the concrete walkway. She stood a head taller than him then, standing on the stoop in the fancy shoes she hadn't worn since the Christmas party at Daniel's office, only days after she learned she was pregnant with Alexis and everyone was still alive and happy. "Thank you. I did have a nice time. Seriously."

"The pleasure was all mine. Seriously."

Claire smirked, shook her head. "Well, good night, I guess."

"Claire?"

"What?"

"I do think I know it all. It's one of my incredibly annoying personality traits, along with four million others that I wish you'll one day get to see so you can tell me over and over how incredibly annoying they are."

"What are you talking about?"

"I want to see you again. Since that utterly disastrous day at lunch, I haven't been able to get you off my mind."

"I didn't even—"

"I know. I know. I can't explain it. But I've been praying you'd call. And praying I'd stop thinking of you if I wasn't going to hear from you again. But there you were, on the other end of the line, when I picked up the other day."

"That's crazy."

"I'm an architect, Claire. I'm about as dull and predictable as they get. I don't have grand schemes, and I don't expect to turn into some middle schooler over a woman I hardly know. But there it is. You're right, it is crazy. And what makes it crazier . . ." He stopped, tugged the sleeves of his jacket, first the left, then the right. Shook out his arms. "What makes it crazier is that I haven't felt this way about anyone since my wife."

"I don't know what to say."

"Say you'll go out with me again. Once more. And if you can't stand me after that, I won't say

175

another word. I'll just wave to you in Price Chopper if I see you squeezing oranges. That's it. I promise one more dinner won't kill you."

She hesitated, watching this accomplished, handsome man quiver in the yellow patio light, pouring out his feelings with a rare honesty, knowing his chances for success were slim indeed. But she found him endearing, and she hadn't been pursued in a long time. It was flattering. "You're right. I think I can handle one more meal with you."

"I know I'm right," Andrew said, his smile all teeth, lips thinning, nearly disappearing. "That's one of my other incredibly annoying habits, that I think I'm always right."

"So, I'll give you a ring?"

"Oh, no. You don't get a chance to back out. I'll call you. 'Night, Claire."

"Good night."

Andrew walked back to his car, jiggling the change in his pants pockets. He didn't look back at her as he slid into the driver's seat, and if he waved after turning on his headlights and backing from the driveway, Claire couldn't tell through the dark windshield. She waited until she saw his car stop at the corner of her street, turn left, and disappear behind the evergreen buffer the developers had planted to separate the neighborhood from the main road.

Inside, she undressed, squirted some baby oil on

a cotton ball and wiped away her mascara—waterproof so it wouldn't wash off—and scrubbed her face with a washcloth. She twisted her hair away from her face, put on a nightgown even though she hated them—they rode up in the night, tangling around her thighs—but all her other pajamas were either in the hamper or too warm to wear. Then she puffed her pillows and burrowed back against them, covered her legs only from the knees down, and turned to the next puzzle in her book. She set the timer, tried to fill in the words, but her eyes kept wandering to her open closet and the dress she'd worn, hanging in the center of the bar between her plain thermal shirts, her cotton sweaters, her printed tees.

Tomorrow she'd go to Macy's for something new to wear the next time Andrew asked her out.

14

Hanna
November 2002

They didn't get the Jesus channel on her television. She searched late at night, when her mother was sleeping, waited until Susan snored and then waited some more, until the snoring smoothed and became one long, rough breath going in and coming back out. When that happened, Hanna could roll out from under her arm without waking her, and if the snoring did start up again because of too much jostling, she waited on the floor until the sleep sound came again.

She knew all the creaks in the hallway's floorboards, the stairs, so she could walk downstairs without stepping on any of the loud places. By her bedroom door she needed to stay close to the floor molding, so close she had to walk on her toes with her back flat against the wallpaper. In the middle she jumped to the opposite side, avoided an area of dark wood outside the bathroom, and then tightroped along the center board until she reached the stairs. She had to skip the top two, swinging herself over them by clutching the banister. Then three more safe steps and a jump onto the area rug in the entryway, closer to the front door, avoiding the very bottom stair.

Most nights she didn't sleep. She tried staying in bed, but there were only so many sheep to count, and when she tried, the sheep morphed into Thin Man, or Fat Guy, or Short One, and then her body prickled with sweat and each hair on her arms and legs stretched up as if reaching for the sky, tugging a little bit of skin with it—and it hurt. And she remembered the smell of the kennel, of her father's blood.

She couldn't lie there with her thoughts. The TV helped.

The closest thing she found to the Jesus channel

was an infomercial for Time Life praise music. Hanna watched people with raised arms, swaying back and forth, tears running down their faces and star-shaped shimmers on their pupils. Were they happy? She couldn't tell, though she thought they must be or they wouldn't be on a com-mercial. No one wanted to buy music that made them sad. At least she figured as much.

Sometimes she watched *Law & Order* episodes; they were on three different stations. Or she turned on QVC or a cooking show or the TV Guide channel. And then she decided to hide the book she took from the basket at Claire's church in the living room. One morning, while Susan took a shower, she used a steak knife from the silverware drawer and cut a slit in the underside of the couch, in the lining hidden by the dust ruffle. The book fit snugly, and Hanna couldn't imagine her mother ever finding it there.

It would have been easier for her to just tell her mother about the book. She didn't know why she thought Susan would be mad. No, *mad* wasn't the right word. She felt deep down, though, her mother wouldn't approve of the book, like she didn't like the Catholics who took up the road when she needed to get to the store.

Like she didn't like Claire.

Hanna reached under the couch and found the book. *New Testament—Psalms—Proverbs*. She had started reading at the beginning, but there was a whole list of names she couldn't pronounce, so she skipped through to the part called Luke because that was her daddy's middle name, and her grandpa's real name, even though everyone had called him Loop and she had no idea why. But she read what she could even though there were lots of words she didn't understand, some really pretty words she wanted to write down but didn't, and the letters were so small. She thought she had a magnifying glass in her bug-collecting kit but couldn't find it. So she held the book close, squinting, learning about old lady Elizabeth's baby leaping for joy when it heard the voice of young girl Mary—Jesus's mother—and Hanna understood something she hadn't before.

Why she loved Claire.

That day on the playground, even before she saw the cross necklace, she had something inside her jump, too, when Claire had asked to push her. It was this, what the book called the Holy Ghost. She didn't know anything about ghosts, but she knew she felt safe around Claire in a way she didn't feel with her mother. Not just safe. Close.

It was too cold to sit outside now. Her mother parked her van in the spot directly in front of the store so she could see Claire and Hanna if they sat at the table in the store window. And that was where they sat, after Hanna ordered her cone and

Claire poured hot water over a tea bag—Lipton, which she said she hardly ever drank because it tasted like dingy water—and covered the paper cup with a lid.

"My mom is mad I'm here," Hanna said.

"Why do you think that?"

"I just know." She'd thought it would be fun to use a straw today, to stick it deep into the ice cream and pull it out, the middle plugged with mint chip, and then suck it out the end. But it didn't work well at all, like a too-thick milk shake. She chomped down on the plastic and scraped out the cream, jabbed the straw in again. "I wanted to go with you by myself. Without her following."

"She's trying to do what's best, Hanna. She doesn't want something to happen to you . . ." Claire stopped, and Hanna knew that she had almost added *again* but stopped herself. "And, really, she doesn't know me. Neither do you."

"I do."

"Not really. I could be . . . not a nice person."

"You're not."

"No, I'm not. But your mother is right to be cautious."

Ice cream dripped over Hanna's fingers. She went to the counter, asked for a bowl, and the teen girl with the messy ponytail and eyebrow ring gave her one, smiling, and a lid, too. "Don't forget a spoon," she said, and Hanna took one.

She turned her cone upside down into the plastic bowl and sat back down at the table.

"You're not hungry today?" Claire asked.

She shrugged, unsnapped her coat pocket. "I took this," she said, gently pushing the Bible toward Claire, the cover curled back, corner creased. Jagged paper triangles stuck out from the pages, like teeth. "The sign said I could."

"That's fine, sweetie." Claire touched her hand. "Have you been reading it?"

"Some."

"Is this what you have questions about?"

Outside the window, a horn blared—two short bursts—and Hanna looked out to see her mother motioning, tapping her wrist.

Claire said, "You'd better go. We can talk Saturday, or maybe next week."

But Hanna shook her head. "You have to tell me first."

"What, Hanna?"

"You have to tell me . . ." She felt a cold puff of air on her hair and heard her mother's voice.

"I know you saw me, Hanna-Bee. We have to go. I have to be at Cindy's in less than fifteen minutes."

Hanna slipped the book from the table back into her pocket, snapped the flap closed with one hand, pushing the metal buttons against her hip until they popped into place. "Claire can take me home."

"Hanna," her mother said, in that *don't start this again* voice. "We have to go now."

She didn't want to leave, but Claire had the same look on her face as her mother—two adults ready to back each other up, like adults do—and so scooted from the booth. Susan closed her coat for her. "Want the rest of your ice cream?"

Hanna shook her head.

"Throw it out, then."

She did, the sides of the plastic sticky with melted green goo, and after pushing the bowl through the swinging door of the trash, she wiped her fingers on her jeans.

"I'll see you later, Hanna," Claire said.

"Okay," she whispered.

Her mother jerked her head toward Claire in acknowledgment and then, holding the door open for Hanna, bumped her through and outside and into the van.

"I told you not to do that again in front of her," Susan said.

"She's nice."

"I don't care, Hanna. You don't know everything. Remember that."

"I know that Cindy canceled. I heard it on the machine."

Her mother turned around, her face scrunched with anger. "Okay, little girl. I don't want to hear another word out of you. You may think you can get away with whatever you want, and maybe

183

I've let you, but not anymore. No more Wednesdays and Saturdays with Claire. I don't care what Diane says. We don't need her. You don't need her."

Little girl. She called me little girl.

She suddenly felt threatened by her own mother, and it scared her. Susan meant nothing with the words—not like *he* did—but it still brought up all the things she'd been trying to push down deep, to keep down deep—like when she had been sick with the flu in first grade, and she had to throw up but didn't want to, because she wanted to go to school that day for the Christmas party, and she kept her hand clamped over her mouth, swallow-ing any tickle of vomit that inched up her throat. She managed then, even ate one of the candy-cane cupcakes Mrs. Torino had made, white with red swirls in the cake, and red icing, too, with crushed candy canes sprinkled all over the top. She didn't know, though, how long she could keep what was inside her now from coming up. Each time Dr. Diane asked questions, it got harder not to remember.

She was so afraid of living it all again.

At home, she ran into the house and slammed her bedroom door, locking it.

"Hanna. Hanna, open up," her mother called through the door, and when she didn't, Susan went away, returning minutes later, and Hanna heard scraping in the doorknob as her mother tried to jimmy the lock. It opened, and Susan came in to find Hanna facedown on the bed, coat on, boots on. Hanna felt her mother touch her back, but she didn't speak, didn't roll over. Eventually Susan left without closing the door. And Hanna waited until she heard the murmur of her mother's voice on the telephone before she snaked her hand into her pocket to touch the little book. Just holding it calmed her.

She had two questions for Claire. She wanted to know if Claire felt it, too—that jump in the womb, that Holy Ghost who wasn't scary at all, the *pull* when she and the woman were together.

And she wanted to know if the friend Claire talked about—Jesus—would still love her if He knew she'd been the one who made the decision to go to the post office first, and not the bank. If she had chosen the other way, her father would be alive.

Oh, Gee. Jesus, I mean. Jesus. Help me.

Only she didn't know what help she wanted this time.

15

Claire
November 2002

Hanna had called and asked her to bring ice cream when she came. The girl could eat ice cream every day and never choose any flavor but mint chocolate chip. Claire had bought her a half gallon of Breyers a few weeks ago, but her mother wouldn't let her have it too close to bedtime, since anything like ice cream or milk had always given her nightmares. She said she didn't mind them, though. "Sometimes it's scary, but fun, too, in a way. Like watching a horror movie." Horror movies and bad dreams must be a welcome relief for her. God only knew what that little girl saw in her head when she was awake.

She said she hadn't liked the Breyers all that much, sort of icy and gritty, not smooth like the mint chip at Stewart's. And not green, either.

Claire didn't care for cold foods since the weather had changed, and autumn had settled over them fully, nights barely above freezing and layers of brown leaves in her yard. She needed to rake, but couldn't find the motivation. Caden had loved ice cream year-round, too, but he'd picked a different kind every time. They would drive past the convenience store while running errands or taking Amelia to occupational therapy, and he'd say, "Can we just stop, please?" And she would let him, of course, pulling in front of the shop with the car running, allowing him to run inside by himself, his coat unzipped, a dollar fifty in his hand and a bit more responsibility growing him taller every time.

Claire took the long way to the Sullers', nearly a twenty-minute drive for a three-mile trip. No left turns. She still couldn't make them, though some mornings, when she sat at the stop sign on the corner of Fifth and Rockland, she'd almost swept the side of her hand down over the directional rather than up, could almost feel her body listing left, waiting to go, wanting to. She could be there for minutes, debating, arguing in her head, until another car rolled up behind her and honked, prodding her to make the right.

Amelia had been left-handed.

She had told Heidi once that her children haunted her. Now, sometimes, she could just have memories of them, little thoughts that made her smile. Like when Caden wanted to make it into the *Guinness Book of World Records* for the longest consecutive days chewing the same piece of gum—after seeing *Willy Wonka and the Chocolate Factory*, of course—and decided to go to bed with the gum in his mouth. He woke up with it in his hair and refused to let Claire cut it out. So she scrubbed with peanut butter, held ice on it, washed his hair in baby oil. Nothing worked. Finally, Daniel convinced Caden a buzz cut was the cool way to go. Claire hated seeing her son's black curls on the bathroom floor, but he gained the swagger of his daddy that day.

Or when Amelia performed in her first dance recital. She had been so proud, and Daniel bought her the biggest bouquet of roses he could put together, driving to every florist in Avery Springs, collecting more than one hundred yellow and pink and red and white flowers. Oh, she had been the envy of her class, and then all the flowers had to be in her room. Claire needed five vases to hold them, and Amelia smelled each one of them every morning until they shriveled and died. They collected the petals in a box, and Claire tied a ribbon around it and tucked it on the top shelf in her daughter's closet.

They buried that box with her.

Sometimes the memories still came with stinging tentacles, wrapped around her limbs and pulling her down, down, down, and those were the times Claire went to bed, forcing herself to sleep, to forget. Or she opened her puzzle books and focused on the clues, the words. The letters. That's what crossword puzzles were, letters in boxes. She had been living her life in those boxes; if she moved outside their black lines, the world came back to her. But she was learning the letters only had meaning when put together in the correct order, written out to match the clues, fit perfectly in the squares. Letters alone meant nothing. Life alone meant nothing. All the crossword puzzles and the fourteen-hour nights wouldn't bring her children back.

But God had given her Hanna.

No, she wasn't her child. But Hanna gave her a reason to get out of bed in the morning. The girl needed her, wanted her around. When was the last time someone had wanted her? Other than Andrew.

Their second date had been nice, as had their third. They spoke on the phone an evening or two during the week, not a long time, maybe a half hour if one of them felt particularly chatty, but both were still trying to find their way in this dance of dating, two adults who'd never expected to have to do the *finding the right one* thing again.

She liked him.

The Suller house came up on her quickly, like always, tucked back behind an island of landscaping. It was on the west side of the city. The money side—where people had driveways and carriage houses and perfectly painted trim around the windows. Susan had started inter-viewing nannies, Hanna told her. *"It's too sad for her to stay home with me. She's going back to work."* And this twinge of resentment built, the idea that she was a better woman to take care of

Hanna, that Hanna needed her more than her own mother, that she deserved the girl's love because she knew how to give love back in the right way.

Parking in the driveway, she prayed, as she always did before seeing Hanna. She knew from Diane Flinchbaugh that the girl had yet to open up about the trauma she experienced. Sometimes Claire thought Hanna wanted to tell her things, would if Claire only asked. But she was afraid to; she didn't want to know what Hanna had gone through, not really. Didn't want to know what men were capable of when it came to innocent children.

Claire had a hard enough time living in the real world without having those pictures in her head.

Still, Hanna had sounded a bit, well, more distant than usual on the phone. She usually spoke little, but there was a hitch in her voice, a distractedness. Claire thought maybe Susan didn't know she was making the call—it was the first time Hanna had phoned her; usually her mother did, if any messages needed to be conveyed—and that would explain the tightness. She knew the girl wanted to talk about something, but with Susan hovering while they visited, she doubted they would have any opportunity to speak openly. She had been surprised to learn Hanna had taken one of those Gideon Testaments but was glad. Claire wanted to buy her another Bible, one written in a translation she could better understand, but also didn't want to do anything to disrupt the precarious balance she found herself trying to keep—building a relationship with Hanna without increasing Susan's clear distrust.

She wasn't doing it all that well.

The light beside the front door hadn't been turned off yet, which surprised Claire. She knew from Hanna it was one of the first things Susan did each morning—it used to be Hanna's job— and she glanced at her watch even though she'd looked at the time seconds ago, before leaving the car: 10:07 a.m.

She knocked on the door, expecting it to open, expecting both of the Sullers to be standing there, Hanna in her coat with a shy smile glossing her lips, Susan trying not to let her daughter see she hated her going out. But no one answered. The half-gallon box of ice cream cold and sweaty under her arm, Claire knocked again, waited, tried the doorknob. It turned—unlocked; also unusual for the Suller home—and she pushed the door open, stuck her head inside, and called, "Hello?"

Silence.

There weren't any lights on in the house, either. Claire felt a spidery sense of concern scurry up from her stomach to her head. "Hanna? Are you home?" She found the three light switches near the door, flipped them all on. The lights came on in the upstairs and downstairs hallways. The closet door was open, and Claire didn't see

Hanna's purple coat. Hangers tangled on the closet floor.

"Anyone here?"

She thought briefly of calling the police, but the idea was so fleeting it left her before she fully knew it was the rational thing to do. Walked down the hallway toward the kitchen. And then she saw it, on the ceramic tile floor.

Blood.

Not slick and shiny, but coagulated, nearly black in some places, gloppy. No neat puddle, either; it looked as though someone had pulled themselves through it, smearing it along the floor. There were half handprints on the counter, the back door-jamb, the wall. On the stove, a cast-iron frying pan lay bottom up, half covering one burner.

Saliva flooded Claire's mouth; she swallowed it down, inhaled and held the air in her lungs until her desperation to breathe overtook her desire to run, to vomit. To scream. She grabbed the pan—had never used a cast-iron one before, so its weight surprised her—and climbed the stairs yelling, "Hanna? Hanna?" All four bedrooms were empty. She checked the closets and under the bed. In the bathroom she hesitated a second, images of *Psycho* in her head, and then pulled the shower curtain back with a quick jerk.

Empty.

Downstairs again, she dropped the pan on the floor. Cell phone. No, her purse was still in the car. She reached for the phone hanging on the wall in the kitchen above some skinny, high-backed stool. Dialed 9-1-1. Gave the information and hung up. Then she called Andrew.

"She's gone, she's gone. And there's blood all over here, and she's gone. Oh, Lord, please let her be okay. Andrew, we need to pray."

"Slow down. Who's gone? Who's bleeding?"

"Hanna. I'm here in their house, and there's blood and she's gone."

"Call the police."

"I did. They're coming."

"Then get out of there, Claire. Get in your car, lock the doors, and wait."

"Sirens. I hear them. Please, come."

"I'm on my way."

16

Molly
February 2009

The ocean had decided to shake off the cold, at least on Dorsett Island. The springlike temperatures had brought people to the town and through the museum. She'd sold a dozen admissions, and three hours still remained until closing. Outside the kitchen window, the round thermometer with a faded smiling rainbow background read fifty-nine degrees, matching the record high.

Dorsett Island was the third and smallest island in an archipelago, the population of all three totaling eleven hundred year-round. The museum was the last building at the end of the island, a converted Dutch Colonial with traditional gray clapboard siding, more gray from the ocean air. In the late 1940s, Mick's father had taken a chain saw to the entire front of the house and installed the huge window after he'd seen a wax figure display on a boardwalk at Coney Island. The House of Wax was Lou's baby; he had traveled all over the United States to buy figures and to see other museums.

It had been popular in the '50s and '60s, when Dorsett Island was popular, when vacations meant summering at a quiet beach in a picturesque location. But now vacations meant Six Flags and Disney Cruises and other places built around constant consumption and entertainment. A small, rocky outcropping in the northern Atlantic could only entertain for half a day, maybe—two dozen photos of lobster boats and wild sea, a clam roll and some homemade saltwater taffy from the quaint local businesses, an overpriced jar of Maine blueberry jam, and tourists had wrung all they could out of Dorsett Island.

She could see a part of the beach from the front window, a small wedge of rock and sand at the end of the street. Two desperate sun worshipers wore bikini tops with their jeans, hoping for an authentic layer of bronze over their store-bought tans, despite the ragged wind. An older couple carried their shoes and stood close to the water, the waves crawling in to lick their toes. One little boy built a sand castle. A girl with white-blond hair ran with a kite—a vibrant butterfly attached to the string clutched in her hand, the purple and blue and orange ribbons twisting from the bottom tips of its wings. Molly watched the little girl run until she had no more room, her path blocked by a sharply rising, forested bluff. She turned and went back the way she'd come, moving fast and careless down a thin finger of granite reaching into the sea.

She'd had a kite once, a plastic one her father bought from the dollar store because she was with him, and she begged, even though he said it would fall apart in an afternoon. She wanted it anyway, picked out one with an American flag design, and he paid for it along with his batteries and paper plates for their camping trip. Then the three of them headed to a campground in Lake George—Molly, her father, and her mother—towing the rented pop-up and playing letter search, trying to find A through Z on the signs they passed, even though it was only a thirty-minute trip. The camping area was wooded, with tall pines and little sky, but Molly ran that kite up and down the dirt road in front of their site, no more than six feet of string behind her, the red-white-and-blue triangle bouncing along the ground more than floating in the air. That had been July. She never would have imagined she had less than a year left with him.

"Oh, awesome! Can we go in? Please?"

Molly heard the voice outside the window, drifting in through the open door Louise had propped open with a chair that morning. A young boy, maybe ten, bounced between two adults, his hair thick gold and windblown, his jacket tied around his waist.

"I don't know, kiddo," the man said. "It looks—"

"—so cool."

"I was thinking infested."

"Oh, please, please? Come on. It's vacation."

"We could see how much it costs," the woman said.

"Awesome," the boy said again, and Molly watched him shake them off, bouncing into the lobby as the man called, "We're just checking." Then the adults, too, were inside, telling the boy not to touch anything.

"I'm not," he said, staring at Elvis. "He looks dead. Like embalmed or something. Can I poke him?"

"No," the man said. "We already told you that."

"It's okay," Molly said, and the three twitched, turning to her as if surprised to see something *alive*. "Just don't poke too hard."

196

"Thank you," the boy said shyly. He stretched up and touched the tip of the wax figure's nose, petted his face. "Weird."

"It's twenty-five for all of us," the woman whispered to the man. "What do you think?"

He nodded, and she waddled to the counter, her pregnant belly swelling from between her mostly unbuttoned cardigan; only the top two were closed. "Two adults and a child," she said, taking out her credit card.

"We're going?" the boy asked. When the man nodded again, he posed with his hands on his hips, squeezing one eye shut so the side of his lip pulled up. "Thank you, thank-you-very-much."

"Funny," the man said.

Molly ran the card through the machine without checking the name, handed it back to the woman, distracted by her face. She looked more than familiar. Known, somehow. Brown hair, layered and slightly wavy to her chin. Thick brows, but not bushy. Dark eyes. Pretty, like Brooke Shields's in *The Blue Lagoon*—a movie she saw late one night on Lifetime. Her voice dislodged something inside Molly, and she thought of ice cream, of the two most important waffle cones of her life —the one she never had that took her away, and the one that brought her home.

The woman signed the credit slip. *Claire Brenneman.*

No. Rodriguez. Claire Rodriguez. It's not her. It's not her.

"Thank you," the woman said, taking the small white paper and folding it, first the long way, and then in half again, before sticking it into her back pocket. "Ready?"

"Oh, yeah," the boy said.

Molly stood there, the phantom scent of mint chocolate chip in her nose, holding the edge of the counter so she wouldn't fall over. Her feet tingled, and drops of sweat slid from her armpit down her side, catching in the band of her bra.

"This way?" the man asked, pointing to the curtained entrance, and Molly managed to nod, croaking out something like "Have a good time," forgetting to give them a brochure or instructions about following the signage.

When they were through the door, Molly's breathing turned loud, shaky, her vision graying over like static on the television. She took some time to straighten up the counter and the lobby displays and then walked through the office to the apartment door, unsteady, her fingers frigid, and went in to find her mother working on the couch, bookkeeping files mounded on the coffee table.

"I heard people," Louise said.

Molly nodded. "I'm not feeling well."

Her mother looked up. "What's wrong?"

"I just need to lie down."

"You look awful."

"I know. Please, will you just do the desk?"

Louise glanced at her pile of work. "Give me fifteen minutes. There are a few things I really need to finish up yesterday."

"Mom—"

"Ten. Okay?" She held Molly's gaze.

"Okay," Molly said, and somehow managed to find her way back behind the counter. She felt like wax, one solid mass of inorganic matter, void of faith or feeling. She couldn't make herself bend to sit down, so she leaned against the stool. Claire would be coming back soon; Molly would have to force a smile, a word or two, but as hard as she tried, there were no words or smiles, or thoughts even. Only the past six years of secrets, dropping away like Shirley's fingers before she could catch them.

Finally, Claire, the boy, and the man pushed their way through the exit draperies, the boy grinning with enthusiasm. "The Chamber of Horrors was so cool. Did you see how that guy's brains totally looked like they were spilling out around the ax? I mean—"

"I think I'm done hearing about brains," the man said.

"Unless you can tell me the three main parts of it," Claire said.

"Mom," the boy said, drawing out the *ah* sound. "It's vacation."

Claire laughed. "Learning never takes a vacation. Tell me and you can pick one of those postcards."

"Even one with the ax guy?"

"I'm afraid so."

"The cerebrum. The cerebellum. And that other one."

"Which is?"

"Um. The brain stem. Does it have a fancy name?"

"Not that you learned," Claire said, laughing again. "Go ahead, pick your postcard."

They ignored Molly, a family, the boy flipping through glossy pictures of movie stars and monsters, the man picking up the wax candy displayed in cardboard boxes on the small souvenirs area—chewable lips and fangs and mustaches. "Claire, do you remember these? I loved these things as a kid," he told her, showing her the Nik-L-Nips, old-fashioned bottle shapes filled with different-colored sugary liquid.

The boy, having decided on his postcard, joined the man at the shelf. "What are they?"

"Candy. You bite off the tops and drink them."

"You had weird stuff back then."

"Do you want some?" Claire asked.

"Nah," the man said, but she took two packages, and the postcard, and brought them to the register.

Molly wanted them gone. She shook open a small paper bag, dropped the items inside, and folded it over, giving it to the little boy, who waited next to Claire. "Free?" he asked.

"Of course not," Claire said. "How much?"

"Uh, one sec." Molly fumbled around for the calculator. She couldn't remember the price of anything. She couldn't make her fingers move. The boy said, "I can do it in my head," and he blinked a few times before blurting, "Four-ninety. Unless there's tax."

"There isn't," Molly said. "Have a nice day."

The woman looked at her, not with recognition but with bewilderment. She scrounged through her purse for a five-dollar bill, held it out. Molly pressed her thumb against a dime in the cash register, slid it up the drawer; it fell under the counter. "Sorry. Let me get another," she said.

But Claire brushed her arm. "Don't worry. Just leave it."

Her fingerprints stayed on Molly's arm, warm in the spot Claire had touched, a place close to her wrist, exposed because she wore three-quarter sleeves. She rubbed at it, trying to erase the sensation.

The boy grabbed a couple of brochures and stood by Elvis, putting his arm around the figure's waist. "Take a picture, Dad."

"A quick one," Claire said. "And then back to Beverly's. I think this nice young lady might want to close up."

The man wriggled a small digital camera from his front jeans pocket, snapped two photos, and Claire told the boy to put his jacket on. "And zip up. It's getting cool." As the boy worked the metal teeth into the zipper, the door behind Molly opened, and she heard her mother's voice. "Moll, I'm done . . . No, it can't. . . ."

In front of her, Claire's lips went white, her face yellowing, and her hand moved to her stomach as she wheezed slightly. She was looking over Molly's shoulder, at Louise. "You."

Molly didn't turn around.

"I'm sorry," Louise said. "I think you must be con—"

"Susan Suller."

"No."

"Claire," the man said, coming close behind her, his hand now on her stomach, too, fingers laced with hers. "What's going on?"

The woman's head pivoted slowly away from Louise. She shrugged off the man's arm and stepped around the counter until she stood just inches from Molly. With cautious fingers Claire touched her hair, dyed brown for the past six years, and looked straight into her face. "Hanna?"

Her mother stepped between them, bumping Claire away. "You've got this all wrong—"

"Yes," Molly said. "Yes, it's me. I'm Hanna."

Silence.

Louise stared at Molly, her proud shoulders rounding forward. Claire slapped at her eyes, coughed. "I went to your house . . . The blood . . ."

"Just go," Louise said.

"I can't leave. I need to know what happened. I searched for you. I thought—"

"Claire," Molly said, and the woman blinked. "Please."

Claire nodded slowly. "Okay. Okay, but Hanna, can we . . . talk?"

Molly breathed deeply, feeling empowered, like her two halves had started melding together. "Yes."

"When?"

"Tonight. Come back at seven. Come around to the side door. It's for the apartment."

"I will."

"No you won't," the man said.

"Andrew," Claire said.

"I don't like it. You don't know—"

"I'll be here." Claire took the man's arm. "Let's go. Beverly's going to be wondering after us."

The boy tore off a small corner of the small brown bag he held—his precious postcard tucked inside—rolling the paper in his fingers and pushing it between his lips. He chewed it, swallowed, ripped another piece. The man took the bag from him and folded it into his back pocket, then spread his arms over the boy and Claire and shuttled them out the open door. Louise pulled the chair away; the door fell shut and she fell on it, her entire body against it, fighting to keep out the past. She twisted the lock, dropped into the chair. Her handprints and forehead prints smudged the dusky glass. "You didn't have to say who you were," she said.

Molly closed her eyes. "Someone needed to."

PART TWO

17

Claire
February 2009

Claire didn't want to be still. Her body had to move in time with her explosive thoughts. She paced back and forth in front of the bed, in the guest room she and Andrew shared, the plush green carpet darkly streaked with her feet's disturbance. Her belly contracted under her palm, the skin pulling tight, hardening with a fuzzy twinge. She exhaled, her mouth starting in a little O, then flattening until her lips pressed nearly together and her breath whistled out between them.

"You need to rest," Andrew said.

"I can't."

"The baby—"

"It's nothing. Just Braxton Hicks."

"Claire, sit."

She did, in the chair by the window, as far from her husband as she could get. He sat on one corner of the bed, near the headboard and nightstand on *his* side. The right side. They both had been sleeping on that side when they married, and she gave it up for him, though she was still most comfortable there, too, and sometimes she started on the right side if she went to bed before him, pretending to be asleep when he finally came upstairs. He would kiss her hair and slip in behind her, and when she snuggled back against him, he'd say, "You always know that spot is yours if you want it."

"This is my spot," she'd tell him, rolling overtop of him, to the left, and burrowing into his chest. "Which side of the bed—that's just geography."

Now Andrew moved around the mattress, sat with his leg touching hers. "You can't go over there by yourself tonight."

"Nothing's going to happen."

"You don't know that."

"Oh, Andrew, come on. This isn't television."

"People don't just disappear when they have nothing to hide."

"I'm done with this conversation."

"I'm not," he snapped, and then quickly softened. "I know you loved that little girl, but think about it, Claire. If they wanted you to know where they were, they would have contacted you a long time ago."

"I have thought about it. I've thought about it every day since I showed up there and she was gone. I used to wonder all the time if I'd see her on the street one day, in the grocery store, in the mall. Early on, that is. I'd look for her everywhere. Then I stopped." Claire winced as the baby inside her jammed its feet under her ribs. "I didn't even recognize her."

Andrew went into the bathroom, came back with a glass of water, and gave it to her. She drank it all—lukewarm, the way she liked it—and the baby quieted. "I need to know what happened. From her," she said.

"Then I'm waiting outside the door for you."

"Okay," she said, "okay." And her husband tugged her from the chair, pulled down the bedspread.

"Take a nap. Please. For me."

"I'll try."

He kissed her, pushing her down into the pillow, and her body went willingly. Then he lowered the shade and switched off the light. "I'll call you for dinner."

She couldn't sleep, Hanna's little-girl face in her mind whether she kept her eyes opened or closed, pale and ethereal and floating between the two metal swing chains, where Claire first met her. Today's Hanna had a longer nose and narrower chin and dark hair. Colored, of course. But her eyes were the same, the palest gray-blue, cataract-like.

How could she not have seen her standing there?

Claire rolled onto her side. A stomach sleeper, usually, she had difficulty finding a comfortable position while pregnant. Sometimes Andrew stacked pillows on the bed, creating a pad for her body from the rib cage up, and from the pelvis down. She'd lie on them, her stomach beneath her in the space between the pillows, her protruding navel just brushing the mattress. She could doze like that for an hour or so, but not a whole night. Plus, baby Brenneman insisted on nestling against her bladder anytime Claire managed to make her way into a deep sleep. She didn't remember peeing so much with her other three pregnancies. Either her memory was going, or her body.

I'm getting old.

They had, for five years, debated having another child—Claire not knowing if she could handle it emotionally, Andrew concerned about Jesse being displaced—working to avoid it but also staying open to an accident. Finally, with indecision pushing her to thirty-nine, and him six years older, they decided that door had closed. "I don't want to be collecting social security the same year my kid graduates high school," he'd said.

But God and His eternal sense of humor had other plans, and Claire bought an EPT after two weeks of craving hot dogs and onions, and another week of vomiting up her tea every morning. She told Andrew she was pregnant after Jesse had gone to bed—no cutesy "To the world's best dad" cards, no Onesie wrapped in a box for him to open; she didn't even save the test stick—and he said, "Are you happy?"

"I think I am."

"I think I am, too."

She couldn't imagine not having this baby now.

Jesse wanted to be a big brother. Andrew painted the nursery three times—first pale yellow, then pale green, then a bright Granny Smith, because neither of them were pastel people, even for a baby's room. And Claire framed the ultrasound printout, adding it to the collection of photos on her nightstand. Caden and Amelia. Alexis's ultrasound, faded gray and hard to discern her head from her feet, but Claire still knew. Jesse's baseball picture, his ears pushed out from the band of his too-big hat, the brim bent into a deep upside-down U, the way Andrew wore his own caps. Her wedding photo.

She got up, went to the bathroom to change from her rumpled clothes into fresh ones and brush her hair. Strands of silver glinted in the mirror, and she pulled several out, along with even more brown hair, and shook the hair off her hand into the sink. Washed them down the drain. Andrew hated that. At home, he kept a Zip-It tool on top of the medicine cabinet because, inevitably, the sink clogged at least once a month. He'd stick the toothy plastic strip down the pipe, pull out the dark, disintegrating hair in clots of foul-smelling mush, and ask her to *please, please* use the trash can instead.

"Mom," Jesse called, barging into the bedroom.

Claire stepped out of the bathroom. "Knock much?"

"Sorry." The boy stepped back into the hallway and closed the door. *Tap, tap. Tap.*

"Come in."

Jesse slipped back into the room, his round cheeks stained with the afternoon's walk. "Dad told me to get you for dinner. Beverly made ham."

"I'm coming," she said.

He looked nothing like Andrew, was every bit his mother. Elizabeth Brenneman died when Jesse was two; he had no memory of her, which made it easy for Claire to slip into the place she'd left. It was more difficult with Andrew. Not for him. For her. She had seen the photos at his home, framed on every wall and in every corner, of his darling Lizzy and her long, firm dancer's body, her face like a Botticelli. She'd died of lung cancer, a smoker during her career, like many ballerinas, the nicotine an appetite suppressant, the cigarettes something in their mouth instead of food. Seven months and gone. Andrew had been devastated.

The depth of Claire's relationship with Andrew had been inversely proportional to the number of pictures he kept out, more frames disappearing with each of her visits to his home, replaced with ones of only Jesse or both him and his son together, until finally even the wedding photo above the fireplace came down the week before he proposed. Claire said yes but didn't understand what he saw in her, after all he had with Lizzy. She still had days when she felt like his second-best wife, though he never did anything to promote those emotions.

She went downstairs and ate the ham, and potatoes and peas Beverly made for dinner, not speaking, listening to Jesse chatter away about saltwater taffy and the beach and the shells he'd found in the sand. When he switched to the wax museum, Andrew tried to hush him, saying, "Nothing gruesome at the dinner table."

"It's all right," Beverly said, her words tumbling lopsidedly from the sagging corner of her mouth, courtesy of a stroke several years ago. She had been the best friend of Claire's mother and was now one of Claire's closest confidantes. "Always fascinated by that place."

"You've been there?" Jesse asked.

"Oh, a few times, when I first moved to the island."

Claire couldn't resist. "Do you know anything about who owns it?"

"Still Mick Borden, I think. He got it from his papa and I haven't heard of it changing hands."

"There's a woman who works there. And a teenage girl?"

"They've been there, oh, I don't know, maybe five years or so. They stay in the house part and run the place for Mick. He can't be bothered with it. Won't sell it, though, because he'd have to split the money with his brother, and he's not likely to do that, ever. Those Borden boys haven't been able to stand each other since the day little Petey was born."

Beverly sipped her iced tea, holding a napkin under the glass to catch the dribbles. "Andrew says you two are having a date tonight?"

Claire stopped her head from whipping toward her husband, pulling the surprise at his lie inward. "Yes," she managed.

"Jesse and I already have plans to play Monopoly into the wee hours."

"Beverly likes it, just like me. I told her you and Dad never play 'cause you hate it so much."

They took the car because the night had frosted, no longer fooled by the sun into believing spring had come, and drove in silence not three minutes down the street. Andrew pulled into the peastone parking place next to the museum, and they climbed stone stairs cut into the hill; at the top the gravel continued on a forked path—one curved left to the museum's porch and front door, the other kept straight before wrapping around the side of the house. Andrew walked Claire to the apartment door, not touching her but hovering, and said, "You have your phone?"

"Nothing's going to happen."

She knocked, and the outside light burst on. Susan opened the door, and Claire slipped past her, into a spotless mudroom area, laundry folded neatly in plastic baskets on top of a front-loading washer. "This way," she said, motioning through the only doorway—a curtained opening in the wall.

Claire went through into a dining area, where three pedestal coffee mugs waited on the table beside a Bundt cake. Hanna stood behind one chair. "Hi," she said.

"Hanna." Claire went to her, drew the girl in, her pregnant belly a rock between them. Hanna was tall now, inches taller than Claire, but still willowy frail, a mix of teenaged growth spurts and melancholy. She wore lean straight-legged jeans, a hooded thermal top, striped socks, and no shoes. She allowed herself to be hugged but didn't relax into it.

"It's Molly now," Hanna said.

"Molly." It felt unnatural on her tongue, as fake as Hanna's brown hair. "You had a cat . . ."

"My aunt did." Hanna hooked the handles of all three cups with one hand and lifted. "Sit, sit. Can I get you some coffee? We have decaf."

"That's fine, Ha—Molly. Thank you."

Claire sat. The girl poured coffee and cut cake, dropping a slice on a creamy white saucer—it matched the mugs—and sliding it in front of Claire, and then sat, too, leaving one chair between them. Susan still stood, close to the curtained doorway. Claire took a tiny sip of her drink, scalding the tip of her tongue. She itched the burn against her teeth. Took a breath. "So, how are you?"

"Good. I'm good," Hanna said. "You?"

"Really good."

"Pregnant."

"Yes, you see that," Claire said, smiling a little. "That's why we're here. On Dorsett Island, I mean. A family vacation before the baby comes."

"You're married again, then. To that man?"

"Andrew, yes."

"And happy?"

"Yes, very much."

"I'm glad for it, Claire. You . . ." Hanna's fingers fluttered around her thin hoop earring. Tugged at it. "I'm just glad."

There were no forks on the table. Claire broke a piece of cake off with her fingers, tasted it, not because she was hungry—the ham had given her indigestion—but for something to do to keep her from falling into the deep, deep moment between their words. She wanted to ask what she knew she couldn't. The answer waited at the very bottom of the chasm, and she wasn't ready to jump down into that dark place with Lord-knows-what-else lurking there.

She only wanted safe answers.

Hanna wasn't ready to go there, either—her legs crossed, her hands trapped between her thighs, her elbows tight to her ribs. Closed off.

"You're eighteen now," Claire said.

"You remember."

"Of course I remember, Hanna. How could I

not? I looked for you. Everywhere. Your aunt wouldn't tell me anything. I went to the police. I thought—"

"Enough," Susan said. "Ms. Rodriguez—"

"Brenneman," Hanna said.

"Whoever you are," Susan snapped, "we left Avery Springs to have peace, to get Molly away from the scrutiny. To make a fresh start. I expect you to respect that. If not, please leave."

Claire brushed crumbs off the edge of the table. "Of course. I apologize."

Hanna shredded her napkin, rolling pieces into tiny wads and piling them on the table by her mug. She sniffled, wiped her nose with the back of her hand. Turned her head away. If Claire wanted to have a conversation with her—a real conversation with the real Hanna—they both had to be away from the girl's mother.

"Ha—Molly, would you have time tomorrow to, maybe, get some dinner?"

"No," Susan said.

"Yes," Hanna said. Her mother squeezed the flap of skin under her own arm, twisted it, sketched eyebrows low.

"Good, okay. I'll pick you up around four? You'll be home from school then, right?"

Hanna nodded.

"Okay. Right. I'll see you then. Hanna?"

The girl looked at her, pale eyes unblinking.

"It was so good to see you."

217

She nodded again, her face crinkling as she pressed her palm to her eye and dragged it over her cheek, toward her ear, swiping her long hair away from her face.

"Tomorrow, then," Claire said.

She left, back through the curtain, a disillusioned Dorothy who had seen the wizard was nothing magical. Andrew took her hand and, walking her back to the car, said nothing. He understood her, could read her body, knew that for all the words she knew and used and loved, none could fill the boxes now.

18

Molly
February 2009

Her mother wasn't speaking to her. She couldn't say she was particularly bothered by the silent treatment or that it hadn't happened before. Louise's favorite weapon was silence, and most of the time Molly gave in first—she couldn't handle the grating tension around her—apologizing for whatever she had said or done or hadn't done. Today, though, she refused to be the one to cry "uncle" with the first words.

I can be stubborn, too.

She used to be feisty. Her preschool teacher had

called her parents in for a meeting not long after the year began, because Molly had claimed the play kitchen area as her own kingdom, and those who wanted to cook play fruit in the oven had to pay half their plastic bounty to her. Her father had told her she needed to share, and she did because he'd asked, and when Mrs. Conroy had thanked her for being kind, she told her, "I'm doing it for my daddy, not for you." But that was when she was Hanna, before her father's death and the kidnapping and her mother vanishing inward.

And then they ran, and Molly dropped little crumbs of Hanna along the way, like Hansel and Gretel, hoping to find her way back. Instead she lost the little girl who wanted to survive and became a young woman who didn't know how to open a door.

She showered, sat on the floor of the tub, and lathering her legs with a bar of Dove, shaved from her ankles to the tops of her knees. When she finished, she toweled dry and dressed in her favorite brown corduroy pants and a cotton turtleneck.

Claire would come for her in seven hours. She had that long to find a way outside. She'd start with the words.

She licked the tips of her fingers and stuck them to a sheet of white paper in the printer, pulled it toward her. Then she fished the scissors out of the desk drawer and cut the paper into strips, at first as thick as her wrist, as long as her hand. Then she trimmed those down to the size of half a playing card, a matchbook, a Chinese-cookie fortune. She could admit she was Hanna now, allow herself to take part in the things that used to be *her*. Like the words. On the smallest paper she wrote *breathe*. Folded it into her front jeans pocket.

Louise, from the kitchen table, rattled the newspaper as she opened it somewhere in the middle. Molly gathered her schoolbooks and went into the lobby of the museum to slump on the stool for the day and wait. She spent the first hour picturing herself holding open the museum's front door, listening to the cackle from the speaker above, saying to Claire, "After you," and then allowing the glass door to puff closed as she let go, leaving the wax behind her. Leaving her mother. Leaving it all.

How did she end up stuck in a museum, inside and alone?

Gradually, like a frog in a pot, the water slowly heating, the amphibian not realizing it was being boiled to death. It started with too much wind and sea and not wanting to be outside with her friends. Even then, though, she could still go places with Louise—to the grocery store, to the mall in Portland, to a diner or movie theater. But those outings soon became more difficult, her anxiety building on the car ride, growing until Molly would ask to ride in the cart, even though her almost-thirteen-year-old legs were too long, but her mother said that was certain to draw attention. So she'd laced her fingers around the thin, cold shopping cart bars until the metal was the same temperature as her hand and she couldn't tell one from the other, sidestepping strangers and formulating plans in her head should someone try to touch her.

There's the closest exit. The best place to hide is in those clothing racks. No one will find me if I curl up behind all those bulk packages of paper towels.

Soon all those thoughts tingled in her skull, working their way down her arms, her legs, making her limbs heavy and numb. Her breath thickened in her lungs like pudding and she was certain she'd suffocate. Every man looked like Thin Man or Fat Guy or Short One. Molly started crying and shaking when Louise made her go to the store with her; once she passed out in the pharmacy section at Target. Those were attention grabbers they didn't need, so Louise let her stay home.

The museum had dead bolts, alarms, and nothing worth taking. Molly locked her bedroom door and pushed her dresser in front of it when her mother had to leave to buy milk or toilet paper, drew her curtain over the window, and balled herself up in her blankets, hoping it would look only like some teenage girl had forgotten to make her bed. She'd stayed there, contending with her hot breath bouncing back at her, filling the blanket tent, heating it until the sweat sprouted between her fingers and toes, until her mother came back. Then she'd jump out of bed, move the dresser, and with a smile help put the food away, shrugging off Louise's concern when she said Molly looked a little flushed.

At least she didn't need to hide in her bedroom anymore.

Her mother realized, at some point, that Molly had stopped leaving the building, even to pull the sandwich-board sign inside during the summer months. And Molly was sure Louise was happier with the situation like it was, her daughter safe from anything in the outside world and, seemingly, never going away.

She opened her physics book and read about states of matter. Solid, liquid, gas. Plasma. Bose-Einstein condensates. She didn't understand that one completely; something about multiple atoms superimposed over one another, sharing the same space as to be indistinguishable. Multiple lives superimposed over one another. Molly over Hanna.

She would have to lie to Claire. She lied every day, every time she told someone her name, every time she answered to it.

"But those things which proceed out of the

222

mouth come forth from the heart; and they defile the man."

The move to Dorsett Island had brought a relief in anonymity, a distance between past and future that comes only when one's past is erased and one's future shimmers in uncertainty. But now, with Claire's arrival approaching like the waves she watched from the window, Molly felt the two halves of herself poised to collide.

Tobias came first, and when Molly saw him walk through the door, panic spurted up her throat, bitter and raw. She swallowed the acidic mouthful back down, asked, "What are you doing here?"

"Nice to see you, too."

"I just mean . . . I thought . . . Don't you have class?"

"Molly, I'm on break. I told you that two days ago."

"Oh, right." She fiddled with a paper clip, straightening the curves, bending it into a circle.

He stretched, arching his shoulders back toward each other; his knapsack—army surplus with ink drawings covering it—slipped down his arms, and he caught a strap in one hand. "I brought a movie," he said, opening one of the pockets. "Popcorn. Yeah, the microwave stuff, but it tastes really good with a whole lot of butter melted over it."

"Tobias—"

"I know, I know. Don't say it. You don't have butter, right? Well, ta-da." He opened another pocket, pulled out two sticks of Land O'Lakes butter and a plastic ice pack. "I'm prepared."

"My mom is home."

"Does she have something against movies and popcorn?"

Something moved in Molly's peripheral vision, and by the time she turned her head toward the window, Claire had entered to the cackle, her cheeks dressed in February, pink and shiny with dry skin. She wore a fleece poncho, shook off the hood and lifted her hair out from beneath the fabric. "I hope it's okay I came in this way. I knocked on the side door, but no one answered."

"It's fine," Molly said.

"I'm surprised you keep this place open in the winter."

"Tell me about it," Tobias said. "Hey. I don't think we've met."

"Oh, sorry. Claire, this is Tobias. His family owns the pizza place across the street. And this is Claire. She's here . . . visiting."

"Nice to meet you, Tobias." Claire extended her arm. "Your folks keep their business open, too, all year?"

"Ayuh, but people gotta eat, locals as well as flatlanders."

"That pesky food thing. Who knew it would be so important?"

Tobias and Claire laughed, and their voices scraped along Molly's spine, vibrated through her pelvis, into her stomach, churning her lunch around until she felt nauseated. She waited for the inevitable, the *How do you know Molly?* question, and it came seconds after she thought it, falling out of Tobias's mouth, smacking Claire in the face. She wrapped an arm around her stomach. "We both lived in Avery Springs, before Hanna moved here."

"Molly," Tobias said.

"What did I say?"

"You said Hanna."

Claire reddened, swatted the emptiness in front of her nose. "Pregnancy brain. Really, half the time I can't even remember my own name."

Tobias looked from one to the other. She saw the wheels turning.

"So, are you ready?" Claire asked.

"I'm not sure I can now," Molly said.

"I'll speak with your mother."

"It's not that. It's just . . . I'm not sure I can now."

"Okay," Claire said. "I don't leave for a couple more days. Maybe tomorrow."

"Maybe," Molly whispered. The room tilted. She smoothed her fingertips over her eyelids, pulling the corners outward until she saw the world through thin, blurry slits.

"Hanna? Are you sure you're okay?"

Tobias scratched beneath his hat. "Why do you keep calling her that?"

"Because it's my name," Molly said.

She sank down against the window, night seeping through the glass, through the thin fabric of her gray shirt, her skin. She hugged her knees and rocked, tears coming hard and fast, her body shaking with the cold and the crying. Claire didn't move, seemed stunned, but Tobias crouched down next to her, cupped his hand under her chin. "Molly?"

"Don't touch me," she shouted. "Don't."

Louise burst out of the apartment, pushed Tobias aside and, falling to her knees, blanketed Molly with her body. "Go away, both of you."

"I don't—"

"Tobias, for once in your life, just leave." Louise's eyes looked past him, to Claire. "You see what you've done?"

"I didn't mean to."

"You see. She was fine before you showed up here. We were fine."

"It was only dinner."

"You bring it all back to her."

"I—"

"Get out."

And suddenly Molly was being lifted, her mother stumbling backward with a grunt, shifting Molly up a little higher with a jostle, bracing her fleshy shoulders on the window for support. Too tall for Louise to carry her, Molly leaned against her, stumbling into the apartment, to her bedroom.

"Lie down, baby," she said.

Molly pushed the blankets aside, crawled into the flannel sheets, her clothes crackling with static electricity, and in the darkened room she saw small sparks of light in between her pants and the bedspread. When she was a child, she'd hide under the covers and try to make the sparks happen. Like fireworks. Like lightning bugs.

Animalia. Arthropoda. Insecta. Coleoptera. Lampyridae.

"Don't go," she told her mother.

"I'll only be a second."

Louise returned shaking an orange bottle. She pressed down on the lid, turned, bounced two tiny blue pills into her hand. "Sleep. It will go away if you sleep."

That had always been her mother's refuge, one or two bitter dots to usher her into forgetfulness. She took them after Molly's father died. She took them during the long days Molly and Louise rattled around the house—after the tutor and their daily walk and television filled up all the time it could, but there was still more, always more, and nothing left to eat the hours. She took them the days Mick wasn't around, pleading a migraine and covering her head with a wet washcloth while she stretched out on the couch. She wanted that escape now, too, letting Louise drop the pills into her own hand. Molly popped them into her mouth, drank the water her mother gave her. "Don't go," she said again.

"I won't." Her mother lifted the blankets and Molly scooted to the wall, giving Louise room to lie down. And it was like before, wedged in the gully between the paneling and the mattress, but this time Molly fell asleep first.

19

Claire
February 2009

Claire left the museum, Tobias behind her, and they waited outside, huddled under the awning, both silent in their own ways—she completely still, him a mass of facial ticks and joint popping. She didn't know what they waited for, but neither spoke for several minutes. When the lights in the lobby shut off behind them, Tobias finally asked, "What is going on?"

"I can't tell you."

"Why not?"

"It's not mine to tell. You need to ask Ha— Molly."

"Hanna. Molly. What is all this? How do you know her, really?"

"I told you. We lived in the same town, when she was a child."

"There's more."

"I'm sorry. I won't say anything else."

Tobias motioned helplessly to the window. "We can't just leave her in there."

"Her mother will take care of it."

"I think her mother's the problem."

Her uterus contracted; Claire inhaled a short, wheezy breath. She needed water. Closed her eyes, leaned back against the door and massaged the twinge in her right side. "No. She's not."

Tobias looked unconvinced. He peeled off his hat, kneaded it between his hands. "She never leaves, you know."

"Who?"

"Molly. Or whatever her name is. She never leaves the museum."

"What are you doing?" she asked. Annoyance oiled her voice.

"Packing," he said, in that way he had—his way, his only way—the one she hated when she was upset, his tone calm, steady, making her feel flamboyant and neon and out of control.

"Why?"

"We're leaving in two days. I thought I'd get a start on it."

"Put them back."

"What?"

Claire gathered her clothes from the open suitcase, dropped them in the drawer, stuffed them down and shut it. "I can take care of my own things."

"I can see that. Very well taken care of." He moved the suitcase to the floor. "Want to talk about it or just throw stuff around?"

"I can't go."

Andrew sat on the bed. "Okay. Go where?"

"Home. I can't leave yet." She closed her eyes, Hanna's crumpled face appearing in her mind, repeating Tobias's words. "She never leaves."

"Who?"

"Hanna. She never leaves that building."

"What are you talking about?"

"I don't know. It's what the pizza boy told me. He said Hanna never goes outside. She wouldn't go with me today. She had this . . . I don't know, breakdown. She . . . she . . ." Claire flailed her arms. "Andrew, something's not right. And I can't go."

"I can't stay. I have to be back to work."

"I know."

"And Jesse?"

"I can keep him with me."

"While you're running around trying to save the world? I don't think so."

"Your mother will take him."

"For how long? A weekend, maybe. She's too old to do much more than that."

"Your sister, then."

"I can ask her. But, Claire . . ." He took her hand, cupping his fingers around hers, like two Js—what he did when he wanted to make her aware he was close. *"This is us, together,"* he had told her the first time he held her hand that way, on their honeymoon night under white hotel linens. "What are you doing here?"

"I don't know."

"How long are you planning to stay?"

"I don't know that, either."

"What do you know, then? Please tell me, because I seem to be missing something. My wife, who happens to be almost seven months pregnant, doesn't want to go home with her husband and stepson, but instead plans to hang around a deserted island town to help a stranger, who may not even want to be helped by some woman from her past."

"She's not a stranger."

"Yes she is, Claire. This isn't the Hanna you knew. This is some other young woman, six years removed from her relationship with you. And you're not the same person who she met then, either. At least, I thought not."

"What's that supposed to mean?"

"That we were past all this. That you were done beating yourself up over things you have no control over."

She shook his hand off, pulled one of her shirts from the drawer. Shook it, trying to flap away the wrinkles, then flattened it on the bed. "I can't talk to you. You don't understand," she said, folding the shoulders and hem toward the middle and then in half again.

"I do understand. That's what you can't handle."

"I shouldn't be long. A week, maybe two." She folded a pair of jeans, a sweater. "You won't even miss me."

Andrew sighed. "Fine. You do what you need to do." And he left the room, closing the door tight behind him.

She kept away from the museum for the remaining time Andrew and Jesse stayed in town, a day and a half of awkwardness, Beverly's knowing eyes following them when they were at the house, Jesse's kid radar tuned in to the tension. He ate paper when his nerves acted up, and Claire found herself reminding him to spit the wad of napkin in the trash, gave him chewing gum to keep the pulp consumption to a minimum. When Andrew loaded their half-empty suitcase into their Mercury Mariner, Jesse squeezed Claire around the middle, both of them in Beverly's living room.

"You're not getting divorced, are you?"

"Oh, kiddo, of course not," Claire said, kissing the top of his head.

"Who'll do school with me?"

"Aunt Sharon will, and you'll have a great time with your cousins. It's just a week or so."

"Promise?"

Claire nodded and squeezed Jesse tight.

When he pulled back—his eyes almost level with hers—she noticed how tall he'd gotten, his jeans short enough that his bare ankles showed above the flip-flops he insisted on wearing—*"I don't care that it's winter. It's the beach."*

She wasn't tall, could fudge five-three in sneakers, but Lizzy had been statuesque, an inch taller than Andrew, so it was no wonder Jesse grew in his sleep like some magical beanstalk. She certainly didn't remember him coming up so high on her last week.

"Don't worry, my love. It won't be long."

He nodded. "Call every night, 'kay?"

"I will. I promise."

Jesse hugged Beverly and dragged his handled backpack down the hall, wheels catching in the fringe of the rug. He pressed the button, pushing the handle down into the case, and picked the bag up instead, pushing the front door open. Andrew met him there, told him to get in the car, and came inside.

"All set," he said.

"Okay," Claire said.

He put his hand on the back of her neck, pulled her into his shoulder. "You are a stubborn, stubborn woman."

"Even if I am, I don't have half as many flaws as you."

"That you don't."

"Thank you for this."

"Was there a choice?"

She took both his hands, held them against her stomach as the baby rolled beneath her skin. "You didn't say no."

"I would never do that." He pushed back a little. "That's not a foot."

"Backside, I think."

"Figures," he said, laughing quietly. "You love me?"

"You know I do."

"Yeah, but it's nice to hear every so often."

Andrew took his hands away from her belly, placed them on either side of her head, squishing her ears. He kissed the bridge of her nose, where it met her forehead, each eyebrow, her mouth, his breath smothered in her cheek. "I love you. I'll call when I get home."

"Be safe."

"Always am."

And he left, too, and Claire was alone in the living room, watching them drive away through the big picture window. Beverly waited long enough to make it seem like she hadn't been listening, then, leaning on her metal four-footed cane, shuffled in to join Claire. "Tea?" she asked.

"I think I'm going to lie down."

"Tired or sad?"

Claire turned to her mother's friend. Her

friend now, in that strange way children grow up and find their identities as adults in a world that had always seemed foreign to them, forbidden, and then one day at eighteen or twenty-one or thirty are welcomed and expected to call all those people they'd previously known as Mr. and Mrs. by their first names.

It felt almost blasphemous the day she'd first called Ms. Watkins *Beverly,* and even today, almost twenty years later, she sometimes had to stop and think about it. Beverly had never married and had no children of her own, so she loved on Claire and her brothers as if they were worth all the time and attention she lavished on them. She and Claire's mother had grown up together, dirt poor on adjacent dairy farms in upstate New York; their favorite times together had involved drinking warm milk straight from the cow and swimming in the muddy creek separating their parents' land.

When Claire's mother died, Beverly had stepped into the role, dulling the loss. But, after the accident, she hadn't been there, was recovering from the stroke that weakened the left side of her body. Claire had felt her absence acutely, angrily demanding why God would not only take her children and her marriage, but deny her the comfort of her pseudo-mother, as well.

"Both, I think," Claire said.

"I can't help with marriage advice, but I can listen."

Claire sat, as did Beverly, on the Victorian-inspired sofa in front of the picture window. "Do you remember when I told you about that little girl in Avery Springs? The one who disappeared?"

"Yes, I think so. You went to her home and there was some sort of . . . altercation there. Or had been."

"That's it."

"That was before you and Andrew married, was it not? Is there a reason it's coming up now?"

Claire sighed. "She's here. In this town. The teenage girl at the wax museum. It's her."

"Oh my."

"Exactly."

"And you're staying because . . . ?"

"Because she needs me."

"Does she?"

"Yes."

"And what do you need?"

"I don't know what you mean."

"Claire, Claire, Claire. I have known you since you were born, and I see this restlessness in you. You're looking for something."

"I have everything I want," Claire said, shifting her pregnant body on the uncomfortable sofa, the cushions too hard, the back too straight. "Andrew. Jesse. The baby. That's my life."

"Then why, my dear, are you still sitting in my house and not with them?"

"The girl, Hanna . . . she's hurting. I feel like I need to stay and do what I can to help."

"At what expense?"

"It's not like that. Andrew understands."

"That man would throw himself under a bus for you," Beverly said, lips loose, a string of drool stretching from the corner of her mouth. Claire reached into the pocket of Beverly's housecoat, found the handkerchief she always kept there, and dabbed. "Thank you, dear."

"I think God wants me to stay. He brought Hanna into my life once. He brought her again. What are the chances?"

"Then I'm praying for you. All of you."

"Bev . . . Thank you." Claire hugged the woman, tucked the hankie back in her pocket. "I need a nap now. And I need to pray, too. I have no idea what to do next."

"We usually don't. And that's usually where God wants us."

20

Molly
February 2009

She wondered if she'd scared Claire away. She knew Tobias wouldn't be back but had expected Claire to be waiting outside the museum when she turned the sign and unlocked the door yesterday morning. She'd glanced up every time a shadow passed the window. Now today, nearly closing, and Claire still hadn't come. She'd said she was going home this afternoon.

Molly thought about trying to track her down. Claire had mentioned staying with a Beverly. Someone would know her; Tobias—though Molly couldn't ask him—or Mick, or perhaps even her mother. She even began going through the phone book, down each column, looking for Beverlys who lived on Dorsett Island; she made it through the Es before giving up, her eyes skimming over names without reading them, having to go back to the top of each column time after time.

She cleaned the lobby instead, down on her hands and knees scrubbing the floor with a stiff-bristled brush and a bucket of water with too much Mr. Clean, each stroke dredging up dark, soapy streaks on the green tile. Her knees soaked up the water, and she breathed in the chemical scent, her head throbbing. When she finished washing, she towel-dried the entire floor, changed her wet jeans, and walked stocking-footed back out into the lobby. She decided to clean the windows next—Windex and three rolls of paper towels—and when she was done, she moved on to the radiators, sliding the wads of paper between the slats.

Louise looked in on her as she ran a hand broom beneath the baseboards. "What are you doing?"

"Cleaning."

"You don't have to do that."

"I want to."

"Moll—"

"Just leave me alone. Please?"

And her mother left the room, closing the office door.

She poked through the dust with her fingers, sliding the dead insects into piles, sorting them. Thirty-two ants. She remembered her father, firing questions at her.

"Kingdom?"

"Animalia," she whispered.

"Phylum?"

"Arthropoda."

"Class?"

"Insecta."

"Order?"

She always forgot the order, no matter what. There were only five kingdoms, or six, depending on the textbook. Her father stood with six. Either way, those weren't difficult to keep in her head. Thirty-six animal phyla or there about, though ninety-five percent of all animals belonged to only nine of them. With her father's specialty, it was always Arthropoda. Again she only needed to remember Insecta. Once she hit order, she had the main ones memorized, the ones her father had quizzed her on most. Lepidoptera for butterflies and moths. Coleoptera for beetles. Diptera for flies.

After that, she had to look them up in her copy of Peterson's *A Field Guide to Insects: America North of Mexico*, the one she bought from Amazon with a gift card Uncle Mick gave her and had mailed to the museum. When she accidentally used her old name and Louise saw it, she shouted about her carelessness—one of the rare times her mother had raised her voice.

Molly had ordered that guide because it was the same book that used to be in her father's office when they had the big house in Avery Springs, the one that Louise packed to send back to the college after his death, the one Molly found before the box was taken away and had slept with sometimes because she missed her father so much. The one she had left behind in their rush to leave.

She left her pile of ants to find the guide in her bedroom, came back and sat cross-legged on the floor and looked up the order for ants: Hymenoptera. She sorted out the houseflies, the ladybugs, the spiders—not insects—and a couple of daddy long-legs—not spiders. All of them crunchy, their organs long mummified inside their exoskeletons.

Like her. She had shriveled up within her skin.

Why hadn't Claire come?

She helped me before. She could help me again.

And Molly realized she wanted that help. Who sits on the floor, picking dead bugs from the dust? She kicked the pile with her foot, scattering the dirt and carcasses, a few ants clinging to her sock by the hooked claw at the end of their legs. The vacuum was in the office, cord looped on the floor. She untangled it, dragged it behind the counter, and plugged in the wire. Sucked up the insects, the dust, the ants on her sock. And then she saw her. Claire. Walking in front of the museum window. No. She was bent at the waist, one hand on her stomach, the other against the glass, stumbling along. And then she sank to the ground, her hair pressed against the window.

Molly opened the door, stuck her head into the air, her shoulders, her torso, all the rest of her still safely warmed in the fluorescent lights of the lobby. "Claire?"

The woman looked at her, face grooved in pain. "Something's wrong."

"What should I do?"

"Call the ambulance."

Closing the door, Molly rushed to the counter, grabbed the cordless phone, and dialed the emergency number. The operator answered, and she said, "There's a woman outside the museum. She's pregnant and said something isn't right."

The woman on the other end of the phone wanted to know her name, kept asking questions—"Is she bleeding? Is she able to communicate the problem? Does she feel like she needs to push?"

"I don't know, I don't know, I don't know," Molly answered. She called out the door to Claire, relaying the questions. Claire's head lolled against the glass. "Just tell them to hurry."

"They're coming," Molly said. And then she found herself outside the door, her body wrapped in February air, and she crouched down, too—crawled, almost—making her way toward Claire. When she got to her, she only sat there; she didn't have a blanket for her, another coat to ball behind her head, or even a word of encouragement. But Claire took Molly's hand and held it against her stomach. "Pray," she said.

So Molly did, asking God to protect Claire's baby, the words safe in her head, the only way she knew how to pray. The ambulance pulled onto the dead brown grass, its red lights staining the road, its siren bringing people into the street. Two men loaded Claire into the back and drove away, leaving Molly on the wood patio, still gripping the phone, still kneeling on the decking.

Still outside.

She looked across the street; Tobias watched her from the window of the pizzeria. She looked to the door, which stretched away from her, like in a cartoon movie, the distance insurmountable. She pressed her back up against the window, flattening herself as close as she could get to the building, and inched along as if she stood on a high ledge, with the street fifty stories below her. She crept toward the door, her head facing the pizzeria, facing Tobias, until her fingers wrapped around the entrance to the museum and she slipped back into the lobby, not opening the door far enough to set the cackling off. Her breath came in rapid puffs. She squeezed her hands into fists, opened them, shook them, trying to warm them.

"Molly?"

Louise watched her from the office doorway.

"They took Claire to the hospital."

"I know. I saw."

Molly didn't move. Couldn't. She sucked in the familiarity of the museum. It replaced the outside within her, filling her with the things she knew. "You didn't come."

"By the time I heard the siren, I thought . . . Well, the EMTs were there, and there was nothing else I could do."

"I want to go to the hospital."

"Baby, that's not really necessary. There's nothing you can do there, either."

"I want to go. Will you take me?"

Louise tugged the waistband of her yoga pants. "Are you sure you can?"

"Take me, please."

"I'll bring the car around front."

Molly waited until she heard the hum of the engine beyond the glass, and then the *ding ding ding* as her mother left the keys in the ignition and the car door open to come get her. Knocking near her head. She stepped away from the entrance so Louise could push inside, hold Molly by the arm. "Come on."

The air didn't feel as shocking as before, and in three strides Molly was in the car, the lock pressed down, her belt holding her against the seat. She sat straight, almost cocked forward, the headrest a boulder against her skull. Louise drove, lifting her hips up to wrangle her phone from her back pocket, and called Mick. He didn't answer; she left a message telling him where they were going and why. Molly closed her eyes, felt the vibrations in her feet, the potholes in her hips. The car made several turns, Molly swaying with them, and stopped with a jerk. Louise turned it off. "We're here."

Molly looked around. They were in the hospital parking lot, their spot directly under a lamppost, the entrance three rows of cars away, plus two driveways and a landscaped median. She didn't unbuckle, only stared at the glass door, opening and closing automatically as a few people went in and out. And then no one.

"Moll?"

"Just a minute."

She thought, *Wrap your fingers around the handle and pull,* but her arm rested limply on her leg. She thought, *Find the red button on the seat belt and push,* but again her hands remained tucked between her knees. She tried to slow her

breaths as a familiar tingle pooled at her collar-
bone, her shoulders, and dripped down into her
elbows, her wrists. She closed her eyes.

"Why don't I pull up front? You can go in and
then I'll park," Louise said.

Molly nodded.

Backing out of the parking spot, her mother
maneuvered around to the entrance, under the
carport. Molly touched the door handle, metal, not
cold like when she first got in the car, but warm
from the heat vent blowing on it for the entire
thirty-minute drive. She pulled slowly.

"It's locked," Louise said, and she pressed the
button on her side, all the latches clicking open.

Molly flinched. "I can't," she said.

"Are you sure?"

She nodded.

"It's okay. We'll go home." Her mother lifted
her foot off the brake and the car rolled forward.
She turned from the parking lot, humming three
tuneless notes over and over, in varying patterns.
She reached over, patted Molly's knee. "It's
okay."

"For you," Molly said.

"Baby—"

"You're happy I didn't go in."

"What are you talking about?"

"You didn't want me in there. You don't want
me to see her."

"I never said th—"

"And you don't want me to be able to do things."

"Things? What sort of things?"

"Go outside."

"Stop. Now. I know you're upset about that woman—"

"Claire, Mother."

"I know her name."

"You never wanted me around her."

"Why are we doing this now?"

"When are we going to do it? When are we ever going to get anything out in the open? You took me away from her."

Louise adjusted the rearview mirror so the headlights behind her weren't so bright in it. "Just stop. You know exactly what happened."

"I needed her."

"You should have needed me," Louise snapped. "I loved you. I sacrificed for you. I went insane every day you didn't speak. I'm your mother. She was some stranger in the park. And still you picked her over me. Why, tell me that? Because of the religion thing?"

Molly lowered her head, thin tears tracing the side of her nose, crawling up into her nostrils as she sniffled. "She was there."

"I was there."

Not the way I needed you to be. But she couldn't say that.

Her mother sighed, softened. "I'm sorry about

Claire. Really, I am. I'll call the hospital when we get back and try to get an update."

"Fine."

"Moll—"

"It's fine."

Louise closed herself in the bedroom, but Molly had no interest in sleep. Or television. Or opening her Bible. Most of the time the Word was a comfort, but times like tonight it became her biggest accuser. Everything she read ignited her past, burning it brightly before her. But the fire never consumed it; those awful things came out the other side of the flames shinier than before.

She didn't want to be angry at her mother.

She didn't want to blame Louise for the life they had now.

She didn't want to be confronted by her own part in it all—her choice to go to the bank after the post office, her inability to be the daughter she should have been, her reaction to Thin Man when he—

No, she wouldn't go there.

Instead, she dug through the junk drawer in the kitchen and found a pocket flashlight, metallic purple, a stocking stuffer last Christmas. She snuck out into the wax museum, through several displays, and sat down near Shirley Temple. The curly-topped kid had always been Molly's favorite, probably because she'd been closest to

Molly's size when they first arrived. She stroked the wax Toto and remembered all the secrets they'd shared, all the times she'd confided that she hated her mother, hated her life, hated herself. Told her about Henry. She tried now to talk to the figure but felt foolish. She had more than that now. Tobias, for one. Perhaps Claire again. Even the girl who left the Bible felt more real than a wax figure. Molly had been swapping bits of her dead life for a living one these past few months. Now she needed to let go of the rest.

"Sorry, Shirley," she whispered.

Back in her room, she dug the Bible from beneath her pillow, opened to the front cover and ran her finger over the squiggle of black permanent marker in the upper left-hand corner. She felt the indentation of a ballpoint pen, barely perceptible. Digging through her pile of school-books, she found her math notebook, ripped a page from the metal spiral, and placed the unlined top part over the marker stain. Gently, she rubbed the side of a sharpened pencil on the paper. A name appeared, and a phone number.

Ellen Josephine Hicks.

555-3127.

Molly went into the office; her mother never shut off the computer. She did an Internet search and found the Colorado Springs area code—719. She slid her hand over the phone.

What am I thinking? What would I even say?

The clock in the corner of the computer monitor read 11:48. She wouldn't be calling anyone this time of night, even with the two-hour time difference. She wrote the phone number on the bottom of the paper, along with the name. Creased the paper with her thumbnail and, holding it tight over the corner of the desk, tore a thin strip off. She folded it in half, and half, and half again until the scrap was the size of quarter. Back in her bedroom, she taped the square to the underside of her top dresser drawer.

Maybe she would call tomorrow.

21

Claire
February 2009

She watched evening television from the hospital bed, local news and reruns. But even with a canned laughter track echoing in the room, she couldn't stop replaying her conversation from thirty minutes ago, as Beverly pleaded with Claire to call Andrew and tell him about the episode with the baby.

"It was just a scare. Nothing's progressing. The doctor is probably sending me home in a couple hours. I don't want to worry him," Claire had said.

"Mmm-hmm. He's not going to be happy when he finds out."

"Are you going to say anything to him?"

"You're not?"

Claire rubbed one eyelid with her middle finger, the other with her thumb, listening to the membranes squish beneath the pressure. "I don't know."

"Think about this one, Claire. If they're releasing you, let me know. I'll make some calls, get someone from the church to pick you up."

She sighed. The doctor had examined her, said her cervix wasn't at all dilated. She'd be monitored for a bit longer, to make sure the baby's heart rate stayed strong and the contractions didn't start up again, but he expected it was a one-time thing, brought on by dehydration, or stress, or overexertion. Perhaps a mix of all three?

"Maybe," she had said.

She closed her eyes. The hospital gown and sheets left her feeling cold, as did the thin cotton blanket the nurse gave her. She wanted to buzz and ask for another, but the nurse hadn't been happy about getting her the first one. Her feet were ice; she covered her right with her left, trying to warm them, remembering when Caden would climb between her and Daniel in bed, his bare feet always cold, and he'd stick them between her legs. "Go get socks," she'd growl, her skin sprouting goose pimples.

"I have none that match," he would tell her.

She adjusted the head of the bed a little higher, pulled the pillow out from under her and covered herself with it.

She wished Andrew were there.

The same unhappy nurse had brought her a newspaper, too, snagged from another room—the Sudoku puzzle half filled, the crossword started, the first five across clues written in, the first two down, and then the fourth, and a half-dozen random words here and there. Most were wrong, and the previous reader had used pen. Claire stretched, her fingertips hooking the strap of her purse on the side table. She rummaged through for a mechanical pencil, licked the top of the eraser, and patted the excess spit onto the back of her hand. Then she erased the inked words, gently, only rubbing one small hole in the newsprint. Started over. She didn't bother to look at the clock; just filled in clues, one after the other, like old times.

She rarely solved puzzles anymore, didn't attend the monthly meetings at the library, didn't write them, except if she was inspired by a theme she found original, which had happened maybe twice since her wedding to Andrew. The crosswords were part of her *old* lives, the one with Daniel and the kids, and then the one after them. Andrew had said to her, "You know, you don't need to write these anymore, if you don't want to. We don't need the extra money." She had taken that to mean, *You're done.*

She and Andrew had married not long after Hanna disappeared—seven months—and with two words she had become a wife and mother again. "I do." *Poof.* She'd wanted to impress her new husband, so threw herself into the proper-wife role with abandon. Schooling Jesse, running errands, having meals on the table when Andrew walked through the door, keeping the house clean, including those pesky tasks she rarely did previously—dusting the ceiling fan blades, wiping down the floor molding under the beds, folding underwear first in thirds, and then in half. By the end of the first year she had exhausted herself, and she cried to Heidi, telling her she couldn't let up because this was what Andrew had thought he married. A dynamo. Not a dud.

"He just wants you," Heidi had told her. "But who is that anymore?"

She hadn't lied to him about who she was, not really. Not intentionally. She'd presented the picture of the woman she strove to be, who she honestly thought she should be. Andrew liked that picture. *"That's just how I feel, too,"* he'd said over and over, his eyes brightening each time the two of them stumbled onto common ground.

Later, Claire found herself not telling him things she thought he might disagree with; she didn't want the light to dim, to lose her chance with him. Commission. Omission. She told herself there was a big difference. *Yeah, two less letters.* Two missing letters in a crossword puzzle meant *unfinished.* Still she ignored the pressure building up, walled herself up into the perfect Christian woman model advocated from periodical and pulpit. After she had worn three-inch wedges to church all summer, Heidi pointed to her feet and asked, "What is that?"

"Andrew likes it."

"There's a big difference between doing something for your husband because he likes it, and doing it because you don't want him to find out you don't."

And her friend's words had wrapped her marriage into a pretty package with metallic paper and ribbon and gift tag—perfect on the outside, but when Claire shook the box, it was hollow.

Empty.

I don't know who I am anymore.

That was why staying on Dorsett Island was so important. A little bit rebellion. A little bit adventure. A whole lot of telling the world, *Yes, I still have a mind of my own.* A chance to get back to the woman she was before her marriage to Andrew. Not that she wanted that whole package—she could do without the loneliness and confusion and TV dinners—but at least she could put on a pair of pants without thinking, *What if he doesn't like me in these?*

A knock on the door. Claire jerked, looked over, saw that pizza boy standing there, the one she'd met the other day at the museum. "Can I come in?" he asked.

"Sure, yeah." She sat up, moved the pillow back behind her. The boy helped her, shimmying it down so it fit in the hollow of her neck. "Thanks."

"No prob. And it's Tobias."

"Sorry."

"No big deal. You just had that look."

"I guess I did. I am really bad with names, like I said."

He swept his hand over his head, removing his hat. Stuck it in his back jeans pocket. "Are you okay? The, you know, um, baby?"

"Yes. Everything's good. False alarm."

"Oh, good. I, uh, hope you don't mind me coming by. I know it's really rude, but I wasn't sure I'd have another chance to talk to you. I guess I'm sorta cornering you."

"I don't know what you're expecting from me. I already told you I can't tell you what you want to know."

"I already know," Tobias said. He unzipped his fleece jacket, took out a thick, rumpled rectangle of white paper. Unfolded it.

"The eleven-year-old girl who recently returned home after being abducted has disappeared again, police said Sunday. Hanna Suller and her mother, Susan Suller, were reported missing by family friend Claire Rodriguez after she showed up at the Suller home for a visit. According to Avery Springs Police Detective John Woycowski, police found blood at the scene, and a van registered to Susan Suller has not yet been located. 'There was no sign of forced entry,' Woycowski said, 'but some sort of struggle took place in the house.'

"When asked if police had any leads, Woycowski replied, 'Not yet.'

"Hanna Suller was kidnapped from FSR Bank when it was held up by three men in May. Her father, Henry Suller, professor of Entomological Studies at Sutcliffe College, and security guard Ralph Pitkin were killed during the robbery. Hanna Suller escaped two weeks later when one of her captors, Bobby Bailey, died of a heart attack. Police are still looking for Bailey's accomplices. 'We're not ruling out the involve-ment of someone with intimate knowledge of the Suller girl's case,' Woycowski said. 'With recent news reports that Hanna had started speaking again, there could be someone out there who didn't want her to talk.'

"Rodriguez could not be reached for comment."

• • •

Tobias refolded the pages.

"How did you find that?" Claire asked.

"I knew your first name. I knew Mol—Hanna's. You mentioned the town you two used to live in. It didn't take all that long." He sniffed. "Molly always says the Internet is her friend. Maybe not now, huh?"

"Are you okay?"

"No."

"Can I do anything?"

Tobias waved the wadded paper at her. "Tell me this isn't true."

"It's true."

"Well, then, what happened?"

"You're looking at almost as much as I know," Claire said, switching her left toes beneath her right, trying to warm them now. "Hanna's aunt would only tell me they didn't want to be found. Beyond that, there's nothing."

"But you came to visit her."

"Yes . . . but they weren't there."

"No. I mean the other day, at the museum."

"It was a . . ." What could she say? Not coincidence. Not fate. *A miracle?*

Was she seeing another? Her proper Evangelical faith was leery of declaring anything miraculous. Oh, she had no problem saying "God did it," but she never meant He reached down His hand from heaven and touched a situation, stirred it, nudged all the pieces exactly where they needed to be.

Not like when He rescued Hanna.

She twisted in the bed for a more comfortable position, for a more comfortable explanation. "I didn't know she was here. We were visiting a friend. My stepson wanted to see the wax figures."

"So it was a God thing."

"I guess." The baby moved inside her; she covered the pulsating spot with the heel of her hand, pressed back a little. "Are you and Ha— Molly close?"

"I want to be."

"You don't know her well, then."

Tobias shrugged, hooked the chair against the wall with his foot, pulled it toward him and sat down. "She moved in six years ago. I barely noticed her. There's a big difference between twelve and fourteen. And she didn't go to school or anything."

"No?"

"Homeschooled. Guess I can see why. Not sure I'd ever let my kid out of my sight if something like that happened to her."

"You said she doesn't leave the museum."

"She used to. I remember seeing her outside sometimes, in front of the place, you know? I didn't even realize she'd stopped going outside until recently when I, you know, started paying more attention."

"To her."

"Ayuh," Tobias said. He hadn't removed his jacket but huddled down into it instead, his chin disappearing into its thick collar.

"She's a special girl," Claire said.

"I know. She doesn't."

Claire nodded. The doctor walked in then, glanced at the monitor printout and said, "Everything looks good, Mrs. Brenneman. We're sending you home. The nurse will be in soon to get you unhooked and ready to go."

She thanked the doctor, and after he left, Tobias stood. "Well, that's my cue, I guess."

"Listen, are you heading back to town?"

"Yes."

"Can I trouble you for a ride? Since you're here."

Tobias nodded. "No prob. Least I can do, since I barged in on you and all. I'll pull the car around front."

"I don't know how long I'll be."

"It's okay. I'll wait."

Forty minutes later, release papers signed and warm clothes back on, the nurse wheeled Claire downstairs to the entrance, where Tobias sat waiting in his car. She lifted her pregnant girth into the passenger seat and buckled the belt under her stomach. "Sorry about that."

"It's all good. I can move the seat back, if you want," Tobias said.

"I'm fine."

They didn't talk about Hanna, or the past, or anything. Tobias drove with the radio on low, more murmur than music, but every so often he'd hum along to whatever he was listening to. Claire closed her eyes and thought about Andrew, about Jesse, and how she wanted to be home. When Tobias turned into Beverly's driveway, he helped her from the car and walked her up the steps, saying, "Careful, they're slick," as she leaned on him for balance. She thanked him and went inside, and when Beverly saw her, she had questions. Claire waved her off. "I'm fine. I just need to sleep," she said. Her friend hugged her and said, "I'll bring tea up to you in a few minutes."

"Don't trouble yourself. I'll be asleep in a few minutes."

Claire climbed the stairs like an old woman, or a toddler, both feet coming to rest together on the same step before moving to the next. She took off her shoes, pants, and bra—nothing else —and climbed into bed. The red light on her cell phone blinked; she flipped it open. Three new voice messages, all from Andrew.

She didn't listen to them.

22

Hanna
November 2002

They drove east first, into Massachusetts, in the dark. Hanna watched the headlights on the opposite side of the highway, not many, one or two every minute, though sometimes they came in bundles. Her mother flipped a lever on the rearview mirror and the bright bursts of light from the cars behind them dulled into pale, smudgy specks. A truck passed them, shaking their van. The driver tossed a cigarette from the window; it bounced over the pavement, throwing off flecks of orange, hot sprinkles of glitter. And then the color died, and once the truck's taillights rounded a curve ahead, there was no warmth on their side of the road. No other vehicles.

"At least no one will miss us, not for a while," Susan said. "Diane will probably give it two appointments before she calls someone to come looking. Maybe three. That's four days or more. There's time."

Hanna didn't remind her mother that Claire would be there tomorrow.

Before leaving town, Susan had stopped at the bank's ATM. She stuck her card in, punched a few numbers, and swore. "There's a limit," she mumbled. She pressed more numbers and grabbed the cash and slip of paper that popped out of the machine. Then they drove into the night.

When her mother turned off on the Barrington exit, she knew where they were headed. Aunt Serrie's farm. Not a farm, really. A big, old falling-apart house with acres and acres of land on which nothing grew. Uncle Charlie called the place Foulton Hollow Farm. Foulton was his last name; he painted a sign for the end of the dirt driveway, big white post and white wood, and bought black stick-on letters from the hardware store. Hung the sign with hooks and eyes so it swayed in the wind, and her cousins would throw crab apples at it to make it shake more. Her, too, when she visited. The last time had been a few weeks before the bank robbery. They used to go all the time, at least a weekend a month when her father was alive.

They drove up to the house, the front porch light on, candles in every window. Not because it was close to Christmas; her aunt kept them all year long. She decorated her entire house like the pilgrims lived there, everything looking old— chipped paint, scuffed floors, worn cupboards, all sanded and prepped that way—or bought old. Primitives, she called them. Susan called them junk. Her mother decorated their house with all sorts of shiny furniture and beautiful, bold art canvases without frames. So different, the sisters. Hanna wished she had a sister of her own.

Aunt Serrie poked her head out the door. "Sue?"

"It's us."

"What are you doing here?"

"We need to stay for a day or two."

"Yeah. Get in here." Aunt Serrie hugged her mother, then Hanna.

"Where's Charlie?" Susan asked.

"Working an overnight."

The cousins came running down the stairs, all three talking over one another, asking their mother why she didn't tell them Hanna was coming, telling stories from that day at school, asking for dessert. Aunt Serrie sent them all into the kitchen. "Get everyone brownies, Paul. And milk. Not soda. There's leftover stew, too, Hanna, if you're hungry."

Paul, only a year older than Hanna, dragged Jensen and Liam down the hallway. She followed. The two younger boys climbed on the counter-top to get plates and glasses from the cabinet. Paul pried off the cover of the brownie pan.

"Two," eight-year-old Liam said.

"Mom said one," Paul said.

"She didn't say any number."

"I want chocolate milk," Jensen said. He stomped his five-year-old feet, covered in his blanket sleeper.

"Mom said white."

"Nah-uh," Liam said, stuffing his second brownie in his mouth. "She didn't say anything about it."

"Fine. Whatever."

Jensen opened the refrigerator and lugged out a bottle of Hershey's syrup, bit off the clear cap and pulled up the spout with his teeth. He squeezed three inches into the bottom of his glass. "My milk, Paulie. I can't pour it."

Paul filled his glass and then three others. Liam added chocolate to his, too, dipped his third brownie into it. "Hanna, do you want one before Mr. Piggo eats them all?" Paul asked.

She shook her head.

"I thought you were talking again," Liam said, teeth dark with cakey mush. "Mom said so."

"She is," Paul said. "Leave her alone."

"I don't hear her."

"Be quiet."

"Mom said you go to a shrink."

"Liam," Paul said. "Shut your trap."

"What's a shrink?" Jensen asked.

"Nothing. Go brush your teeth."

"Mom didn't say we had to," Liam complained. "Go."

"No."

"Now or I'll tell Mom you ate three brownies."

"I don't care."

"And I'll tell Jessica Clark you still wear Pull-Ups to bed."

"Stupid," Liam said, but he went.

"You too," Paul said.

"You won't tell Mom I had chocolate milk, will you?" Jensen asked.

"Not if you head upstairs right now."

Jensen saluted. "Aye, aye, Captain," and he ran out of the kitchen, skidding on the smooth hardwood floor and crashing into the banister.

"You want stew?" Paul asked Hanna.

She shook her head again.

"You are talking, right?"

"Yeah."

Paul stacked the small saucers in one hand, managed to collect three of the four glasses in the other, his fingers inside them, holding them together, and dropped them all in the sink. Wiped his hands on his jeans. He left her milk for her, but it was too late to drink it. She'd have night-mares.

Probably would anyway.

Aunt Serrie came in, with Susan. Her mother's eyes were glazed over, rimmed with red. Her aunt's lips were white, really white, like she had eaten a powdered donut and not wiped her mouth. "We have a dishwasher, you know."

"I know," Paul said, though he didn't move to load it.

"Where are your brothers?"

"Washing up."

"You too. Get your sleeping bag. You'll

sleep with them. Hanna has your bed tonight."

" 'Kay."

"Take Hanna up with you. And change the pillowcase."

He turned to Hanna. "C'mon."

She followed Paul through the house to his bedroom, the attic room, the ceiling low enough she could touch it if she stood against the sidewalls. He stripped off the blue pillowcase, dropped it on the floor near some sweatpants and socks. "Flannel or regular?"

Hanna shrugged. "I don't care."

"Flannel's warmer," he said, and shook open a plaid case with a big black bear in the middle. Threw the pillow on the bed. "You want me to change the sheets, too?"

"No."

"You got pajamas?"

"My bag is still in the van."

"I'll get it."

She rinsed her face in the bathroom and dried it on her shirt. The tub was the old-fashioned kind, white with feet. The sink, too, hanging on the wall without a pedestal or cabinet. She heard footsteps, went back out and sat on the bed. Paul set the bag next to her. "Your mom's crying."

"Oh." What else could she say?

"Is it about what . . . happened to you?"

"I don't know. Maybe."

"My mom's cried about it, too. I guess there

were . . . bad things . . . you went through," Paul said.

"Yeah."

He looked away, crossed the room to the dresser, fished out a pair of camouflage thermals. Wadded them against his belly. "I know."

"Paul?" Aunt Serrie called up the steps. "You can talk to Hanna tomorrow. Get down here and let her sleep."

Her mother slept with her for most of the night. She came late, jostling Hanna's eyes open as she climbed under the blankets and left sometime before Hanna woke. Hanna spent much of the morning in bed, listening to the boys run around the house beneath her, occasionally opening the door to the attic, hinges groaning, and trying to tiptoe up the steps to spy on her. She wasn't sure they ever made it to the top, heard Aunt Serrie shouting at them to shut the door and stay out of there.

She smelled Susan, her perfume, coming up the stairs before her. Miss Dior. Her father had taken Hanna to Macy's every Christmas to buy it for her mother, had the lady at the counter wrap it in thick gold paper and stick a red bow in the middle. When was the last time Hanna had smelled her perfume? She must have been wearing it in the weeks or months since Hanna had been home. Must have. Why would she start today? But Hanna never recalled waking or eating, or walking past her mother as she sat watching television, and catching a whiff of the scent, not since she'd been home. Maybe the smell made Susan feel safe, like it was something she knew. It made Hanna feel that way. If she could have, she'd have rolled up in her mother's neck and stayed there in the familiar scent of her parents' love.

Her mother smoothed Hanna's hair from her face, touched her back. "Baby, get up. It's late. There's pancakes downstairs. Get dressed and come down to eat."

She did, wearing yesterday's clothes, and her mother didn't say anything about it when she sat down at the table. Susan stood at the counter; Aunt Serrie filled a plate with pancakes, layered thick pats of butter between them. "Real syrup or Aunt Jemima?"

"Aunt Jemima isn't real?"

Her aunt laughed. "Should have known with you, Sue."

"Henry did all the pancake cooking. I had nothing to do with it."

Serrie squeezed stripes of the brown syrup from the Aunt Jemima bottle, zigzagging them over the pancakes. "There you go."

Hanna cut them into triangles, ate two at once, before they got soggy. She hated soggy pancakes, especially cold, the syrup squishing over her mouth, the pancakes disintegrating around her teeth so she didn't even have to chew. Her mother poured her a glass of orange juice. "I thought we'd stay here a few days. Would you like that?"

She nodded, then the clock caught her eye, on the microwave over her mother's shoulder. Nearly eleven thirty. Claire would have come to the house already, to bring Hanna the ice cream she asked for yesterday and to spend time with her.

Susan followed Hanna's eyes, saw the clock, and her body stiffened. "It's Saturday," she said.

"What?" Aunt Serrie asked, peeling Jensen off her leg. He wanted a fruit punch drink box; she told him they were for school lunches. He wanted one anyway.

"Pleeeeeeese," he whined. "Just one."

"And then your brothers will want one, and that will be three." She took a green Tupperware cup from the cupboard. "You get apple juice."

"We have to get going," Susan said.

"I thought you were gonna stay the weekend," Liam said, barging into the kitchen. "I'm thirsty."

Aunt Serrie took out another cup, this one yellow. Poured juice into it. "Here. Sue, what's going on?"

"We have to go."

"Now?"

"Yes. Hanna, go get your bag."

"Liam, Jensen, go up to your rooms," her aunt said.

"Mom, you said Hanna was staying the whole weekend," Liam said. "She slept all morning. We didn't even get a chance to see her."

"Get upstairs now," Aunt Serrie said, her voice raised—something she never did; the two boys looked at each other, then scrambled out of the kitchen.

"Go, Hanna," Susan said.

She climbed the stairs to the first landing, waited, listened. She couldn't hear enough, murmurs with the occasional word or phrase, mostly in Aunt Serrie's voice. ". . . do anything wrong . . ." ". . . need . . . call . . . understand . . ." ". . . enough already . . ."

She whirled as something touched her arm. Paul. He put a finger to his lips and bobbed his head toward the bedroom. So she went up the remaining stairs to the attic, where he pointed to the phone on the desk beside the computer. "Hold the mute button down before you pick up."

Hanna hesitated, did what he said. A conversation was already in progress between her mother and a man, who said, "—know where you are."

"We're staying at my sister's house in Great Barrington."

"Take a few days. When you're back, come in and make an official statement."

She recognized the voice. Detective Woycowski.

"You have my statement. We're not coming back."

"Mrs. Suller, I realize you're upset—"

"You have no idea how upset I am."

"We can have a patrol car—"

"No. You can't do anything for us." Hanna heard a soft cough, a deep swallow—the sounds her mother made when holding back tears. "I'm sorry. I just need to keep her safe."

The detective sighed. "Give me your number. We'll stay in touch."

Hanna gently replaced the receiver. She curled her finger up and down; it had cramped from her pressing it so tightly on mute. Paul sat in a monstrous leather swivel chair, staring at the computer monitor, clicking matching sets of colored jewels and watching them disappear. "So?" he said.

"I think we're staying for a while."

23

Claire
March 2009

She rested for a day, sleeping, lounging in the bedroom, roaming the kitchen, watching Beverly bake cookies for the church fellowship supper, her steady right hand scooping lumps of oatmeal raisin dough with a metal tablespoon, her shaky left fingers pushing it onto a greased pan. She left each lump where it landed, the baking sheet patterned like a minefield, random blobs here and there, some touching, some close enough to grow into each other as they baked.

Claire offered to help.

"No one complains about ugly cookies," Beverly said. "Just as long as they taste good."

"These do," Claire said, swiping a bit of dough.

"Shame, shame. You should be resting."

"I'm fine."

"Mm-hmm."

Claire threaded her hand through the handle of her mug of tea. No dainty china cups for Beverly. All her beverages were served in sturdy, thick-lipped stoneware, dark, earthy colors with the glaze dried dripping down the sides. They'd been handmade by a potter acquaintance years ago, Beverly had told her yesterday, even though Claire knew that already. Her friend repeated things more often, forgot things. Age? The stroke? Something else? That Claire didn't know. But she worried about Beverly. Stubborn as a boar, she'd been on her own all her life and would never admit to needing help, even as she opened the oven and, arm shaking, slid the baking sheet inside without wearing an oven mitt because she couldn't put it on herself.

"These will be done in fifteen minutes, if you want one cooked," she told Claire.

"I just might. I'm going to call Jesse now, though."

"And Andrew."

Claire didn't answer, carried her mug upstairs, settled in on the made bed, on her side—the left side—and used her cell phone to dial her sister-in-law's number. Jesse talked excitedly about all the things he'd been doing with his cousins, playing soccer in the snow, helping the neighbors with maple sugaring, and riding the four-wheeler.

Jesse wasn't an only-child type kid, entertaining himself for hours in his room with Legos or model airplanes. He was Mr. Social, like his mother, and Claire was his secretary, juggling play dates and trips to the museum art program and Tae Kwon Do classes and basketball at the YMCA. Every day something else. Even with the new baby, he'd still be an only. Two only children, almost eleven years apart.

"You are doing school out there, too?" she asked.

"Of course I am. Aunt Jane is more of a stickler than you. She makes me do all the problems in math, not just the odd ones."

"Really."

"And I got a ninety-eight on my last test. Multiplying fractions."

"Maybe I should start making you do all the problems, if that's the results."

"Mom."

"Just thinking out loud," Claire said, laughing. *He's such a light.* And he was—the stepson she couldn't love more if he were her own, the one who could make her smile just walking into the room. "Anything else?"

"Simon's doing a poetry unit, and I'm doing it with him."

"Hmm. How's that going?"

"Fine, because I missed all the boring stuff and we're doing the fun stuff, like writing limericks. Want to hear one?"

"Should I be scared?"

Jesse giggled. "Okay, here goes. There once was a woman named Claire, who kept tripping all over her hair—"

"I'm not sure I like where this is going."

"Just listen, Mom."

"I am. I am. Go ahead."

"She took out her knife, and for the rest of her life, poor Claire had to walk around bare." He laughed some more. "And that's not even my best one."

"Spoken like a true ten-year-old."

"I gotta go. Simon and me are heading to the Robinsons' to sled."

"Simon and I."

"Mom," Jesse said, and she could hear his voice roll with his eyes. "We're done with school for the day."

"School is never done for the day. You know that."

"Do you want to talk to Aunt Jane?"

"No, I'm good. You have fun, and be careful. I don't want your poor aunt to have to rush anyone to the emergency room for stitches or broken bones."

"The hill isn't that big."

"Well, be careful anyway."

"I will. Love you."

"Love you, too," Claire said, unsure if the boy heard her before he dropped the phone. She pictured him struggling into his snow pants and cramming his double-socked feet into his boots. He'd put his gloves on first, like he always did, because he wanted them to stay under the cuffs of his coat, but then he wouldn't be able to zip, so he'd ask Jane to do it because Claire wasn't there.

What am I doing?

She looked at the numbers on her phone's screen, blinking, indicating the nine-minute call had ended. It was nearly one o'clock. She scrolled through her contacts and dialed Andrew's office. His assistant answered.

"Uh, yes, could you tell me if Andrew Brenneman is in his office?" Claire asked. She deepened her voice a bit.

"I'm sorry, he's at a lunch meeting, but I'll put you over to his voice mail."

Andrew's recorded message came on, the same one he had when they first met. When his voice ended, another electronic one began, giving Claire all the options she already knew, and she pressed one. A beep and then, "Hi, Andrew, it's me. How are you? Lisa said you're in a lunch meeting, so I guess we'll catch up later. I just talked to Jesse and he's having a great time. This is good for him, I think." She hesitated. "Anyway, we'll talk later. Have a good day. I miss you, you know. Bye."

She closed the phone, left it on the bedside table, and wriggled her swollen feet into her shoes. Downstairs, she snagged a cookie from the plate in the kitchen. "I'm going for a walk."

"Where?"

"Maybe on some of the walking trails."

"Not the ones along the bluffs."

Claire shook her head. "I wouldn't worry you like that."

"Hmm. Do you have your phone this time?"

"Yes."

Beverly slid the spatula under a cookie on the baking sheet, transferred it to the plate. "If you're going to the museum, I think you should take my car." She didn't drive anymore but kept her Olds in the garage, lending it out to people whose vehicles were in the shop or who temporarily needed a set of wheels.

"I'd like some air."

"Remember what happened yesterday."

"I'm good to walk."

"You're stubborn."

"You'd know."

"It's fine on your own time, my dear, but don't be stubborn with that baby you're carrying."

Claire sighed, closed the top three buttons of her coat. "Where are the keys?"

"Good girl. In the drawer right on the end there."

"Bev," she said, slipping the ball chain around her finger and closing her hand around the keys, a mix of shiny silver and dull brass. When she opened her palm again she could smell the warm, sweaty metal. "It's a small island. Do you know anything more about Hanna, at the museum, or her mother?"

"Just gossip."

"Gossip you can repeat?"

Beverly added more dough to the cookie sheet. "I've talked to the mother several times. She's friendly and personable and I know has helped with several town fund-raisers—for the library addition and such—and has some closer friends on the island. Linda Johnson's daughter was killed in a car accident, and she's helped her a lot. People ask her for decorating advice all the time. I've never met the girl. She's quite shy, I hear. And I believe there was talk of them moving here to get away from some past drama, to start over. Perhaps an abusive husband or boyfriend. I never bothered with the details. That's about it."

Outside, Claire yanked up the garage door, pushing it over her head. It rocked down again and she caught it, nudged it up more gently. It stayed, and she started the car, let it run for a minute, then backed it out into the road. Left the garage door open. She wouldn't be out long.

She drove to the museum, parked in the lot again, but walked over the frozen lawn rather than taking the path. She knocked, waited. A shadow passed by the window. The door opened, and Susan stood there, staring back at her. "Molly's around front."

"I'd like to talk to you, if you have a little time."

"Time's about all I have these days."

Claire followed Susan through the mudroom, this time piled with boxes instead of laundry. Boxes lined the dining room table, some taped shut and labeled, others open and half filled.

"Going somewhere?" Claire asked.

"It's not what you think."

"I don't know what to think anymore."

"I'm getting married. We're moving into my fiancé's place. Well, he'll be my husband then."

"Hanna's going, too?"

"Molly. Yes, she's going." Susan stacked a pile of DVDs in her arms, dropped them into the cardboard box on the coffee table. "What do you want from us?"

"I'm worried about your daughter."

"That's right. My daughter. Let me worry about her."

"She needs help."

"Playing savior again?"

"Is she in counseling?"

"What business is it of yours?"

"So she's not."

Susan looked as though she wanted to snap back another retort but instead closed the box in front of her, overlapping each of the flaps, folding the last one under the first so it stayed shut by itself. She sagged, motioned loosely around her with a flap of her hand. "For better or worse, I've done what I thought was best. Please, just forget you've seen us and leave Hanna alone."

She called her Hanna.

Claire watched the woman in front of her, thicker than she remembered from six years ago, eyebrows penciled on, hair dyed the same color as her daughter's, but still well groomed and well dressed in dark-wash jeans and a camel-colored duster, belted at the waist. As Susan stared down at the creased cardboard box, inspecting it as if it were the most important thing on earth, Claire saw she was terrified—of her, of what she could do to her. The woman had lived the past six years pulled into her shell, Hanna crammed in there with her, two snails sharing the same protective coating. And here came Claire with her two-pronged escargot fork, ready to pry them from the safety of their home, sauté them in garlic and butter, and serve them up to whoever waited on the other side of their past.

"I'm not planning on saying anything," Claire said, and she heard the way the words came out, coated in a threat she didn't mean but left hanging there because it served her purpose. *I'm not planning on saying anything. Not planning to, if I get what I want, if you answer my questions.* "But will you tell me . . . Does Ha— Molly leave the building?"

"She went outside for you."

And Claire heard it in her voice, the same feeling that had come over her when Caden was three and he had fallen on the cement, scraping his knees and, with blood trickling down his chubby legs, had run to Daniel. He scooped the boy up as she watched from the lawn, stunned that her baby had chosen his father over her.

It was the first time and she didn't know what to do with the intensity of her—what? Disappointment? Displacement? Plain ol' hurt? It was ridiculous, she knew, resenting Daniel for, in that moment, usurping her place in the pecking order. He was her husband, for crying out loud. And Caden's father. But her heart didn't care. Her body had carried Caden. She rocked him through his colic and nursed him night after night, sacrificing her sleep and her perky breasts and daily showers and waistline. She was the most important person in his life.

And then she wasn't.

Susan had that look, the one that cried out, *It's*

not right. She did for you what she won't do for me. It was how the woman must have felt the day Hanna spoke to Claire, on the swing, and every visit afterward.

"I guess she did." Claire hadn't fully appreciated it at the time, seeing the girl inch out on the sidewalk, shoulder and hipbone pressed against the glass, creeping unsteadily toward her. The pain, the worry, it was all too great. But afterward, in the ambulance, once the contractions lessened and the oxygen cleared her head, she blinked and thought, *Dear Lord, she crawled to me.* And now, because it was the only thing she could think of to add, she said, "I'm sorry."

"Yeah, well, you always had part of her."

Claire thought she wanted to add more, but Hanna came through the door, calling, "Mom, do you think we can . . . ? Claire."

"How are you?"

"No, how are you? Is the baby okay? Oh, I'm such an idiot. Of course it's okay or you wouldn't be standing here."

"The baby's fine."

"I wanted to make sure . . . We called the hospital, but you had already left. Mom thought she knew who you were staying with, but I wasn't sure I should . . ." The girl's voice faded and she tucked her hair behind her ears. "I was worried."

"I'm fine."

"Good. That's good. I was really worried."

"It's close to dinnertime, so I should get going. But, can I go through the front?"

Susan sucked her upper lip into her mouth until it disappeared, emitting a long, soft squishing sound. But Hanna nodded, motioned through the office door.

In the lobby she unlocked the dead bolt. Claire touched her arm. "Thank you . . . for yesterday."

"I didn't do anything."

"You did. You did." *Just say it, Claire.* "The other evening, you know, after I came and you . . . Well, I spoke to . . . Oh, what's his name again, the pizza guy. Thomas?"

"Tobias."

She nodded. "Yes. He said that it's hard for you, sometimes, to leave the building—" The girl opened her mouth, but Claire shushed her. "So I know . . . I *know* that yesterday was . . . a big deal."

"Claire?" Hanna said.

"Mmm?"

"I want to go down to the beach."

"Okay," Claire said slowly.

"With you. Now. Before I change my mind."

"Are you sure?"

"I think I have to. If I wait, you might go home. He sent you to me again. He's giving me a chance." Hanna wrinkled her forehead. "I don't want to be stuck here forever."

She was the girl on the swing then, frail, broken. But Claire also saw a glint of something more, a bubbling potion of bravery and tenacity and hope. "Well then. How about a coat?"

24

Molly
March 2009

Molly was careful not to jangle the hangers in the office closet, and with movements as smooth and precise as neurosurgery she slipped on her mother's long wool peacoat, drowning her thin frame. She wrapped a scarf three times around her neck and pulled it up over her mouth, breathing into it until it became damp. "My mom's," she told Claire when she stepped back into the lobby. "I don't have a jacket. Haven't needed one."

"It's not that cold out there."

"I'm always cold."

Claire held the front glass door open; Molly waited at the threshold, closed her eyes. She inched her foot over the metal frame, feeling around, as if looking for a drop-off or a step down. Her breath wheezed in the back of her throat, but she brought her other leg forward, stood outside for a minute, eyes still scrunched closed. "It's all spinning."

"Take your time."

She noticed the air first, how it felt in her throat, cold and raspy, like the salt from the ocean had been taken up into the sky, and she breathed in the grittiness of it, scraping down into her lungs. The world was gray around her—the sky, the clouds, the water, even the sand. She wanted to run back into the museum, to grab the bright red knit hat Mick had given her for Christmas last year, the one she knew he bought at Dollar General as an afterthought. She wanted color out here. She wanted something vibrant to focus on, something to remind her of who she used to be. But Claire took her arm and crossed the street with her, then let her go, starting down the steps to the beach. "Coming?" she asked.

Molly nodded. She didn't want to be alone so followed Claire down the stone stairs, her bare hand on the wooden banister, smoothed by years of other hands sliding over it.

Gloves would have been a good idea, too.

Claire waited for her at the bottom, where the steps turned to gravel, and they followed the path past the cement barriers placed at the road's end, the yellow-and-black-striped reflectors a warning for cars to stop before careening down the rocky embankment into the sea. And then the gravel gave way to sand, to uncertainty. There was nothing more uncertain than the path of a grain of sand. It might be taken up by the wind, carried away in the tread of a shoe, in a dog's paw. Shoveled into a bucket and moved down the beach. Clutched by the waves and carried . . . well, wherever the water went when it left the shore. As her feet sunk into the granules, she pictured the sand holding her there. She wanted to be held there.

"I can't."

"Yes you can," Claire said. She took Molly's elbow and tugged.

The sand shifted under her feet, into her sneakers. She had to think about walking, told her legs to move. *Why am I out here?* She trembled, everything so wide open. No, she needed to be kept inside. Caged.

"A safe place," Thin Man had told her.

"Claire, I need to go back. I need to." The tears came now, the shaking.

"No. Not yet. You're so close."

"I'm out here. It's enough. Please."

"Just touch the water."

"I can't."

Claire took her gently by the shoulders. "You know He helped you escape, Hanna. Do you think He did that so you could lock yourself up somewhere else?"

Help me, Gee.

She still found herself calling Him that sometimes, like a child's pet name for her older brother, created when she couldn't quite form the letters of the real name. Sometimes those names stuck forever. Did God consider the name sacrilegious? She didn't mean disrespect at all. She meant it in love, because it reminded her of the time she needed Him and He answered. She asked herself sometimes why He didn't answer her prayers like that anymore, with immediacy, with clarity and theatrics. And then she answered her own question.

She had stopped expecting Him to.

Without realizing it, Molly had convinced herself she was only allowed one miracle. She'd used up her allotment and didn't deserve any more. That preacher, that day, had said if people didn't ask, they wouldn't get. Molly didn't know how to be afraid then, afraid of *not* getting. But once she had gotten, then she knew it was possible. And if she asked and her prayer wasn't answered, then surely it meant she'd fallen out of God's favor. She couldn't handle that. She couldn't take the risk of trusting and having that faith be broken. If He didn't answer, maybe it meant she was as bad as she thought she was.

It was easier to trust with nothing on the line.

"Okay," Molly said. "The water. I can do that."

"He'll help you."

She focused her eyes on the waves, listening to the sound they made as they leaped toward the shore, thundering like a herd of wild gray stallions, jumping and rolling and frothing. Just five yards. Each step brought chest pain, and she recalled the story of *The Little Mermaid*, not the sanitized Disney story, but the original, where the mermaid was given her legs but it felt as if she walked on scissors, her feet bleeding. The pain had been worth it to her, for her chance at love, of gaining an eternal soul, instead of ceasing to exist in the sea foam.

"I'm dizzy."

"Close your eyes. It might help. I'll guide you," Claire said.

"I don't think so."

"Try."

She forced her lids together, covered them with one hand. Claire took the other, her hand warm against Molly's skin, and walked. Molly had to move or fall over from the tugging. It did help, reducing the huge outside world to only a sound —the ocean—and a sensation—the wind over her face. The rest was blackness, and the dark never scared her. No one could find her there.

Claire stopped.

"We're here."

Opening her eyes, Molly looked down first, her feet on the packed sand, the surf just brushing the rubber toe of one sneaker. Then she looked out, at the ocean, at all its vastness. It had been more than four years since she'd been down to the beach, that last time with her mother, who had somehow lured her from the museum with a picnic lunch, though she remembered how she had kept looking over her shoulder, stuffing the chicken-salad sandwich in her mouth as quickly as she could so she could get home all the sooner.

"It's so big." Without thinking, she bent down and put her hand in the water. It stung, like ice, but she held it there until her fingers numbed. She touched them to her lips, tasted the salt, thought of the day she tasted another forbidden water, the holy water at Katie's church, the day she saw Jesus for the first time as a man, not a life-sized plastic baby in the Nativity scene outside St. Catherine's every winter. She had forgotten the saltiness was so strong.

She kicked off one shoe, balanced on her left foot, and stripped off the sock, too, cramming it under the laces so it wouldn't blow away. Stood with her bare foot in the air, like a crane, and then slowly stepped into the wet sand. It enveloped her foot in a clammy cast, and the water slid down into the divot her footprint made, filling the spaces around her toes. She sucked the air between her teeth.

"That's cold."

"You'll get used to it," Claire said. "Roll up your pants. Let's walk a little more, if you want."

Molly nodded. She stripped off her other sneaker and sock and cuffed her jeans to her knees. Claire didn't remove hers, stayed in the dry places, but Molly kept moving closer to the water, until the waves bit at her ankles, her calves. She focused on one feeling at a time. The wet. The cold. The shivering air. The almost pavement-like firmness of the tide-packed sand; she stomped down to make a footprint in it.

And then she started running. She couldn't say why. The thought didn't pop into her head to run. It just happened, her legs extending as far as they could—she felt the muscles stretching, tearing almost, in her thighs—and her arms pumping, urging her forward. And then she was at the rocks, climbing them, slabs of metamorphic-derived sandstone that looked so much like petrified logs the tourists all took photos in disbelief. She felt her lungs swell with an exertion she hadn't experienced in years and gasped at the grayness around her, her mouth dry, her cheeks hot. She brushed her frozen feet over the little patches of yellowish seaweed. The little girl had run here with her kite into the sea, the rocks forming a natural jetty of sorts. But Molly could go no farther. And, as she stood with her hands clasped behind her head, she heard someone say her name.

Tobias was there, off a little ways, at the bottom of the rocks, knee-deep in the water. He wore a wet suit, a surfboard under his arm.

"You're crazy," she told him.

"You're out," he said.

She was embarrassed, like he had seen her naked. In a way she was, no longer wearing the walls of the museum. He looked at her lovingly, the way her father had peered at his most prized Lepidoptera, the Madagascan sunset moth, its gorgeous wings shifting from blue to gold-green to yellow and fuchsia as the viewing angle changed. The wings were pigmentless, the rainbow a refraction of light on its ribbon-like scales.

She had the color she had been looking for now, in her memory. In her father.

Tobias anchored his board between some stones and climbed up to her.

"I thought I was hallucinating from the cold when I saw you."

Molly poked the lichens with her toe. "I came out with Claire."

"Now you don't have any excuses. About going places with me, I mean."

"I wouldn't go that far."

He smiled. "No, I guess not."

"Walk me home?"

"Do you have to go back right this instant?"

She glanced around. Her pants were wet, sticking to her legs, her skin tightening in gooseflesh. The waves suddenly sounded louder, menacing. And she was so high up. "I think, maybe, I do," she said, tugging at her hair.

"Ayuh," he said. He peeled off his wet suit and stood for a moment shivering in his swim trunks. Giving her a quick smile, he pulled on his clothes and then held out his arm to her. "Take my hand?"

She looked at it, hesitated, and oh, part of her was ready to grab on to him. But that part couldn't eclipse her past. "Not today."

He nodded, and they climbed down the rocks together, Molly concentrating, praying, not with words but with her body, each step a praise, a relinquishing of her fears to God. And then Claire came up on the other side of her. They retraced their steps, sand, then gravel, then street, Molly's eyes on the window of the museum, the huge painted letters. And then she was there, and inside, and she breathed back in all the familiarity.

It felt so good.

"Okay?" Claire asked.

"Yes."

"Really?"

"Really, really."

A noise in the office doorway. Louise, clearing her throat, standing against the jamb and backlit from a lamp on the desk behind her. "Mom?"

"I cooked." Her mother's voice cracked.

"Can Claire stay? And Tobias?"

"Mick is coming, should be here any minute. Put on something"—Louise glanced at her sandy feet—"dry. And sweep up that mess you dragged in."

"I will," Molly said as her mother closed the office door.

"I'll help," Tobias said, but she shook her head.

"It's fine. I got it. I'll see you later."

"Tonight?"

She laughed a little. "Tomorrow. Maybe."

"I'll be here," he said. Now he took a turn scuffing the toes of his boots in the wayward sand. "I'm glad I saw you today."

"Me too."

He opened the door. No cackle. Looked up at the silent speaker. " 'Ding, dong the witch is dead,' " he said. "Nothing to hold you in here anymore, Moll."

Molly watched him jog across the street, hands in his pockets, hem of his jeans matted under the soles of his boots. She felt a smile tiptoe to her mouth, tried to hide it by rolling her lips together, but Claire noticed and said, "He's a keeper."

"Yeah."

Tobias turned and waved before disappearing into the pizzeria.

She waved back. Then she looked at the closed office door, and heaviness pressed down on her shoulders again. "I'm sorry about my mom. She—"

"No apologies. You and I both understand. It's okay. More than okay."

Claire wrapped her arms around her, pulled her as close as the pregnant belly would allow. This time Molly squeezed back. "Thank you."

"Ice cream next time," Claire said. "And maybe a short walk down the road. There's someone I really want you to meet."

And then Claire left, and Molly took off her pants to keep the sand from spreading, buttoning the coat to wear as a temporary dress, dropping the scarf on the front desk. She vacuumed the dirt instead of sweeping—knowing from years of tourists that dustpans and brooms did little to remedy the sandy floor—and wrapped her jeans in a plastic bag before carrying them through the apartment to the laundry. Then she joined Louise and Mick for supper.

25

Hanna
December 2002

They stayed with Aunt Serrie and her family through Christmas.

Hanna thought of it as a vacation, even though Susan bought workbooks at Borders for Hanna to do school—one for math, one for social studies, one for language arts. She also bought a science encyclopedia and a Webster's college dictionary, though Uncle Charlie had both on the bookshelves in the living room. Hanna did two or three pages each day, watched the Discovery Channel, wrote out her multiplication tables, and copied entries from the encyclopedia, drawing pictures to go along with it. She focused on the insects because they grounded her in the past, in a home and a family with a dad and mom, a hope and a future. When Susan saw the drawings, she turned away, told Hanna she had dust in her eye. And when her cousins came home, Hanna ran around with them, playing, laughing even. She learned to drive the mini-snowmobile and built Lego empires.

Her mother used the time to "get things in order." She put the house in Avery Springs on the market, and when Hanna protested, she held up her hand like a traffic cop. *Stop. I don't want to hear it.* And Hanna didn't bother trying to argue. Susan also sold the van. Hanna woke one morning to an engine purring in the driveway; she tried to picture her mother's red Windstar in her head, but it wouldn't come. She snuck over to the window, floorboards frigid on her bare feet, and pulled aside the denim curtain. A dusky gray car sat below, wipers swishing back and forth, with a delay in the middle, swatting away flakes of fat, blue snow. Swish. One-one thousand. Two-one thousand. Three-one thousand. Swish.

The engine stopped, and her mother stepped from the driver's door, Uncle Charlie from the passenger side. They disappeared beneath the house's overhang. Footfalls on the porch steps. A slammed door. Murmurs. Hanna jumped back under the sheets, chilled from being exposed to the attic air, turned on her side and pulled her feet up so she could rub them. Her heels were rougher than the rest of her skin. She picked at one hard spot, her thumbnail clicking against it.

There were murmurs all the time. Adult conversation. Plenty of "Go play in your rooms until we call you." But there was also Christmas, with Aunt Serrie's brined turkey and sausage stuffing, mashed potatoes, homemade cranberry compote, green beans with rosemary and garlic. And yeast rolls—the kind Hanna loved, crust glazed with butter and slightly sweet. They watched *Miracle on 34th Street* and *It's a Wonderful Life* and *A Christmas Story*. Susan gave her a Timex watch with a stretchy purple band and a button that made it glow green in the dark. A butterfly ticked around the face on a clear disk as a second hand.

Hanna gave her mother a tiny bottle of Miss Dior—Uncle Charlie took her out to buy it—this time wrapping it herself. She tied her own gift tag to it, made from an old holiday card; she cut out the picture of Santa wearing a candle wreath on his head, used Aunt Serrie's scrapbooking scissors to scallop the edges, and wrote a note on the plain white back. *Mom, I love you. Hanna-Bee.* Susan opened the gift and tried not to cry.

"My favorite," she said.

"I didn't forget."

"No, you didn't." And she dabbed a bit of the liquid behind her ears. "Your daddy taught you well."

It all went away the next day.

Hanna and the boys played video games in the family room, and the doorbell rang. Liam pushed the woven curtains aside to peek, and shouted, "Mom, some guy's at the door."

Aunt Serrie walked past the room and called in, "Mute that for a minute. I can't hear myself think." And as Paul turned the sound off, she opened the front door and asked, "Can I help you?"

"Yes, good morning. I'm looking for Susan Suller."

"I'm sorry. Who are you?"

"I'd rather tell that to Mrs. Suller directly."

"You have the wrong house."

"I know she's here, Mrs. Foulton. I just want to speak to her. I'm with the *Avery Springs Register*—"

The man's voice disappeared in the slamming of the door. "Go upstairs," Aunt Serrie said. "Now."

The boys hesitated. So did Hanna.

"Now," she said again, clapping her hands.

They scrambled upstairs, Paul herding the younger two into the room they shared, nodding at Hanna as she paused on the landing. After Aunt Serrie passed into the kitchen, Hanna crept back down to the hallway and scrambled back to the family room, through to the laundry room, which also had a toilet, sink, and two doors; the second opened to the kitchen.

She breathed quietly, slipped into the space between the dryer and the wall, and listened.

"A reporter?" Susan's voice.

"That's what he said." Aunt Serrie.

"We can't stay here any longer."

"Sue, just think for a minute—"

"I am," her mother said, voice firm and jittery at the same time. "If he found us, that means anyone can."

"You're overreacting."

"She's not your daughter." A sigh. A sniffle. "I'm sorry. But we have to go."

They left the next morning. Aunt Serrie gave her a hug. Uncle Charlie, too. And her mother pushed her through the door, down the snowy steps and into the old-new car; it smelled like French fries and a musty garage, neither covered by the evergreen-tree air freshener hanging from the rearview mirror.

"Buckle," Susan said.

"It's cold."

"Small car. It will heat up quick." Her mother turned around in the driveway, drove slowly onto the snow-slicked road but skidded as she accelerated.

Hanna wriggled her knees up into her coat, only her toes exposed, and her head and hands, stayed that way until pins and needles filled her feet. Stretched out, keeping her legs as still as she could; each pothole bounced her boots, shocking her with tingles that made her want to laugh and cry all at the same time. Finally her feet felt normal again. She stuffed her legs back beneath her jacket. "Where are we going now?"

Susan didn't answer.

They drove for two hours and stopped at a Walmart to buy groceries and hair dye and scissors. Then they checked into a motel north of Boston. Susan cut Hanna's hair to her chin and colored it brown; she cried while Susan hacked away—skinny, silent tears sliding down her face from one eye only, each one using the same path, each one traveling a bit faster than the last, like sleds in the snow.

"It will grow back," Susan said, covering Hanna's head in the plastic cap and using a gloved finger to rub a bit of dye into her eyebrows. She colored her own hair, too, the same shade, number fifty-eight, medium golden brown. "Now we match."

The Travelodge only had doors and staircases on the outside, each room opening out to a sidewalk or a balcony, depending on whether it was on the first or second floor. Theirs was on the second, right next to the soda machine, number 217. It had a key with a turquoise tag attached to it, longer than Hanna's hand, the number printed on the plastic. It looked like 2 7, the 1 so faded she could only see it if she looked really, really hard in the light, and even then she probably was imagining the shadow. All the other hotels she'd ever stayed in had had those credit-card keys that were swiped in the door, making the green light blink and the lock open with a *chink*.

Their room was the Sleepy Bear Den, light blue curtains and double bedspreads printed with clouds and a cartoon bear dressed as a porter and doing various childhood activities. The carpet was plush green, the bathroom had no tub, just a stand-up shower—which was fine with Hanna because she didn't take baths anymore. They reminded her of the bath Short One had given her.

There was a little kitchen area with a micro-wave, tiny refrigerator, and table for two. It had two Bibles in the nightstand drawer, both bigger than the Bible she took from Claire's church, which Hanna had to leave behind—stuck under the couch—when they fled their house. She thought the police might have found it, if they searched the house, like they sometimes did in the movies, overturning furniture and poking in all those secret places.

The motel Bibles had bigger print, too, which she liked, and they had more stories. But the pages were the same, thin and crinkly. Both had an Old Testament to go along with the New one. But one of them had a hard, slick cover with flowers on it and was easier to read, without all the *eth* endings and with very few words she had

had to look up in the dictionary. Most of the time she didn't even bother but did what Ms. Holiday had called making an educated guess. She figured this was okay since it was a schoolish thing to do.

Inside the cover, someone had written:

God says, "Thou shall not steal."
But we want you to take this book!!!!!
It can change your life. If it does, let us
know, please.
Write to P.O. Box 1286, Colorado Springs,
CO 80906

So she took it, and started reading the Old Testament. She sometimes started at the beginning with the creation, with Seth and Noah and Abraham and all those men who kept having more sons. Sometimes she hopped around and started reading, and if she liked it she found the beginning of the book or at least the story. The battles and rules and lists of names bored her, but she enjoyed the girl stories about Ruth and Esther, and even Sarah.

Every day since she had gotten the New Testament from Claire's church, she had read about Jesus, just a little part, and it was easy to find because all His words were in red ink. And before going to sleep, she'd said the prayer Jesus told people to pray, since she didn't know any others, and He said it was good to do what He commanded, anyway.

"If you love me, keep my commandments."
She wasn't sure about that, the loving part. How did she love someone she didn't know or had never met, who was floating in heaven—wherever that was. In the sky? That's what the movies always showed. And what did the love feel like?

With her daddy, it had been warm and snuggly and secure, a hug and a whiff of his aftershave, the scratch of his mustache. With her mother, it was more messy, sort of like a Rubik's Cube, but without a doubt Susan would do whatever necessary to keep Hanna protected. She showed that, right in front of Hanna's eyes; with one action she surrendered everything for her daughter. But Jesus . . . ? Well, Hanna kept saying, over and over, "Help me. Help me," the way she had the day Fat Guy died. And Jesus, who made promise after promise about asking and helping and giving, seemed to do nothing—not like before.

Except maybe it wasn't nothing.

Hanna didn't know how to explain it, except in the words of Genesis from the easy-to-read Bible. *The Spirit of God was hovering over the waters.* That was how she felt, like He was hovering over them all the time, guarding them, and when she doubted—when her mother was out and she was all alone, listening to the noise in the street below, the creak of the bedsprings, the phantom sounds that seemed to have no reason to exist, other than to frighten her—that gentle

300

pressure settled on her and she did all she could to push back into it.

Perhaps that was love, to a child. The parent guarded, the child recognized that guardianship, trusted in it, a blind faith eventually outgrown. In that sense, she did love Jesus. She began writing out the commandments she found, numbering them, so she would remember them all, keeping the list folded up and tucked in the safest place she knew, taped to the underside of the dresser drawer.

They spent a week in that motel near Boston, her mother collecting apartment-finder magazines and classifieds in the newspaper. Susan used her laptop to search for jobs in the area, ones that would pay well but also allow some measure of anonymity. She considered traveling down to Brooklyn or the Bronx.

Then one day her mother shook her awake, early. "Baby, get up."

"What's wrong?" Hanna pawed at her eyes in that uncoordinated morning way, limbs still numb with sleep.

"Nothing. But I think I found us a place. A good place we can stay."

"In Boston?"

"No."

"Where?"

"Maine."

Hanna sat up, scraped her hands over her face again. Half covered her mouth as she said through a yawn, "What's in Maine?"

"A job, I think. I have to meet with the guy in a few hours. It's a bit of a drive."

"There's a big city there?"

"No, not really," Susan said, and Hanna saw the weariness that had come over her the past months, painted on, like her eyebrows, hasty and dark and uneven. "Hurry, and we'll drive through Mickey D's for breakfast."

They packed what little they had in minutes, her mother throwing everything from the bathroom into a plastic grocery bag, and any food that wouldn't spoil into another. She let Hanna wait in the room as she went outside to start the car and scrape the ice off it. Hanna stuck the easy-to-read Bible in the bottom of her bag, in the leg of her jeans. She hoped Jesus wouldn't mind. There was still one in the room, she figured. And the inscrip-tion told her to take it.

She also took her list from beneath the drawer.

She watched at the window until her mother motioned for her to come, belted into her warm seat, and when they pulled through McDonald's she asked if she could have two hash browns instead of one.

"And OJ, and an Egg McMuffin," Susan said into the speaker.

"With no egg," Hanna said. She didn't eat eggs

anymore, not since *that day*. She had two *that days* now, and while they were separate in her head, they had the same name. *That day*. When Thin Man took her. And when she and her mother left everything.

"With no egg," her mother echoed.

They drove three hours, ate Wheat Thins and dry Life cereal for lunch, and Hanna had the last two Fruit Roll-Ups. Finally, her mother veered into a small town, pulled to the side of the road. "One more thing. You'll need a new name."

Hanna didn't protest. She made a silent list of girls she knew from school or television, and one bounced to the top. "Molly," she told her mother.

"Molly? Are you sure? Aunt Serrie named her cat Molly."

"I like it."

"But will you remember it?"

"I'll remember."

"Fine. Molly." She paused. "You might have it for a while. Be sure."

Hanna nodded.

Susan slipped a sheet of paper from her visor, read it, then tucked it into her lap as she turned back onto the road. She drove a few miles, made a few turns, then crossed a bridge into a wooded area, a mix of lush pines and tall leafless trees. Hanna watched the buildings as they drove. Neat clapboard-sided homes, both large and small, most painted gray or blue-gray. House trailers, their lawns stacked with woodpiles and tires and metal. A tiny elementary school. A small market and deli. And several other businesses, large signs in their windows declaring Closed for the Season.

They crossed another bridge. The trees thinned. More houses. A large hotel with rows of glass windows—Reopening April 1st. A white chapel. And shoreline. Just beyond the buildings on the right side, Hanna could see the ocean, gray and foamy, spraying icy drops into the air before collecting them back into itself. Then a third bridge, and driving over land so thin there was only room for the road, the shoulders rocky and tumbling into the sea. Red and brown shacks with nets and compact buoys of every color draped over the walls, stacks of cages next to them. "For catching lobsters," Susan said.

There were boats on the water, despite ice crusts close to the shore and snow in the weeds. Buildings were built over the water, too, on long stilts. A candy store, closed. A gift store, closed. Several seafood restaurants, all of them closed.

"What is this place?" Hanna asked.

"Dorsett Island."

"It's small."

"And empty most of the year. Just what we need."

"What about when it's not?"

"Tourists. They don't pay attention to anything."

Susan finally stopped. She had to; the road ended at the sea. ——

"Come on," she said, motioning to the green-roofed building with the words Lou's House of Wax painted in huge letters over the windows. "This is it."

Hanna zipped her coat and wrapped her scarf around the bottom half of her face, pulled her hat down low like her mother expected. She didn't put on her gloves but balled her hands up into her sleeves and bumped the car door shut with her hip. She walked next to Susan, and together they hurried across the empty street, up the path, Hanna almost jogging. A man in dirty jeans and a black jacket opened the door to the museum. "You must be the gal who called me yesterday," he said.

"That's me," Susan said, offering her hand. "Thank you for meeting us, Mr. . . . ."

"It's Mick." He pulled at his jacket so the snaps popped open, took it off and tossed it on the counter in front of the window. It knocked the little metal service bell onto the floor. He wore a wrinkled T-shirt and suspenders. Hanna stared at his forearms, bulging like Popeye's, with thick straight hair at his wrists, almost bald skin in the middle of his arms, and then, starting at his elbows, sparse, wiry curls that disappeared beneath his sleeves. He reached out and tugged Hanna's scarf down from her mouth. "Uncle Mick, to you."

Susan's arm went around her.

"Well, this is it," Mick said. "You read the ad. Stay here, rent-free, and look after the place. I'll pay you, too, five-fifty a week, which comes up pretty good if you factor in the rent you're not paying. The apartment's through there. Ain't pretty, but plenty for the both of you. And mostly furnished. I'll show you."

Hanna held her mother's hand as they followed the man through a door marked Office, where there was a desk, sofa, and television, through another door into an apartment that looked like the motel they'd just left. Her mother glanced around. "What happened to the other caretaker?"

"Fool ran off and got himself married," Mick said.

"When do you want us?"

"Soon as you can. I like to keep this place open every day except Christmas and Thanksgiving. Even in the off-season. You'll get vacation, though. What's your name again?"

"Louise," her mother said, squeezing Hanna's arms. "Louise Fisk."

"Ha. Ain't that a kicker. You seen the name on the window. Place was named after my pops, and he was a Lou, too." Mick slapped his thigh. "Guess it's meant to be."

"Molly, go to the car for a minute."

Hanna stood there.

"Molly."

She jerked her head around. "Sorry."

"Go to the car and wait for me."

She did, running across the street without looking, her heart racing because she forgot who she was supposed to be, and she locked the doors in the car, piling the blankets on her. She watched the minutes on her watch, pressing the glow button every three or four breaths.

After eleven minutes, the door opened. "Molly."

Hanna took the blankets off, her hat coming off with them, her hair crackling with static around her face, sticking to her skin. "I'm sorry. Really."

"It's fine. Everything's fine."

"Are we staying here?"

"I think so. I told him I would decide by tomorrow."

"I don't like it."

"You don't have to. But it's for the best." She started the car. "Let's find a room for the night, and dinner. You can pick the place."

Hanna pointed to the Island Pizza & More sign not far from their car. "How about pizza?"

"Pizza it is."

26

Claire
March 2009

"We're walking?" Molly asked, her face creasing with concern as she looked out the window.

"We don't have to," Claire said. "But I thought it would be nice. It's not quite half a mile."

"If you want."

"What do you want?"

Molly nodded slightly. "We can walk."

The girl seemed agitated, flicking the plastic buttons on her mother's long wool coat, tugging on them, absently twisting them. One came off in her fingers. She squeezed it, plunged both hands into her pockets.

"Are you okay?" Claire asked.

"Fine. Really."

"We can take the car. I'm parked right over there."

"No. I want to do this."

"No rush."

Molly took her hands from the pockets, removing a pair of stretchy one-size-fits-all gloves. "I remembered this time," she said, wriggling them on.

Once, Caden, Amelia, and Claire all had gloves

like that. Claire had bought four black pairs one year at CVS, when she went in to pick up an amoxicillin prescription for Caden's strep throat. The gloves, she'd thought, were the perfect remedy for their typical "getting ready" routine— all three of them digging through pockets, coat sleeves, baskets, and bedroom closets, each trying to find any matching gloves. Often they went out with mismatched mittens, or none at all. But if they all had the same and an extra pair, too, it might stop the frantic searching five minutes before leaving the house. The gloves had been on the store's clearance table for $1.99, so she dropped them on the counter with the medicine and a bottle of ginger ale.

They'd misplaced them all by the end of the month.

"You're not meant to have warm fingers," Daniel had said, laughing one morning as they bundled up for church, gloveless, Claire telling the kids to pull their coat cuffs over their hands.

Jesse never lost his gloves. Andrew tied a piece of yarn to the plastic loops on each one, strung it through one of the jacket's arms and out the other so that the gloves dangled, waiting for Jesse's hands to show up. Lizzy had taught him to do that.

Claire missed them both, hadn't realized how much a part of her they'd become. Silly, she knew. They'd been together nearly every day for six years. And yet she still hadn't spoken to Andrew since he left. Though they played telephone tag, he had talked to Beverly, and while she didn't disclose their conversation, Claire certainly understood her friend's silent message. *He needs you. He's worried about you.*

What are you running from?

Claire wasn't quite sure.

She and Molly stepped out onto the low wooden decking in front of the museum, the girl drawing a sharp, surprised breath. Her hand snaked back to the metal door handle and squeezed. Her eyes shifted around in their sockets, darting from one object to another, drawing it all in.

"How you doing?" Claire asked.

Molly pulled her coat tight around her, holding the extra fabric at her neck, her waist. "I'm good."

They strolled, not speaking, Hanna watching her feet now, concentrating on each step. Arriving at Beverly's home, Claire opened the door without knocking, called, "We're here."

"In the kitchen."

She had warned Molly days earlier about Beverly's stroke, about her loose lips and mostly paralyzed left side. And when Beverly saw the girl, she didn't hesitate to put her good arm around her and say, "Welcome, welcome. You are a beauty, just as Claire said. Sit. Have tea. It's warm. Let me take your coat."

"I'm good," Molly said, sitting at the table, the wool thick around her. She did take off her hat,

310

unwound her scarf so it only looped her neck once. Reached for the tea bags, in a small wicker basket at the center of the table, her hand snapping back as soon as her fingers brushed the paper wrappers. Claire slid the basket closer, nodded to her, and Molly plucked the first bag she touched, opened it. She picked up the earthy stoneware teapot and poured water over the bag in the matching cup. Claire did the same.

"You sit, Bev."

"I am. Just takes a minute to get there." She moved to the table, dragging one leg, and inhaled deeply. "Ah, you chose the almond tea. My favorite."

With deliberation, Beverly's hand flopped across the table, twitching, curling, until finally she knocked the basket over, a dozen tea bags pouring out.

"Here, let me get one for you," Claire said.

"No, no. I could do this right-handed just fine, but it won't do me any good to leave the left side idle." She sifted through her choices, found another almond, and labored to open it. "I will let you pour the water, though. I've scalded myself enough times."

Claire filled Beverly's teacup and added honey to it, and to her own. Molly stared into the brown liquid, tapping the handle with her finger, setting the surface vibrating. Claire touched her hand. "Are you okay?"

"I feel . . . nervous."

"Understandable. When was the last time you were this far from home?"

"Always," she said.

Beverly, perceptive and generous, knew the girl needed some conversation in which to hide. She and Claire made small talk, telling humorous tales of when they were both young and out of parental eyesight, stories about daring, stupid things—jumping from haylofts, swinging from branches into shallow streams, eating all manner of creepy crawly things. That made Molly smile.

"You live here all alone?" she asked finally.

"By myself but not alone," Beverly said.

"Do you ever, well . . . Are you afraid? I mean, maybe of something happening and no one knowing?"

"For one, my dear, I am too stubborn and independent to be afraid of much these days. And too old." Beverly laughed, wet and low. "For another, God always knows, and I've learned it's better to leave those details up to Him. He took care of me when I had my stroke, and hundreds of times before and since."

Claire tried to nudge her friend with her eyes—*tell, tell.* But Beverly didn't need her direction; she felt the Spirit in the room, too, and began recounting the events of all those years ago.

"I walked every day, five a.m., and got home

when my neighbor was leaving for work. Never missed a morning. And then I did. I got up, got dressed, went downstairs to drink my Tropicana . . . and don't remember anything else until waking in the hospital. My neighbor found me, not that first morning, but a day later, when she realized it had been two days since she saw me. Found me on the floor in a swamp of orange juice, the refrigerator door open, my eyes open. Said she thought I was dead.

"The doctors didn't think I'd recover. It had been too long, too much time without treatment. Told my sister to make plans to move me to some long-term care facility, if I lived at all. But she got her church to pray, got them all to come and lay their hands on me, anoint me with oil, and spent hours by my bedside seeking the Lord on my behalf."

" 'Ask and it will be given to you,' " Molly whispered.

"That's right, and that's what they did. I remember coming back. I remember hearing them, the murmurs. I remember trying to speak, but I couldn't. I had words in my head, but my tongue wouldn't move. Nothing would move, but I was there. And then they sent me to a nursing home, far enough from my sister that she couldn't come visit all that often, so I spent my time praying, reciting the Bible over and over in my mind. All those times I got sent to bed with no supper for not learning my verses? I was thankful for that then."

Molly hesitated. She pulled the tag of her tea bag from the string, folded it in half. "But you're better now."

"A long road, but I'm better enough not to be a burden to anyone, which is probably all I ever wanted." Beverly brought her cup to her lips with her good arm, sipped her tea. A bit dribbled from the corner of her mouth, and Claire wiped it away with a cloth napkin Beverly had set out, in another basket, all white with tatted edges and rolled with mismatched jeweled napkin rings. "Thank you, dear."

"Would you call, what happened to you, I mean, a miracle?" Molly asked.

"Oh, absolutely yes, and there is more to the story, if you'd like to hear it."

Molly nodded.

"Well, in the nursing home, I had a roommate who was dying. I could hear it in her lungs, her voice. Sometimes she had a daughter sitting by her side, but often she was alone, and she'd cry at night. Moan. And my heart broke for her. I prayed because I could do nothing else. My speech hadn't returned; I was only just beginning to be able to communicate through blinks and hand squeezes. And then I heard God tell me, 'Sing.'

"I said, in my head, mind you, 'Lord, are you crazy? I can't make anything but garbled sounds.

I'm not going to be able to sing anything at all.'

"And He just said again, 'Sing.'

"Now, I'm usually not one to argue with my Lord, so I opened my mouth, and a song came out. I heard it clear and strong with my ears. If it sounded that way to the woman in the bed next to me, I don't know. But she calmed. Her moaning and tears stopped. The rustling and bumping of the bed stopped. And when my song ended, I heard her breathing smooth and light. And I fell asleep, too.

"She had passed on by morning."

Claire batted at her eyes. She'd heard the story dozens of times—told it to others dozens of times—but it never failed to move her to tears. A testament of God's goodness and providence. Another miraculous sign from a loving Father, like Hanna's—*It's Molly now. Molly. She wants it that way*—escape. Like their meeting on the playground. Claire had seen so much of the sacred, and yet she forgot so easily, falling back into old patterns of self-pity. Why was that? She'd been given blessings as numerous as the stars.

Forgive me.

Molly stirred more sugar into her tea, despite having added spoonfuls already. She hadn't even tasted it. "What did you sing?"

Beverly leaned back in her chair, and her voice came, deep, slow, majestic and full of nursing-home memories.

" 'Man of Sorrows,' what a name
For the Son of God, who came
Ruined sinners to reclaim!
Hallelujah! what a Savior!

Bearing shame and scoffing rude,
In my place condemned He stood;
Sealed my pardon with His blood:
Hallelujah! what a Savior!

Guilty, vile and helpless we;
Spotless Lamb of God was He;
Full atonement! can it be?
Hallelujah! what a Savior!

Lifted up was He to die,
'It is finished' was His cry;
Now in heav'n exalted high:
Hallelujah! what a Savior!

When He comes, our glorious King,
All His ransomed home to bring,
Then anew this song we'll sing:
Hallelujah! what a Savior!"

"I have no doubt I had that stroke so I could be
in that bed, that day, to sing to a woman I'd never
met."

Molly's face waxed over—Claire could only
liken it to one of the figures in that museum of

hers—and she turned inward again. Claire and Beverly continued for a little longer with pleasantries, and then the older woman apologized for her age and exhaustion and went through the curtained pocket doors for a nap. Claire straightened the kitchen while Molly swished her cold tea, and when she asked if the girl was up to walking back home, Molly nodded.

Twilight touched the edges of the ocean, the horizon curling under in a hazy gray. Their shadows stretched ahead of them, gliding over gravel and sidewalk crack with a grace only shadows could muster. Claire's silhouette showed no protruding belly, no clunky extra-forty-pound gait. And Molly's shadow betrayed none of the hesitancy the body beside Claire clearly felt, all stiffness and twitches and nervous snorts.

As they approached the museum, Claire touched Molly's arm. "Are you okay?"

"I don't know," the girl replied. "I think . . . I feel . . ." She shook her head.

"Do you want to go inside and talk a little?"

"No," Molly said. Her back was to the museum window. She didn't look at it. On purpose.

Claire nodded across the street. "We could sit in the pizza place."

Molly shook her head quickly.

"How about the car?"

"Okay."

She unlocked the passenger door, closed Molly

inside. Crossed around the front and settled behind the steering wheel. "Heat?"

"I'm good."

Claire waited. She sensed Molly needing to take the lead on the conversation, was reminded sharply of another time, when Molly-as-Hanna wanted to ask her questions but did not have the opportunity that afternoon in the convenience store.

And then she disappeared.

Obviously remembering the same thing, Molly said, "That day. The last day we saw each other. I wanted to talk to you."

Claire nodded. "I know."

"What Beverly said . . . It all came back to me. Do you think she's right? Did God give her a stroke so she could sing to that woman?"

Claire didn't have to be brilliant to follow Molly's rabbit trail. She'd been in the same place, still found herself there, wondering those same things and finding only dry, tasteless responses. A mouthful of unseasoned bread crumbs. Nothing to fill the hungry places. Nothing satisfying.

"You want to know if He put you in the bank that day for a reason."

The girl trembled. "Yes," she breathed. "Yes. Because if He did, then it wouldn't be my fault."

"Your fault. Ha—Molly, what are you talking about?"

"I picked." The tears spilled down her face.

"Dad asked where I wanted to go first, and I picked the post office. If I . . . if I hadn't . . . he'd be . . . he wouldn't . . ."

Her words disintegrated in great quaking sobs. The temperature inside the Olds warmed with the crying—thick, foggy veils of grief coating the windows. Molly dove against Claire's shoulder, clinging to her, and Claire rocked the girl, stroking her hair and saying "Shhh. Shhh." Six years of bottled-up guilt exploded out, sour and fermented. "Shhh."

"I didn't mean to," Molly said, hiccupping. She sniffled, pulled away, her face blotchy, her eyes puffed up, as if she were having an allergic reaction to her memories.

Stung by the past.

"Sweetie, it wasn't your fault."

"Then whose? God's?" the girl rubbed her face in her scarf. "I don't understand. Why did He take my dad? Why did He let me get kidnapped if He was just going to save me? It all hurts so much."

She began to cry again, quietly this time, shoulders bobbing up and down. Claire touched her knee, hidden beneath the huge black coat. "I killed my children."

Molly's head snapped toward her, pale eyes even icier with fear. "What?"

"You knew my son was dead. Caden. But he wasn't my only child. I had a daughter. Amelia. There was a car accident. I was driving. I turned left and pulled out in front of a truck I didn't see because of the way the sun was shining. The other driver was going too fast, too. Both my children were killed. And I lost the baby I was pregnant with. Her name was Alexis.

"I've asked myself all the questions. What part of it did God make happen? What part of it did He simply allow to happen? Did He set the sun to blind me to oncoming traffic so I veered into the truck's path? Did He know the crash was coming because speeding and windshield glare happen in a fallen world, and He sat back and allowed it because doing so would bring His purpose to pass? Was it some combination of both or an entirely different reason?

"I have no idea, Molly, but here's what I am sure of. I know God is good. I know His ways are perfect. I also know only He gives and takes life. No one else has ultimate control of that. So it doesn't matter why or how the accident happened. My children's days were fulfilled, their purposes accomplished.

"And even though I know that, it still hurts. There's no way around it."

Claire exhaled slowly, kneading a tight, bulging spot low on her belly. She pushed in, felt the baby's entire body shift, fluttering upward. "Here," she said, taking Molly's gloved hand and holding it to her stomach. The baby responded, bumping against her touch.

"Boy or girl?" Molly asked.

"We'll find out April thirtieth. Or thereabout."

"You miss your other children?"

"Every single day," Claire said. "With everything I have."

"Yeah," Molly said.

The baby kicked again. Claire squeezed her fingers. "Yeah."

27

Molly
March 2009

When she told Tobias she wanted him to take her to church the next morning, he nearly crowed with delight, like Peter Pan, grinning and tossing his knit cap into the air. "Oh, wicked. We can walk down together. Or I'll drive, if you want. Can't say the car will warm up before we get there . . . Oh, shoot. It's my grandmother's mass."

"What?" Molly asked.

"Every year my grandfather has a mass said for her, on a Sunday near the anniversary of her death. I always go. I promised him, when I started attending the Baptist church. Dad didn't care about me going any other day, just that one."

"I'll go to the mass."

"Nah. Don't worry about it. Maybe we can find

a service tonight, if we call around quick, or one really early. Not here, but maybe in Duncan. There's a couple bigger churches there."

"No, really. I want to go."

"Seriously?"

Molly nodded.

"Well, all right," Tobias said, shrugging. "If you say so."

"I do."

"You ever been to a Catholic mass before?"

"A couple times. When I was a kid."

"Okay then. Just want to be sure you know what you're getting yourself into. I'll pick you up at quarter to ten."

She thought she should wear a dress, but didn't have one. Didn't have anything but a couple pairs of jeans and her favorite corduroys, none of which she would have worn to services, even if she went only with Tobias. But with his family, on such a special day? She sighed, wondered what he would be wearing. She could call him, ask.

Yeah, right.

Louise was out with Mick. The *uncle* part had been dropped in Molly's mind since the engagement; she just couldn't fathom having an uncle and stepfather rolled into one. It gave her a creepy feeling.

In her mother's bedroom she slid open the

mirrored closet door and pushed through the hangers, found Louise's skirts in the back, all three clipped onto one hanger. Molly didn't remember her mother ever wearing any of them. Two of them buttoned and zipped and would never fit, but one of them was linen, yellow with gray flowers, and had an elastic waist. She grabbed it, carried it into the kitchen and took a serrated steak knife from the block, poked the sharp tip through the fabric inside the waistband, and sawed. Hooking the elastic with her finger, she scrunched the linen to one side, sliced through the exposed elastic and tied it to make the waist small enough to fit her. In her bedroom she paired the skirt with a gray cable-knit sweater. They looked silly together—the summery bottom with the bulky winter top—but the sweater was the only thing she had that even remotely matched.

She ironed the skirt and hung it on the inside of the closet door. She did have tights—on cold days she wore them under her jeans—and held both the black pair and the ivory pair up against the patterned fabric. Neither went well, but she decided on the black, and her black mules.

Her mother and Mick came home; she heard them fumbling in the other room, tripping over something while trying to find the lamp on the end table. Boxes, probably. For all Louise's zeal over moving, most of the boxes sat half filled and half stacked around the apartment. Molly didn't know why she had stopped packing and taping and labeling, and didn't ask.

The silences had grown longer between them, Louise seemingly avoiding her. Or maybe she just imagined it, her mother simply preoccupied with Mick and the new life finally coming to her. Molly didn't want to spend too much time wondering but pushed the worry away, like she'd been trying to do with the fact she wouldn't be sitting on the sofa watching television church for an hour tomorrow morning before wandering into the museum to open the door to no one. She'd have to tell Louise before she left. Or maybe she'd just leave a note.

Tobias picked her up outside the side entrance, like she'd asked him to. He must have driven around the island several times, because hot air brushed by her as she opened the passenger's side. She was glad, as she hadn't wanted to wear her mother's bulky coat, had put on gloves and a scarf but no other outerwear. She sat, closed the door, and then tried to wiggle into a more comfortable position on the seat. Couldn't. She had closed her skirt in the door, but before she had a chance to free herself, Tobias pulled out onto the street and started toward the church. She belted up, her knees trapped—one against the door, the other against the one—knobby bones grinding painfully with each bump and turn.

"You look nice," Tobias said. He wore his everyday jeans with the faded thighs, a frayed hole here and there—whether intentional or simply from overuse, Molly didn't know. He wore his everyday shoes, black and chunky and creased, like boots cut short, dark laces specked with gold. And his hat. His coat was flung in the back seat. He wiped his damp forehead, shoving his hair up under the hem of his hat.

"Are you hot?" Molly asked.

"I'm good. Unless you are. Then I'll turn it down."

"If you want to."

"Molly," Tobias said, "I'm asking you."

She shrugged. "I'm okay. But you're sweating."

"I'd sweat in a blizzard."

They drove to the church without any more talking, Molly sensing something different in Tobias, something tense and uncertain. She'd never seen him that way before. Was it going to mass with his family, or her presence in the car? She traced the outlines of the flowers on her skirt with her finger. When he parked, she nearly jumped from the passenger seat, stretching her cramped legs, glanced down. The bottom of her skirt was wet with dirty road slush. Tobias came around and draped his jacket over her shoulders.

"I don't—"

"Just take it," he said.

She didn't slip her arms into the sleeves but held the zipper closed with both hands from the inside. They walked around the front of the building, a small white chapel with curls of loose paint dangling from the clapboard here and there, latex caterpillars waiting to be scraped away in the spring. Molly had hoped for a stone building, like St. Catherine's, pointed and arched and grabbing at the sky above. The front, however, had an uncovered porch constructed of old New England stone, and carved into each of the steps' risers was a different biblical word or phrase. She climbed them, reading—*prepare, repent, believe, redemption, salvation, praise, do justice, love mercy, walk humbly, eternal life*. The Ts in both *salvation* and *redemption* were damaged.

In an awkward moment Molly tangled with Tobias as he tried to reach from behind and open the door for her. "Sorry," he said, moving aside quickly and giving her space to enter the building, maybe remembering the day the King fell over.

She stepped onto carpeting. Not the low, flat cardboard kind usually found in places where many people walked. This rug, plush and blue, squished under her feet like seaweed, trapping the dampness of the ocean in its fibers, releasing a puff of saltiness with each of her footfalls. Tobias motioned to a full pew, and Molly recognized his brother, Frank, and both parents. She'd seen them plenty through the window, and Frank had delivered food to the museum more than once. The grandfather was there, too, on the end, narrow-shouldered and long-faced, like Tobias, his hair shiny black and waxed to his head. Tobias hugged him, both men slapping each other on the back before parting, and the family scooted down the row, making room for them to sit. Molly claimed the first seat, on the aisle, keeping the warm coat around her.

The pews had kneelers attached to them. Tobias knelt for a moment, crossed himself, but Molly didn't move. The chapel was not only small but plain. It had no crucifix above the altar, no colored glass in the windows, no saints peering around at the hundred-person congregation. There were candles, though, flickering in red votives.

She wanted to go home.

"Tobias . . ."

He glanced up from his hands, folded in his lap, pointer fingers extended, tips touching, the rest of his fingers folded down between one another. "Are you okay?"

"I think I need to—"

The organist blasted a chord through the sanctuary, then another. She announced the hymn and everyone stood. The processional paraded down between the seats, one altar boy and a baby-faced priest, both with Skechers poking from beneath their robes. Tobias whispered, close to her face, "Are you okay?" and she nodded because the desire to flee had somehow been carried away with the organ's voice. She fumbled around for the missal, but Tobias handed her his, and she mouthed the words of the last verse and then sat again.

The priest—Father Gino, Tobias had told her yesterday, *"Pops likes him. Gets him out of church in forty-three minutes and has a good Italian name"*—mumbled through the mass, tripping over words but plowing forward, as if he had somewhere to be before the end of the hour. Molly followed along the best she could, her fingers splayed in the leaves of the missal, keeping the pages marked so she could flip between the readings and the songs. Standing, sitting, kneeling—it had all seemed less complicated as a child.

" 'Lord, I am not worthy to receive you, but only say the word and I shall be healed.' "

The words stirred Molly as the congregation recited them together. They reminded her of similar words somewhere else, not from her visits to St. Catherine's, but where? Then it came to her; it was in one of the New Testament books, she couldn't remember which, had very little memory for chapter and verse, but it was in there. A centurion, a servant, an astonishing faith.

She closed her eyes, let the Spirit consume her. What believer didn't think—*know*—Jesus could heal? Molly had experienced healing on many levels, she thought, but now she inventoried those moments—when the broken became whole, when the fear receded and peace overtook, when for a never-long-enough time belief was total and unconditional—and knew all those moments had been surface moments. Only the first level. Only dealing with the immediate, like an argument with her mother or an odd person in the museum who made her nervous. It never went deeper, to the places she really needed it.

She didn't want it to.

She was scared. Her healing would come with a probing, painful cutting away. She could picture it in her mind, hear Christ's knife scraping the rot from the bone. Because that's where it was, in her bones, all sunk in and deep in the marrow. She would have to allow God in there if healing was to come. She would have to listen to Him say the word, watch Him snip away the sutures with which she had hastily, tightly, bound up the past. She'd need to peer into each one of those gaping wounds, put her finger into them, confront them, and let them close up in the long, slow way these types of hurts close.

And she would begin today.

I'm ready, Lord. Say the word.

Communion began, and people shuffled sideways from between the rows and into the aisle. Tobias's family squeezed past them; he shifted his knees into hers to make room, and she swung her knees out of the way, too. They sat together for, well, not long, barely two lines of whatever song the organist sang, and there was a gap in the Communion line. Molly stood and slipped into it.

"Where are you going?" Tobias whispered, coming up behind her. "You're not Catholic."

"I know."

"Molly, you don't even—"

"I can see what to do."

And she could. Right hand under left. An *amen* and pop the wafer into the mouth. Just touch the wine to the lips and don't take a huge gulp. She took the bread not from the priest but from a regular guy dressed in a wrinkly plaid shirt and navy jacket, gold buttons etched with anchors. No tie. She couldn't bring herself to chew the white circle so plastered it to the roof of her mouth with her spit. It stuck there, a small amount flaking off when the woman with the cup tilted it up too far, flooding Molly's mouth with wine. She swallowed, the wafer soggy but still stuck. She tried to keep her tongue away from it, but couldn't help rubbing at it every so often, checking to make sure it was there, even though she could feel it.

Tobias's family knelt in their row, so Molly continued walking to the back of the church and went around, back to her seat on the outside. Tobias went in next to her, tugged the kneeler down and she followed. She didn't know what she was supposed to be thinking or praying, so she concentrated on the wafer, on the disintegrating flecks falling into her mouth, which she swallowed.

The mass ended with a blessing, and most people waited for the priest to pass. Tobias's grandfather embraced him again and patted Molly's cheek before making his way out to say good-bye to Father Gino. His mother made sure to remind him not to be too long. "I'll just drop Molly home and be in to work," he said.

They shuffled out with everyone else, Molly still in Tobias's oversized coat, but somewhere during the service she'd slipped her arms into it, the sleeves flapping like penguin flippers. Her hands covered, she didn't reach for the holy water, probably wouldn't have anyway, even if she could. Tobias held the door open for her, and the sunless light outside still made her squint; no blue or yellow broke up the sky, only a pale gray-white melting over everything. She crossed her arms over her midsection to keep the cold air out of the unzipped coat and walked, slightly behind Tobias, back to the car.

She made sure not to close her skirt in the door again, crossed her legs and sat with her hands between them, shoulders folded forward. Her posture was bad all the time. When she stood straight and flat and open, it felt as if she were showing herself to the world, a billboard, easy to see and read. She tried not to look so slouchy when people were around, when she worked

331

behind the counter, but softened back down when alone.

Tobias said, "There should be heat soon. The car wasn't off very long."

"Forty-three minutes," Molly said.

"Forty-one today." He gathered his hair at the back of his neck with one hand. Released it. "Was the mass okay?"

"Fine. I enjoyed it."

"I was really, uh, surprised about the Communion part."

Immediately her tongue went to the roof of her mouth. She had forgotten about the wafer; it still clung there, but when she touched it, the small bit of pulp fell to the back of her throat. She tried to quietly keep from swallowing it, but it slipped down to her stomach. She could feel it moving, tracked it all the way down until it disappeared somewhere behind her rib cage.

"Only say the word . . ."

"I just thought I'd go," she said.

"I'm not . . . It didn't bother me or anything."

". . . and I will be healed."

She used to have so many words—the ones in her pockets, the ones she spoke. As a young child she'd had too many. Her father would come home from the university and her mother would say, "You talk to her awhile. The kid never stops." Then Susan would shut herself in the bathroom for an hour while Molly chatted about her preschool class and peanut butter and the commercials she saw on television. She talked in her sleep, too. Or used to. Not that she ever heard herself; both parents told her that. She had sometimes wandered into their bedroom at night and burrowed into the blankets between them, and when they all woke she'd asked if she had said anything during the night. Her mother and father looked at each other and started. "Oh, yes," her mother said. "You told us your secret mud-pie recipe. The one you sell to the frogs each spring."

"And," her father continued, "you let me know what you were making me for Christmas. And my birthday. And Hanukkah."

"We don't celebrate Hanukkah," Molly giggled.

"Hmm. Then why are you making me a gift?"

The words went first when she had been taken, and she hadn't gotten them all back, even now. Some days she spoke to no one. Other days she wished she could speak to no one, all her words like rusty gates or slaughtered lambs. Her healing would come with them, though. Not one word. Words upon words. She imagined them growing out of the Communion wafer planted in her belly, the vines curling up, each leaf inscribed with a story. She needed to tell. It had started two days ago when she poured herself out to Claire in the car.

It had to continue.

Tobias slowed the car in front of the museum.

The lights were on, the sign in the door read Open, and Louise passed in front of the window. He'd forgotten to pull up to the side door. The engine hummed, and Tobias hummed, under his breath.

"Thanks for bringing me today," Molly said.

"Next Sunday we'll go where you want."

"You have to go now?"

"Deliveries are calling."

"I don't want you to go."

"I have a few minutes. I could come in."

"No, here is fine."

"Uh, okay," he said, drawing out the *a* sound. "What's up?"

"I want to tell you about my dad."

Shifting the car into park, Tobias turned in his seat to face her. "Sure, yeah."

"He's dead."

"I'm sorry . . ."

"He loved me. He loved my mom. And he loved insects. He was an entomologist at the university. Not around here. We would identify bugs together. It sounds creepy, but it wasn't. After he died, everything changed. Mom was a wreck. I still don't think she's over it."

"Or you."

"I guess not."

"No wonder you know all that stuff about beetles and whatever."

"It kinda stuck with me." The slush on the floor mat shimmered with streaks of color, muted rainbow tones. She'd stepped on some leaked motor oil, she guessed, tracked it in on the bottom of her shoe. "And then there was the time after my father."

Tobias gripped the steering wheel with his left hand; Molly watched his knuckles whiten, the skin thinning, the veins pushing up to the surface.

"Before you moved here."

She nodded, and Tobias's hand released the wheel, limp, lifeless, like a bird being shot from its perch.

"Say the word . . ."

She was going to tell him.

"My father was killed in a bank robbery. I was there. And they took me."

Tobias half slid, half hopped his hand toward her. One finger stroked the side of her thumb. She resisted the urge to bury her hands between her skirted thighs, to clamp them away from his touch, and when she didn't move, Tobias looped his finger around hers. Squeezed.

And so the story came. No details. Just in the plain language of the child she'd been back then. She'd stop every four or five sentences, and after the silence had thickened with too much time and condensation, Tobias would gently squeeze her finger until she spoke again, tugging it almost, milking it, drawing the words from her.

When she finished, she couldn't bring herself to move, to look into his face and see . . . What?

Pity. Disgust. She stared instead at his one finger curled around hers, twice the thickness of her own, with a heavy, dark nest of hair under the first knuckle. And his nail was long, a deep U, shiny like the inside of a seashell.

She didn't want to leave the car. The heat had made her lethargic, sleepy. She could have closed her eyes and dozed, listening to the air blowing around her. She loved to be warm; better too hot than too cold. She'd step from the shower with reddened skin and sleep with the electric heater in her room cranked up so high she would wake with her throat scratchy and dry, drink the lukewarm water she brought with her to bed the night before filled with ice.

Most of all, she didn't want to go back into the museum, didn't want to see her mother. Louise wouldn't say anything to her. But the *looks* would come, speaking more loudly than any argument. Things were so tense between them since Claire came. Since Molly went outside. She hated the discord but had no idea how to fix it.

"Do you have to go to work now?" she asked him.

Tobias said, "Look at me."

Without moving her head, her eyes shifted as far left as they went. She could only see him with her left eye; the bridge of her nose hid him from the right one's view. Her eyeballs ached, a long, pulling pain like short muscles being stretched.

"Look at me," he repeated.

"I am."

He moved his hand from the steering wheel to her chin, turned her face to him. Her eyes dropped back to their fingers. "Thank you. For telling me."

"You already knew."

"Some. That day, when that woman kept calling you Hanna, I went home and found some news articles online."

"Claire didn't tell you?"

"No. She wouldn't." Now he glanced at the museum windows. "I thought your mom was abusing you."

"My mother . . ." Molly hesitated. "No. My mother has given everything for me."

Tobias pinched the hair at his chin. "You could come. When I make the deliveries, I mean. If you want."

"I do."

So he let go of her hand and made a U-turn in the street.

Tobias used his back to push open the restaurant door, three insulated bags in his arms. More people ordered pizzas on Sundays than Molly had expected. She opened the car door to get out and help him, but he shook his head. "Stay in, stay in," he said, sliding the red bags onto the hood of his car and pulling open the back door. The pizzas went into the back seat.

They were regular customers, most of them. Tobias knew the houses and the orders by memory, telling Molly a bit about each of them. "Mr. Burke—his wife left him last fall, and he doesn't cook. Always gets the Hawaiian. He's the reason it's on the menu. Pops always said no self-respecting Italian would put pineapple and ham on a pizza. But Mr. Burke orders it at least three days a week."

"There are worse things to put on a pizza."

"Such as?"

"Tuna fish," Molly said. "It's popular in Germany, I guess."

"That's gross."

"I know."

Tobias eased into the driveway. "You can come with me."

"I don't know," Molly said, but she opened the door and followed him to the small shingled house, battered by sea air and time. It looked like a home that had been left, too, any woman's warmth packed up and taken away.

The man who answered the door had a clean, groomed look, with hair and mustache clipped short and sharp creases down the front of his navy blue trousers. "I wondered what took you so long," he said, glancing at her. "Training someone?"

"This is Molly," Tobias told him.

"Well, Molly, take my advice. Don't make a

customer wait forty-five minutes for a pizza or you won't get a tip," the man said. He took the box and shut the door.

"Um. Wow," Molly said.

"No biggie there. That's just Mr. Burke. He's always spleeny and conjures up some reason not to give me a tip."

"Spleeny?"

"You know. Cranky."

"I've never heard that one before."

"That's because you're a flatlander," Tobias said, laughing. "We have our own language."

"Ayuh," Molly said.

Tobias laughed again. "Not bad."

They spent the afternoon driving between deliveries and the pizzeria, making light conversation or listening to the radio. Molly didn't mind the silence with Tobias, though he never really was silent. He hummed with the music or drummed on the steering wheel or twisted his wrists until they popped. He sucked his drink through a straw until only ice remained and then sucked some more, the air rattling around the frozen cubes. Or he pointed out things in town and told amusing stories about them.

She found herself falling in love with him—the real Tobias, not the one she imagined while reading the romance novels.

"I should get back," she finally said.

"Okay. One more house, then I'll drop you off

when I go back for the next bunch of pizzas."

"I suppose you'll be glad to be off to school and done with this soon."

"You know, Moll, I think God puts us where we're supposed to be, when we're supposed to be there. If I'd gone away to college after high school, you and I . . . well, we wouldn't have become friends. And, yeah, being a pizza delivery guy isn't saving lives, but God still uses me through it. It might seem dumb, but I pray for the people I bring food to. Maybe it does some good, you know? Maybe it doesn't. But I do it because that's what being faithful means, using each situation in a way that's pleasing to Him."

She'd never thought about praying for the tourists who came through the museum. She didn't pray much at all anymore. Why had she stopped?

Because I used up my prayer quota.

They stopped in front of a bungalow with heart cutouts in the wood shutters and window boxes painted to match, not filled with flowers now but with evergreen branches left over from Christmastime, faded red bows tied in the middle of each bundle. Molly carried the insulated pizza bag, and Tobias held her elbow, ringing the glowing orange doorbell button after they climbed two concrete steps to the front door.

" 'Bias, bro, how are you?" the man who answered the door said. He looked not much older than Tobias, with the same cool, slouchy jeans, the same style of striped thermal shirt. He held an older infant in a long-sleeved Onesie, unbuttoned at the crotch, diaper saggy between the legs.

"Dillon, doing good." Tobias shook his hand. "Haven't been here in a while."

"Yeah, man, Kat and I have been gone, down to Hartford with her mom. You heard what happened?"

Tobias nodded. "Frank told me. I'm sorry."

"Well, you know. This crud happens and you gotta roll with it, know what I mean? Kat's okay, she's dealing. And now we got Dakota." Dillon nodded toward a little girl, maybe nine years old, staring at the television in the other room. She sat on the floor, chubby shoulders rounded, arms strapped across her shins, feet bare. Her long straw-colored hair nearly touched the carpet, her face a mask of freckles and loss. "Linda helps as much as she can, but she couldn't keep up with a kid, not with her Parkinson's."

"What happened to the dad?" Tobias asked.

"Didn't want her. No surprise there. Liz tried for years to get anything from him. Time. Money. Man, a phone call now and then would have made Dakota happy." Dillon snorted, shook his head. "Nothing."

"That's hard."

"Tell me about it. I've barely gotten used to this one," the guy said, bouncing his baby on his hip. "How the heck am I gonna take care of a nine-year-old whose life has been torn apart?"

Tobias stuck out his hand, and Dillon shook it. "I don't know, Dill. But you call if you need anything. I'll help if I can."

"Thanks. Tell Frank I said hey."

"Will do."

Dillon took the pizza from Molly and shut the door. Back in the car, Tobias exhaled deeply. "You okay?"

"Why wouldn't I be?" she asked, shaking from within. She'd been that little girl, was still that little girl.

"Nothing," he said.

Tobias dropped her off at the side entrance, his upbeat mood all but evaporated, his dark eyes flat. "Hey, Moll . . . ?"

"Hmm?"

"Nothing. Never mind. I'll see you tomorrow, okay?"

She nodded, unsure of where the two of them stood. She slipped into the apartment, changing from the skirt to a pair of clean jeans she had left folded on the washing machine before making her way into the kitchen area. Mick and her mother were eating at the table, jotting notes on identical turquoise Post-it pads. Louise was laughing. *Laughing.* Molly half smiled at the sound while bracing herself for her return to bring a scolding and the end of the happy atmosphere. But it didn't. When Mick saw her, he said, "Miss Molly Macaroni, how was church?"

She hesitated. "Good."

"Good. Great. Come sit and eat." He tapped the red-and-white bucket of KFC.

"How come you always bring chicken?"

"Why, because I know the way to a woman's heart is through her stomach, and your mother loves this stuff."

She does? And Molly realized right there that despite living the past six years packed together in a broken-down wax museum, their lives inextricably knotted to each other, she didn't know her mother at all.

"That's okay. I'm not hungry."

Mick shrugged, throwing up his hands and bringing them back down with a slap on his meaty thighs. "You never eat. Louise, she never eats, not a bit."

Her mother laughed again. "That's why she wears a size three."

She's happy. Molly had the beginnings of happiness stirring inside her, too. She didn't want it to disappear, and she didn't want her mother to lose it, either. They'd both been trapped in wax for too long.

"I guess I will have some," Molly said. She sat across from Louise, grabbed a chicken leg and scooped a mound of mashed potatoes onto a paper plate.

Louise met her eye, and nodded.

28

Claire
March 2009

"Andrew, you're here."

She'd returned from the grocery store—picking up a few things for Beverly—and found him in the bedroom, his presence unexpected, like discovering an army of fat black ants when opening a brand-new bag of sugar. He squinted at her. "Why wouldn't I be here? This is where my family is." He shifted her toiletry bottles around the top of the dresser, pushing the cocoa butter stretch-mark cream back against the antique mirror and stacking her perfume atop a container of salted peanuts she'd been snacking on last night. "You are still my family, correct?"

"What are you talking about?"

"I've been trying to call all week, Claire. You can't return my voice mails?"

"I did."

"Yes. You left me messages when you knew my phone would be off."

"That's not how it is, Andrew."

"Then how is it? From where I'm standing, I would think my wife is trying to avoid me."

"Because I knew you'd want to know when I was coming home."

"You're right."

"And I just don't know yet."

He sighed. "What's going on? Talk to me."

"Nothing."

"Nothing? You've been here more than a week and nothing has happened?"

"I thought you meant with us."

Andrew sat hard on the bed, first smoothing the wrinkles in the floral duvet, then chopping at the fabric with the side of his open hand, creating lumpy waves in the feather comforter.

She loved this room, with the simple painted-wood furniture, the misty blue walls, the fresh whites and tender grays. The closeness of the furniture in the small space. But it was a woman's room, and Andrew looked out of place.

"I'll take anything at this point," he said.

"Hanna went outside. For the first time in four years. She walked on the beach. She came here to see Beverly. We've talked, a little."

"So things are good."

"They're better."

"Which means what?"

"I can't go yet."

He opened a second button on his shirt, fingers of one hand mauling the fabric until the smooth plastic slid through. Always overheating, Andrew liked having two buttons undone. Claire hated it. She thought he looked like one of those television Mafia men, collar wide and chest hair curling out. Instinctively she stepped to him and closed the button. He took her hands. "I don't think this is about the girl anymore."

"Of course it is."

"No, it's about us."

"There's nothing wrong with us."

"You're here. I'm in New York. Our son is in Vermont with my sister. You end up in the hospital because of problems with our baby and you don't tell me? There is absolutely something wrong."

"The baby's fine. It was a false alarm."

"That's not the point."

"What is the point, Andrew?"

"I love you," he said. He still sat, peered up at her, a starving man searching her face for the tiniest crumb of reciprocation.

"No you don't."

"What are you talking about?"

Claire pulled away from him. She wanted to stand, to stay taller than him, towering over his seated form, but her back ached and her shoes pinched her swollen feet, and she felt so tired all of a sudden. She pressed into the wingback chair in the corner, remembering Molly in the car, crying up her past. Claire's own haunts were ready to show themselves, and there was nothing she could do to stop them.

She didn't know that she wanted to.

"You don't love me. You only love the Claire

you think you know. The one I've been showing you these past six years."

"And who is that, Claire?"

"The one who wears the sandals you like and the blouses you like and puts on mascara every day because you like it. The one who cooks the foods you like, and who hasn't changed the stupid color of the bathroom—even though I hate it—because you picked it out. Or the ugly striped comforter on the bed. Or the dishes that you bought with Liz. The one who never tells you how I really feel because I don't want you to look too close at me and see who I really am."

"You're my wife."

"Will you stop being so insanely calm? I'm telling you I'm a fraud. I'm telling you I've kept huge parts of myself locked away from you so you wouldn't wake up one day and realize . . ." She started to cry. "And realize what a huge, dumb mistake you made in marrying me."

She went to him now, despite her brain repeating *Don't go, don't go, don't go,* wanting her to prove she didn't need him at all. They rolled back onto the bed, his hips against her tailbone, his arm threaded beneath her neck and folded up to her shoulder.

"This isn't a mistake. You're the prize, Claire. Not what you do. Not what you like. Just you."

"No."

"Yes. You hate the dishes? Gone. You hate the

bathroom color? I'll paint it polka dots if you want. I don't care. I want to serve you. I want to know you. Nothing you tell me will shock me or disappoint me. I'm so sorry if I ever made you feel like you weren't enough." He came up onto his elbow, took her chin, and turned her face toward his. "So go ahead. Lay it on me."

"What?"

"Tell me what you've been keeping from me."

"I can't."

He laughed. "After all this drama, you're going to waste the opportunity to say whatever it is that's on your mind?"

She took a breath, shifted her eyes to the window, to the eyelet drapes, counting the lacy holes. "I miss my clogs. And those long cotton dresses I used to wear, even if they make me look completely shapeless. And I want to write puzzles again."

"I never asked you to stop."

"I know. This isn't about you, Andrew. It's me. I wanted to be perfect for you. And I didn't want to bother you with all my crud about . . . you know . . . The accident. The divorce. I didn't want you to know how much I still had to work through. Still am working through." She wiped her eyes on the pillowcase; its edging matched the curtains. "I didn't realize it myself until this week, really."

He tilted her face back toward him. Kissed her.

Dabbed her remaining tears with the cuff of his shirt. "Come home. I need you. Jesse needs you. The rest of it? Eh, we'll figure it out."

"You think you're so smart," she said, smiling a little.

"One of my most annoying personality traits."

She nodded. "Okay. Let's go home."

Andrew stayed behind to fix Beverly's leaky kitchen sink. When Claire left, he was wearing one of the elderly woman's short-sleeved house robes over his pants; Beverly had made him take off his good shirt so he wouldn't ruin it. He worked like an auto mechanic beneath a car, his feet, legs, and most of his torso outside the cabinet housing the plumbing, his face turned up toward the PVC pipe, water dripping on his face. Claire saw one of his socks was inside out, the green toe seam showing. She chuckled to herself and shook her head. This was the man who bought only dark socks so it didn't matter which ones he put on in the morning, even if the lengths or ribbing didn't match.

She borrowed Beverly's Olds and drove to the museum, after a detour to the mainland and the first gas station mini-mart she saw to buy a pint of Ben & Jerry's Mint Chocolate Cookie—the only flavor remotely close to Molly's favorite.

The girl beamed when she came through the

door, and Claire jumped as the recorded witch's cackle echoed down on her.

"Sorry. I forgot to disconnect it."

"I'm surprised someone hasn't had a heart attack." She shook the plastic bag. "Ice cream? It's the best I could do without driving all the way to Straightham."

Molly opened the bag. "It's perfect. Thank you. Wait a minute." She went through the door marked Office and returned moments later with two spoons and two coffee mugs. "All the bowls are in the dishwasher."

"Oh, I don't need any," Claire said. She patted her stomach. "This little one doesn't like dairy all that much, and doesn't let me forget it."

The girl laughed, opened the container, and stuck the spoon into it. Took a bite and dug out another scoop. "It just doesn't seem right if it's not green."

"You'll have to come visit me in Avery Springs, then, and I'll take you out for some of the real stuff at Stewart's."

Molly's spoon stopped mid-flight. "What do you mean?"

"I'm going home tomorrow."

"You just got here. I mean . . ." Her face crumpled, and she dropped the spoon onto the container lid. A white blob dripped onto the counter. "You can't go."

"I have to, Molly. Andrew and Jesse need me

back. And this baby has a mind of its own. It could decide to make an early entrance, and I'd like to be home if that happens."

"I don't want to lose you again."

"Oh, sweetie," Claire said, pulling the girl close, knocking the spoon onto the floor. Mint Chocolate Cookie splattered on her jeans. "That won't happen. You can call me anytime. And I promise to come visit again after the baby's born. If you want me to."

If you're still here.

Molly disentangled herself from Claire. She bent to retrieve the spoon, jammed it into the softening ice cream. Opened the drawer beneath the cash register and removed a wad of napkins. She dropped them to the floor, using her feet to rake them over the spill and stepping on them to soak up the stickiness. An impression of the bottom of her sneaker imprinted into the paper. "Can you stay a few minutes longer? Because there's one more thing."

Claire nodded. "Okay."

The girl looked back at the door, then motioned toward the display entrance. "In here, though."

She followed Molly through several rooms, until she stopped in front of the Shirley Temple figure. Stared at her. "She was always my favorite. I whispered it to her. And I wrote it for . . . someone. But I've never told anyone real."

"Told what, Molly?" Claire asked. She rested her hand lightly on the girl's back, and Molly closed her eyes.

"Why we left."

29

Hanna
November 2002

She had seen Dr. Diane that morning but said nothing to her, even though it was a day she had quite a bit to say—all about how her mother didn't want to let her see Claire anymore, was threatening to end the visits. But she'd been watching Dr. Diane as much as the psychologist watched her. She knew talking wouldn't get results.

But silence . . .

She spent the entire session staring at her hands. She didn't nod. She didn't make eye contact. She didn't color. She didn't even shift in the hard plastic chair when her hipbone started to ache. She counted the clicks of the big wall clock, knowing after sixty of them she could go home. It was boring but worked as she had hoped. After forty-eight clicks, Dr. Diane excused herself to talk with Susan. Ashley, the intern, tried to engage her with a yarn-haired puppet, but Hanna blocked her out so she could listen to her mother and the psychologist speaking in the other room. She could hear both of them, not their words but their tone, with voices raised. And when Dr. Diane returned at fifty-five clicks, she wished Hanna a pleasant weekend, reminded her of Monday's appointment, and asked her to say hello to Claire on Saturday.

Hanna smiled against the sleeve of her sweater.

As soon as she arrived home, she ran upstairs, swiped the cordless phone from her mother's bedroom and, locking the bathroom door, dialed Claire. She had memorized her phone number, just in case. When Claire answered, Hanna flushed the toilet to muffle her voice and hastily asked the woman to bring ice cream tomorrow. She didn't care about the treat; she wanted to be certain Claire still planned to come. Susan had been on her cell phone when Hanna left Dr. Diane's office, and she wondered if her mother hadn't decided on her own to end Claire's visits, despite the psychologist's recommendation.

By the time her mother called her to the table for lunch, Hanna had returned the phone and washed her hands, confident she'd still be seeing Claire tomorrow.

Then the knock came. Susan went to answer the door as Hanna ate her cheese, biting the rectangles into animal shapes before swallowing them between bites of Granny Smith apple. She only liked the green ones, tart enough to suck the spit from her cheeks and make the inside of her mouth dry up. Before she was taken, her mother rarely had them in the house because she and Henry liked Red Delicious better, and used to only buy apples in bulk bags, never individually. Hanna couldn't eat an entire five-pound bag of green apples before they went bad.

Now her mother made sure to have the Granny Smiths in the fridge. She made sure to have most things Hanna liked around the house—smooth peanut butter, frozen toaster waffles with chocolate chips, microwave bacon. Lucky Charms, of course. And plenty of cucumbers.

"I told Detective Woycowski that you need to call first," Susan said, her voice floating back to Hanna.

"I'm so sorry, ma'am." A man's voice. "But given the nature of this new information, I thought it best to come down here straightaway."

Hanna froze. Her bladder released, the heat and wet spreading under the backs of her thighs, soaking into the kitchen chair cushion. She squeezed her cheese animal in her hand.

"I understand, and I know you have a job to do. I just would have liked to have prepared her first."

"I could come back in an hour or so."

"No, no. Don't do that. Hanna's eating lunch. I can call her into the living room."

"I'd love to sit and chat with her for a few

minutes, if that would be all right with you, Mrs. Suller. It may allow her to be more comfortable. I know she's been working with Woycowski, so this is a change. I can't imagine Hanna does well with change at the moment."

"You're right, Detective. That would be fine. Please, follow me."

Susan came back into the kitchen and Thin Man followed. He wore a suit and tie, and as soon as he stepped through the door, he adjusted his jacket. Hanna saw a gold badge pinned on his belt, and a pistol holstered at his side. "Hanna-Bee, this is Detective . . . I'm sorry. What was it again?"

"Detective Mahoney."

"Detective Mahoney," Susan repeated. Her mother was charmed by him, she could tell. "Detective Woycowski transferred to another case, so Detective Mahoney is in charge of . . . everything now."

"Pleasure to meet you, Hanna."

She squeezed harder. Cheese seeped between her fingers.

"Please, sit," Susan said. "Can I make you something? We're having breakfast for lunch today. Except Hanna-Bee couldn't wait and needed a snack."

"No, ma'am, but I appreciate the offer." Thin Man grinned, and she saw rows and rows of big, white, pointed shark's teeth. He would devour her, given the chance. Her teeth began chattering; she bit down, hard. Her head bobbed instead. "Hanna-Bee, huh? That's an adorable nickname for a little girl like you."

"Her father gave it to her. Baby, you want your yolks runny?"

She couldn't speak. Her mother glared at her, probably thinking she was still in silent-protest mode from the appointment. She managed to shake her head the smallest amount, more a tremble than an actual movement.

"I was hoping you could answer a few questions for me, Hanna. Detective Woycowski said you were talking again."

"She is. Must be shy today." Susan sucked her cheeks in, opened her eyes wide behind Thin Man's back, mangy eyebrows raised. She mouthed, *Answer him.* "Are you sure I can't at least pour you a cup of coffee?"

"Now, that would be lovely. As long as it's no trouble."

Susan opened the cabinet, removed a tall ceramic coffee cup. "It's already made and still warm from this morning." She poured the coffee and gave it to him.

"Thank you kindly, ma'am."

Susan carried the skillet from the stove to Hanna's plate and, careful not to touch her with it, slid the eggs out in front of her. "Hanna, Detective Mahoney said they think they may

356

know who was at the bank that day. I believe he has some more photos for you to look at."

She said nothing, hands still fisted on either side of her plate, heart hammering against her rib cage so loudly she didn't know how no one else could hear it. A drop of water-thin mucus formed in one nostril and, slow as a slug, crept over the top of her mouth and spread into the crack between her lips.

Her chin quivered.

Her mother hesitated over her, touched her cheek, and Hanna stared back, willing all her fear into her eyes, thinking, *It's him, it's him, it's him,* as if somehow the words would shoot, like a laser beam, into Susan's brain. Susan glanced down into Hanna's lap, saw the wet spot—now cold—on her jeans. She reached down, touched it, brought her fingers to her nose. A quick, all but unnoticeable motion. Hanna crossed her legs. Her mother nodded, set the pan on the table, pried open Hanna's fist, and taking the napkin from beside the plate she wiped the crumbled cheese away.

"Over easy," Susan said, grabbing the handle of the fry pan again, her skin white around the cast iron. She stepped back toward the stove. "Hanna's favorite."

"Well, they look delicious on her plate. I don't mind waiting until she's finished to—"

In one swift, smooth motion, Susan brought the pan down on Thin Man's head.

Hanna's entire body jumped, startled by the movement, the sound of metal against skull. Thin Man fell off the chair, hitting the floor with his hands, his arms pinned under his torso.

"Wait . . ." he croaked, trying to turn over but couldn't before Susan hit him again—this time a chopping motion, like an ax in wood, the way her Papa Loop used to hack at the logs in his yard, the ones he used to burn in his woodstove for winter. He'd set those logs on an old stump, split them in two with one blow. *Thud. Thud. Thwack.* Thin Man's head split the same way, blood pouring out onto the kitchen floor, trickling toward the sink because the floor tilted. Every time Hanna dropped a grape or spilled her juice, it rolled that way, too.

"You sick—!" Her mother swore. The pan hung by her side, and with her other arm she wiped her sleeve over her face. Blood had spattered on her, teeny pinpricks on her forehead, her cheeks, her shirt. And then her contorted face slackened, the anger draining away.

She jabbed him with the pan, let the skillet drop back onto the stove, wrong side up. Let out a deep, rickety breath.

"Mom?"

"It's okay, baby." Susan pulled Hanna from the chair and hugged her fiercely, led her upstairs. "Let's get you cleaned up."

"But—"

"Don't worry about him. He can't hurt you anymore." Her mother sat her on the toilet. "Wait here. I'll get a change of clothes."

Hanna waited, the bathroom quivering around her. She closed her eyes, hard, an attempt to blink away the cottony confusion filling her head. Susan returned and helped her out of her soiled jeans, washed her legs with a warm cloth. Hanna stepped into the fleece jogging pants, her body moving independent of her mind, her brain slow to process what had happened downstairs only minutes ago.

Her mother zipped a matching hooded jacket over the fresh T-shirt and then rinsed the washcloth and used it on her own face and neck. Susan kicked her specked shirt against the tub, slid a purple cowl-neck sweater over her head. She ran her hands under the faucet and, after shaking off the excess water, patted them over her hair to control the static-charged flyaways.

"I need to call the police now," Susan said.

"No!"

"It's okay, Hanna."

"You'll get arrested."

"I won't. It's not like that."

"You ki—"

They heard a noise then, like someone stumbling. And then a slam. The bathroom window shook.

Hanna began to cry.

"Lock the door, Hanna."

"Mommy, don't go."

"I'm locking the door. Do not let anyone in. Understand?"

She nodded.

Then Susan left her alone. Minutes. Hours. She didn't know. The handle of the door jiggled, and Hanna backed against the far wall, sank down and crouched behind the toilet. The push lock popped up, and the door opened; it was Susan, kabob skewer in hand, fear in her face.

"Come on. Now."

Hanna stumbled along behind her mother as she dragged her down the hallway into Susan's bedroom, where Susan yanked a small suitcase from the top shelf of the closet—she stood on a stool to get it, shaking, swaying, and Hanna thought she'd fall off—and threw handfuls of underwear and socks and shirts into the case. Then into Hanna's bedroom, leaving Hanna on the bed with the bag, coming back with an armful of clothing she dropped into the suitcase. Zipped it.

"Your coat. Where's your coat?"

Her mother lugged the bag from the bed, pulled Hanna behind her again, back down the steps, into the hall. Hanna glanced toward the kitchen.

Thin Man was gone.

Every nerve in her body splintered with panic. "Where is he?"

"Just keep moving, baby," Susan said, throwing

open the coat closet and giving Hanna her jacket. She knelt, tried to zip that closed, too, but her hands shook now, and she just patted down the Velcro tabs, grabbed Hanna's hair, and twisted it into a makeshift bun before stuffing a knit hat over her head. "Let's go."

Susan put the suitcase in the van, put Hanna in it. She turned the key and sat for a moment, the engine idling, the fasten-seat-belt icon blinking. In the rearview mirror, Hanna watched the gray exhaust swirling over the back windows.

And her mother backed out of the driveway, turned toward the highway, and drove.

30

Molly
March 2009

"And that's what happened," Molly said, eyes still focused on the wax child standing in front of her. She reached out and fluffed Shirley's ringlets. "That's why we're here. Mom was afraid he'd try to find us again. Or the other one would. She wanted to keep me safe."

"I tried to find you. I knew you were okay. I mean, I knew you were alive, at least. But the police couldn't tell me where you went, and your aunt wouldn't, either." Claire shifted her purse from one arm to the other. Unzipped it. "I'm sure it was a relief for all of you when they were arrested."

Molly swallowed. "They who?"

"The men who robbed the bank—they're in prison. A few years ago one of them came forward and confessed."

"That's not possible."

"It was all over the news—"

Molly shook her head, cheeks wiggling. "No, you're mistaken. Aunt Serrie would have contacted my mom. Or the detective. He knew where we were."

"Hanna—"

"It's Molly." She raised her arms up and out, knocking Claire's hands from her shoulders. Stepped away. Her voice rose, loud enough that Claire flinched. Molly's stomach twisted inside her, spiraling tighter and tighter, a cotton dish towel being wrung over the utility sink, all manner of filth squeezed out down the drain. But she had no drain; the bile simply pooled in her gut. "Why can't you get that right? Hanna is gone. She stayed in the house when my mother drove away."

She finally looked at Claire, the angel God sent to her twice, now her adversary, whispering things she wouldn't allow herself to hear. The woman gazed back at her with clear, dark eyes, moist with pity. She stood with one hand in the crook of her back, the other supporting her pregnant stomach, her skin tired. Claire knew sorrow. Christ knew sorrow.

And yet Molly had never been more alone.

"You don't understand. He has to be still out there. If he's not, we've been trapped here for nothing." She averted her eyes again. "Please go."

Claire didn't protest. She removed a small, square envelope from her purse and set it against Shirley's foot. Then she left. Molly heard the recorded *hahahahahahaha* as the door in the lobby opened.

HahahahahahaHanna.

I'm not Hanna. I'm no one.

She left time behind. She lost awareness without losing consciousness. Her entire being unplugged from her brain and descended as deep into her core as it could burrow, the place where all her most terrifying memories lived, where not even she could find herself.

When she finally became cognizant of the world again, the first thing she noticed was the air. Stale. Dusty. Clotted with a certain hush she recognized as pulseless—and how could it be anything other than that, in a roomful of wax people, Molly included? Even though she took in oxygen, it had been a long, long time since she'd actually lived.

Her limbs unfroze, and she went into the office and closed both doors—the one to the apartment and the one to the museum. Clicked on the Internet. If he had been arrested, if it had been reported as Claire told her, she would find the article online.

Her thumbs waited on the space bar, and she saw the letters in her head, the ones she needed to type. The middle finger on her right hand pressed the *f,* lowercase, not wanting to waste energy stretching her pinky to the Shift key. Then an *s,* and *r.* And then *bank robbery avery springs.* Hopped her little fingers over two keys and pressed Enter.

Eight thousand results.

She went back and added quotation marks around the town name and *"bank robbery,"* then as an afterthought added *"hanna suller."*

Three hundred and nineteen.

She scrolled down the first page until a headline caught her eye. *Local Men Charged in FSR Robbery, Murder.* In the text beneath the underlined hyperlink, her name glared back at her in bold letters.

She clicked on the story. Thin Man's face appeared in the upper left corner of the monitor, one of those police photos, the height lines visible behind his head, face grim, jaw set, right eyelid drooping slightly.

She didn't remember that.

Below his picture, another mug shot. Short One. The article, dated 2006, stated Kenneth Karey of Albany, New York, had come forward to turn himself in for the 2002 robbery of the Avery Springs FSR Bank. During the interview, he implicated his accomplice, the ringleader of the plot, William P. Martin of neighboring Redfield. Karey also accused Martin of shooting the bank security guard and a patron, and kidnapping a young girl.

Hanna Suller.

Martin denied all charges.

Molly returned to the search listing, found another article dated eight months later. *Martin Sentenced to Life.* Thin Man had been found guilty on two counts of second-degree murder, one count of robbery in the first degree, and one count of kidnapping in the first degree. He would be transferred immediately to an upstate New York prison.

Karey had made a plea bargain with the district attorney in return for his testimony against Martin. He was serving fifteen years at Daawkill Correctional Facility. She printed the story.

Once again she hit the back button and scanned the articles. She clicked on one more, an exclusive prison interview with Kenneth Karey, where he was asked why he turned himself in.

"I just couldn't live with myself anymore," he'd said.

Molly gathered the two printed pages from the

printer and went into the apartment. Louise stood at the stove, mixing something in a bright yellow saucepan. A housewarming gift from Mick, for when she moved into his place. She'd kept the rest of the set packed in the original box but wanted one to use until then.

"Baby, set the table, will you?"

"Is Mick here?" She took paper plates from the package on the table. Most of the kitchen had been packed and labeled and moved to the other house.

"Running late. Some heating problem at one of his other properties."

"Oh."

"You feeling all right? You look awful."

Molly held the pages out to her. "Read this."

"Ever heard of please?" her mother asked, one eyebrow raised in amusement.

"Please."

"Seriously, Molly. Are you okay? You're pale as—"

"Just"—Molly raised her voice enough to get her mother's attention—"read it."

Louise frowned. She switched off the stovetop and gently slid the pot from the hot burner to an unheated one. Held out her hand. "Give me."

Whatever she saw first on the paper—the headline, the photos—made her stop. Her hand shook. Her eyes met Molly's. "Claire," she said.

"Claire."

Her mother pulled a dining chair from its tidy place beneath the table, its legs scraping the tile, and flattened into it, folding the printed pages in half, smoothing her thumb over the crease once, twice. "I never meant to keep it from you."

"Three years ago they were put away. Why are we still here, still hiding? Why didn't we pack up and—?"

"What? Go back to Avery Springs? To pick up where we left off? We made a life here, Molly. Going back would only mean more scrutiny for you. More questions. I thought it best we stay."

"We didn't have to go back home. We could have gone anywhere."

"What's the difference between any other place and here?"

"Because *here* meant we were trapped," Molly said, and the tears came. "*Here* meant we couldn't leave, because *he* was out there. *Here* was a reminder, every day, that our lives were ruined because I was with Dad, and I picked going to the post office first. If I'd chosen differently, none of this would have happened. *Here* meant *my fault*."

She dropped hard into the chair beside Louise, her body droopy and without the strength to do much more than slump in half, her chest to her thighs, her head resting on her crossed arms and knees. Her back bounced up and down as she cried, silently, except for a wheezy gasp of breath every now and then. Her mother moved to the floor, kneeling at her feet, their heads pressed close together. Louise threaded her arms around her daughter and rocked her.

"I didn't know, baby. I had no clue you blamed yourself."

"How could you not?" she mumbled against her shirtsleeves.

"Because I was too busy blaming myself."

"You?" Molly lifted her head. "You gave up everything for me."

"No. I was afraid." Louise wiped the wrist cuffs of her blouse under Molly's eyes, down her cheeks. "We could have gone home and just . . . faced things. But I had so much fear inside me. Fear you'd be taken again, or worse. Fear you'd never heal, or I'd never heal. Fear of *dealing* with everything in front of us. But running only brought us closer to it, not farther away."

"I love you more than anything, Mom," Molly said, and her mother squeezed her close.

Louise nodded. "I know. Time to stop hiding now. Both of us."

Thank you, Gee.

Louise called Mick and told him not to come, and they talked a long time, over pizza, her mother's beef stew forgotten on the stove, both their faces throbbing with emotion. They swallowed Tylenol to help with the headaches, and the words poured out of them.

Louise apologized for her irrational jealousy of Claire—"You were all I had left. And you wanted her. People can do and think some stupid, stupid things when they're broken."

Molly said she wanted to make the move to Mick's place—"It's time for a change."

It felt like midnight when they decided they'd talked enough, throats irritated and eyes burning, but the clock read a little past nine. It happened like that during the northeastern winters, days so short darkness came by suppertime. Molly tossed their paper plates and claimed the bathroom first, brushing her teeth and flossing crust out from between her bottom teeth. She found Louise wrapping the leftovers in aluminum foil and asked if she was going to bed now, too.

"In a few. I'm going to call Serrie first."

Molly squinted. "You've kept in touch with her all along, haven't you?"

"Not in the beginning. She knew how to reach me if she needed to, but we didn't start talking regularly until I learned . . . of the arrests."

"Tell her I said hi," she said with a nod of understanding.

Her mother smiled a little. "I'll do that."

In her bedroom, Molly changed into flannel pajama bottoms and an oversized MAINE sweatshirt, then tugged open her top dresser drawer. Ran her hand along the underside and dislodged the paper she'd taped there, with the name and phone number of her Bible's previous owner. Then she turned off the light and climbed under her down comforter, waiting for her mother to go to bed, the folded square flat between her palm and breastbone. She heard Louise hang up the kitchen phone, saw the shadow of feet at her bedroom door, and then more noise as her mother shuffled to her own room. Molly lay still awhile longer before taking her watch off the nightstand and lighting its face.

Ten thirty.

Only eight thirty in Colorado.

She slipped into the office, feet bare, wishing she'd kept on her socks. The computer was on; she tapped the space bar for light, sat in the chair crisscross-applesauce, toes nestled behind her knees. Without giving herself time to reconsider, she held the paper near the screen so she could read it, and dialed the number.

Three rings and, "Hello." A man's voice.

"Um, hi. Is Ellen there?"

"Who's calling, please?"

"Well, I, uh . . . This is Molly, and I found the Bible she left in a hotel room drawer. In Boston."

"How did you get this number?"

She spoke quickly. "Sir, I'm sorry I called. I know there was a PO Box I was supposed to send a letter to, but I've had the Bible nearly six years, and I wasn't sure it would still be open. The name in the cover was blacked out with marker, but I . . . I was still able to see it. And the number was there, too. I'm sorry I intruded. I just wanted . . ." Molly thought she would cry. "I just wanted to thank her. I needed it."

The man laughed. "Oh my. I can't believe it. Six years, you say?"

"Yes, sir."

"That girl," he said, and she could hear the delight in his voice. "Her mother and I were so angry at her when she told us what she'd done. Docked her allowance until she'd earned enough money to buy herself a new one. Ellie didn't mind one bit. No, she said she was certain the Lord had told her to leave the Bible there, that someone would be coming along who had to have it more than she did. Molly, you said?"

"Yes."

"Where you from, Molly?"

"Maine."

Another laugh, low and friendly. "I cannot wait to tell my wife. And Ellie. She's away at college. I'll give you her number, but if you don't mind—" he cleared his throat—"could you wait a day or two before you call? I'd really like to give her the news myself, first. I have to admit, I have some crow eatin' to do."

"I don't mind."

"Molly from Maine. You'd think I'd know by now the Lord works in His own ways."

She wrote down the phone number the man

gave her, and after a few minutes more of his incredulous chatter, hung up the receiver. His joy had been contagious, though, radiating through the phone lines and warming Molly's cheeks until they puffed and burned. She rubbed at them as she returned to bed, unable to squish away her smile.

31

Claire
March 2009

Andrew loaded their bags into the back of the Mariner, slamming the tailgate closed and adjusting the magnetic New York Yankees emblem Jesse had purchased at his first live game last autumn. He'd bought a foam finger, too, paid nineteen dollars for the navy blue number-one sign Claire had seen in marketing catalogs for a buck apiece. But Jesse wouldn't be deterred; he pinned the finger to his bulletin board, wore it during the spring training games he watched on television, and waited impatiently for his chance to go back to the stadium.

They planned to pick up Jesse from her sister-in-law's house that evening.

Claire hugged Beverly and promised to visit soon. The elderly woman rested both her hands on Claire's belly and prayed over the baby. Then

Beverly patted her cheek and said, "You did good."

"We'll ring once we get there."

"Don't forget. It doesn't matter the time."

In the car, Andrew adjusted the heat, positioning the vents toward the ceiling on both the driver and passenger sides. For him, because he hated the air in his face; it dried out his contact lenses. For her, because her pregnant body was its own travel furnace. They both knew better than to keep the air off completely, though, especially today when the sharp coastal winds passed seemingly unobstructed through metal and glass.

"Do you want to stop?" Andrew asked. He backed out of Beverly's driveway.

Claire shook her head.

"You're sure?"

She shrugged. "I think so."

"That means no," Andrew said.

"You think you know me so well."

"I do, don't I? That must be really annoying."

And then he turned the car around.

"Andrew . . ." Claire said.

"You need to do this. Humor me, okay?"

He parked outside the wax museum, and when he asked if she wanted company, she shook her head. He left the car idling as she squirmed out of the seat. The sign on the door read Closed and the lobby lights were off. Claire cupped her hands around her eyes and peered through the unpainted parts of the window. She saw no one and motioned to her husband that she would try the door around the corner. Knocked. This time the door opened, and Susan Suller—or whatever name she went by now—stood there. "Molly said you'd left."

"We're going now. I just wanted to say good-bye, if she's up for it."

The woman nodded. Hesitated. She picked at her eyebrow and then, as if realizing what her fingers were doing, quickly stuck her hand in her pocket. Finally she looked at Claire, her pores clogged with six years of concealment, her eyes yellowed with six years of tears. "Thank you," she said.

Claire nodded.

Susan went inside, and Molly walked into the entryway moments later. She wore her hair pinned back from her face, blond roots beginning to show at her forehead and ears. "You're here," she said, delight in her voice. "I wasn't sure I'd see you again before you went home."

"I couldn't go without a good-bye."

"I read your card. It meant . . . a lot to me."

Claire had set the card at Shirley Temple's feet with the hope the girl wouldn't be so angry and distraught she'd destroy it without opening it first. She told Molly the things she treasured in her heart from their days together, things only Andrew knew, about how God had stirred her to offer a push to a young child on a swing, and the encounter—no, the entire, entirely too short relationship—had been aloe on her wounds. Hanna had given her the chance to reopen all her clamped-down places to someone, and in doing so, light and air and life circulated through the necrotic tissue, reviving it. Hanna had made it possible for Claire to allow Andrew and Jesse into her life. Hanna showed her she still could love someone as fiercely as she had her own children. She had focused so much energy on *helping Hanna*—both times—she continued to stumble over the obvious, the gym shoes dropped in the middle of the room she refused to pick up, until now: God had sent Hanna to help her, too.

"We're just finishing up the last of the packing, but you can come in, if you want," Molly said. "Mom's getting married, so we're moving. Just to another island about twenty-five minutes from here, but it's good to start fresh sometimes. I think so, anyway."

"I'd love to, but I left poor Andrew in the car waiting for me."

The girl hesitated. "You'll still visit Beverly, right?"

"I'll still visit you."

Molly smiled. "And I'll write. Or email. But maybe not call so much. I hate the phone."

"I'd really like that," Claire said. "Tell that cutie of yours to take good care of you."

Blushing, Molly said, "I will."

They embraced, more clinging to each other than a hug. The girl still felt delicate beneath her arms, but no longer fragile. A sturdiness had come into her bones, calcified with her conquered battles of the past two weeks.

She'll be okay.

Claire stretched away, smoothed her fitted maternity tee down over her torpedo-shaped belly, navel poking through the plum-colored fabric, the cool beach breeze tickling a narrow patch of exposed skin at her beltline. With her other three she'd had a compact bulge, no larger than a soccer ball beneath her clothes. She buttoned the chunky sweater around herself; she'd bought it at a craft fair and couldn't get the musky wool smell out of it.

"It's like when John leaped in his mother's womb," Molly whispered, eyes on the over-stretched sweater. "Their souls knew each other."

"You take care," Claire said, sniffling.

She waddled back to the car. Had to pee. Andrew stopped at a gas station, and she used the bathroom while he refueled. He paid inside, bought her an iced green tea and lemon pound cake. Before pulling onto the highway, he took her hand. "You good?"

"Yes," she said. And meant it.

They arrived at sundown to pick up Jesse. He threw his arms around Claire and squished her until she had to say, "Enough, Jess. I can't breathe." Andrew's sister invited them for dinner. After eating, the three of them sat on the porch, despite the bite in the mountain air—Jesse snuggled against Claire on the wooden porch swing, Andrew in the rocking chair, coffee cup between his knees. When the baby kicked, she took her stepson's hand—*No, he's my son*—and said, "Feel."

Jesse laughed. "So cool. It's like an alien."

"Sometimes."

"I still think it's a girl."

"Well, we'll see soon, won't we?"

The boy leaned close, lips nearly pressed to Claire's side. "Hello in there, baby. It's your big brother. We can't wait to meet you." He looked up at the only woman he knew as his mother, eyes round and hazel, a perfect replica of the one he didn't remember. "She can hear me, right?"

Claire nodded. "She, or he, will definitely know your voice."

"You're sure loud enough," Andrew said.

Jesse giggled. "I'm supposed to be loud. I'm ten."

"Almost eleven. And eleven-year-olds are decidedly not loud. Especially eleven-year-olds who have napping infants living with them. Maybe you should start practicing now."

"Dad."

"Just saying."

"Okay, you two," Claire said. "We should probably say good-bye and be on our way. I'm ready to be home."

Jesse ran into the house to get his bag and books, slamming the door behind him. The porch light flickered from the vibrations. Andrew offered Claire his hands, tugging her out of the swing, resting his chin on the top of her head. "I think it's a girl, too, you know. And I'm always right, remember?"

"You *think* you're always right."

"There's a difference?"

Claire laughed. "Come on."

She tried to pull him toward the front door, but he held her still. Kissed her. "You're wonderful. And I *am* right about that."

"We're okay?"

"More than okay."

"I love you," she said, and it overwhelmed her. She couldn't help but thank God for all He'd given her.

He kissed her again. "I know that, too."

32

Molly
May 2009

She and Tobias sat on the beach, jeans rolled to the knees, feet buried in mounds of damp beige sand. Castles, Dakota called them, decorating each pile with pebble windows and seaweed moats, a flagpole twig pointing from the top. Neither Molly nor Tobias had the heart to move and destroy the nine-year-old's architecture. So they sat, trapped, listening to the waves and watching Dakota's latest game—throwing random washed-up things back into the water. *Sea gifts,* Molly thought. Little treasures of glass and wood and shell, deposited on the sand for someone to find and marvel at. *God's gifts,* left around for His children to pick up, brush off, and recognize they came from Him.

"I'm gonna try the kite now," Dakota said. "Help me, Tobias."

"At your command," Tobias said. He gently removed his feet from their encasement, but as soon as he did, the pile of sand collapsed. Dakota didn't care; she called for Tobias to hurry, tearing open the package. "Don't let the wrapper blow away," he said, but too late. The cellophane cartwheeled down the beach.

"Sorry," Dakota called as he ran after it, eventually stomping on one end. He rolled it up, crammed it in his pocket, and made his way back to the girl.

Molly watched as Tobias flattened the kite on the ground, one knee on each corner to keep the wind from carrying it off, too. He inserted the support sticks into the proper holders, attached the tail, and tied the string to the center flap. "You're all set," he told Dakota. She ran down the shoreline, kite bobbing behind her on two feet of twine.

Tobias came back to Molly, offered his hand. She took it and he pulled her to her feet. She wiped off the seat of her jeans. "Follow her?" he asked, and she nodded.

They walked close to the surf, and he found Molly's hand again. She laced her fingers with his. *Here's the church, here's the steeple,* she thought. She liked her arm to be behind his, her palm facing forward. She'd tried it the other way—her arm in front, palm back—but it wasn't nearly as comfortable; she felt as if her elbow would twist out of joint.

"I'm free to paint tomorrow," Tobias said.

"I haven't picked a color yet."

"I thought you wanted lavender."

"I did," Molly said. "Now I don't know."

She and her mother had moved into Mick's house three weeks ago, after he and Louise were married in the town's court building. Their marriage license listed the bride as Susan Suller, but Mick still called her Louise.

Molly had a huge bedroom of her own and a private bathroom, and the go-ahead to decorate them however she liked. She wasn't used to having choices, so the walls remained white, despite the stack of paint chips Tobias brought her from Home Depot. He taped them to the walls, creating various shapes—trees and peace signs and smiling faces—hoping to inspire her.

In the days since Claire's departure, the chasm between Molly and her mother had closed and begun to heal, wounds sutured together with ugly black thread. Their relationship in an adolescence of sorts, they fought more and with all the dramatics that came in those preadult years, sometimes shouting at each other from across the house or slamming doors in grand exits.

"I feel like I'm living with two teenagers," Mick said, more with amusement than complaint.

But they talked more, too, and deeply. Molly told her mother some little things about Tobias—though she guarded most of those feelings, unsure of what they were and how to express them. Louise shared memories of her father, and Molly loved that, could listen to those stories all day.

Her mother spoke of Henry with such tenderness Molly couldn't help but ask why Louise had married Mick, what she saw in him?

"It's always been your father," she said, eyes wet with loss, "so there's no sense looking for someone to fill his place. But I'm lonely, Hanna. And tired. Mick's a decent man, and I enjoy him, and that's enough for me."

Yes, she'd called her Hanna. She did that sometimes now, too.

Molly tried not to dwell on the past too much. She wanted to be like Tobias, like Beverly, eyes always turned toward the brightest point and focused on the growing list of things gained.

Dakota.

The girl had worn a short, ruffled cotton skirt, despite it being early May in Maine, and a thin tee. When she got cold, Tobias had given her his hooded sweatshirt, rolled the sleeves until they mushroomed at her wrists. She pumped her stout legs, tossing the kite in the air as she stumbled along, bare feet kicking up foam. The plastic triangle dove nose-first into the sand.

"Stupid," Dakota said, kicking it. "I can't do it."

"Try again," Tobias called over the wind.

Beverly's words still resonated intensely in that place Molly knew only the things of the Spirit were sown, a sweet-smelling, earthy place way down deep she needed to keep cultivating so the soil wouldn't turn rocky or thorny or too hard to penetrate. *"I have no doubt I had that stroke so I could be in that bed, that day, to sing to a woman I'd never met."*

Molly did have doubts. She looked at the jumble of her life, all the heartache, and despite God's Word's assertion it all worked together for the good of those who loved Him, suffering's residue blinded her belief. But He cradled those doubts in His tender hands, turning them this way and that, until the haze evaporated from the blurry pieces and Molly could *begin* to see how the puzzle fit together.

The bank. Her father's death. The commercial on the television. The preacher. Her prayer and escape. That day on the playground with Claire. That day in the kitchen with Thin Man. The museum. Intersecting lines, intersecting lives, all purposing toward a cup of tea with an old woman she'd never have met otherwise, who told a story of Providence she'd never have heard, stirring her to see the first gleam of feathers rising from the ash. Another little girl who'd lost her mother had stared at a television across town, her worried aunt and uncle unable to break through her wall of mourning. But Molly knew she could, because she'd been there, too.

She began by meeting with the girl at her home after school most days; Tobias drove her there, and at first they just watched episodes of *The Suite Life of Zack & Cody* in silence. It didn't take long for Dakota to share a few things about her mother, and when Molly spoke about losing Henry, the kindredness of loss built a bridge between them. "I can't believe how much better she seems after she spends time with you," Kat told Molly when they'd picked Dakota up earlier that afternoon. "Thank you for doing this for her."

"It's a start," she'd replied. "There's still a long way for her to go."

Molly knew that all too well.

She moved forward and she stayed stuck. Yes, she went outside now, and occasionally into stores. She could hold Tobias's hand—sometimes. She went to church each Sunday with him; they brought Beverly with them and had lunch with her afterward. She had emailed Claire a dozen times in the past five weeks; her friend was eight days overdue and absolutely miserable. "This baby needs an eviction notice," she wrote. Her mother took her to test for her instruction permit, and she passed the written exam easily, the name *Hanna Suller* printed on the card.

But she never left the house alone. Some days she still couldn't leave her bedroom. She startled at all the unfamiliar noises in Mick's house, from creaky floorboards to microwave timers. Some days she asked Tobias to take her back to the museum for a few minutes, a few hours, so she could breathe the familiar air, be cradled within the well-worn walls.

She had no *place* now. She pictured everyone in the world fitting perfectly in their own contoured space, a dimple in the atmosphere enveloping them as they moved and worked and lived. She had vacated two of those places—the one for Hanna Suller and the one for Molly Fisk. She needed to carve out a new spot, but she had no idea how to manage that on her own.

Help me, Gee.

They stopped in front of the beach's famous shipwreck. When Tobias first told Molly about it, she'd expected an actual boat embedded in the sand, but a hundred years of sea and sun had a way of picking things apart, and only a short portion of the ship's hull remained, weathered wood rising up like a moss-covered dinosaur rib cage.

"Counseling today?" Tobias asked.

"It got moved to tomorrow," Molly said. "I know you have class. Mom's taking me."

He drew a circle in the sand with his toe. "So, uh, how's it going?"

"I've only had two sessions."

"I know," he said, smiling sheepishly. "Just wondering."

She let go of his hand, brought two fingers up to his chin and touched that small triangle of beard. His soul patch. Hesitantly, she slid her thumb up, over his bottom lip, chapped skin as rough and pleated as her own.

Dakota burst between them, frustration reddening her face as much as the wind. "I can't do it very good," she whined, sand in her hair, kite dragging behind her.

"It's breezed up quite a bit," Tobias said. "Maybe too much."

"Let me try," Molly said.

She took the spool of string—yellow, with a handle for ease of holding—and gripped the kite's crossbar. Ran.

She heard Dakota shout, "Let go, let go," so she did. She unwound the string, felt the pulling behind her lessen, looked up. The kite had caught in a current; it rose, dipped, rose again and held, twisting against the olive sky.

Tobias trotted down the beach, Dakota on his back. Molly gave the handle back to her, and she slipped to the ground.

"Look at it," Dakota said, laughing, her permanent front teeth gappy and still too large for her mouth, her stringy hair flapping across her face. And Molly saw herself there—what could be, what would be—as she kept her face turned toward the light.

Acknowledgments

With a humble and grateful heart, I would like to thank:

Karen Schurrer, my editor, whose valuable input has made all my novels better than they ever could have been without her.

The entire Bethany House Publishers family, for their patience and understanding.

Bill Jensen, my agent and, more importantly, my friend.

Jack Merry, whose miraculous true story I made Beverly's story, and his wife, Marilyn, one of the most beautiful souls I know.

Laura Combs, MS, LMHC-P, who advised me on the clinical and psychological aspects of this story.

Members and friends of Clifton Park Center Baptist Church, for embracing my family as their own.

Everyone who prayed me through this book, and who prayed for Claire and my family as we crossed from *the worst of it* into *better than we imagined*. I can't name you all, don't know you all, but your prayers sustained us when nothing else would.

My parents, Ann and Joe Parrish, for your endless support, and for the weekends we flop at your house watching cable television.

My family—Chris, Gray, Jacob, and Claire—you make me better every day. I love you all.

About the Author

Christa Parrish is the author of three novels, including *Watch Over Me*, winner of the 2010 ECPA Fiction Book of the Year, and *Home Another Way*, which was a finalist for the 2009 ECPA Christian Book Award. She lives in upstate New York with her husband, author Chris Coppernoll. They have three children in their blended family.

Center Point Large Print
600 Brooks Road / PO Box 1
Thorndike ME 04986-0001 USA

(207) 568-3717

US & Canada:
1 800 929-9108
www.centerpointlargeprint.com